What was it about her?

She tried so hard to appear disinterested in him, but when they kissed, her body language told him otherwise. And thinking that . . .

Quinton narrowed his eyes. "If I kissed you right now, what would you do?"

Expression arrested, she asked, "Scream again?"

"You aren't certain?" He stepped closer. She didn't back away, but she did plant her feet as if preparing for a confrontation. He didn't want to rush her or scare her off.

Without touching her, he suggested, "Maybe we should find out."

She stared at his mouth. Her lips parted on a shaky breath, then slowly curved in a sexy female smile that reeked of confidence. "Yeah," she whispered. Her gaze drifted to his. "I have a few minutes, so why not?"

LORI FOSTER

Murphy's Law

ZEBRA BOOKS
KENSINGTON PUBLISHING CORP.
www.kensingtonbooks.com

ZEBRA BOOKS are published by

Kensington Publishing Corp.
850 Third Avenue
New York, NY 10022

All Kensington titles, imprints, and distributed lines are available at special quantity discounts for bulk purchases for sales
promotion, premiums, fund-raising, educational, or institu-
tional use.

Special book excerpts or customized printings can also be
created to fit specific needs. For details, write or phone the
office of the Kensington Special Sales Manager: Attn. Special
Sales Department. Kensington Publishing Corp., 850 Third
Avenue, New York, NY 10022. Phone: 1-800-221-2647.

Zebra and the Z logo Reg. U.S. Pat. & TM Off.

ISBN 0-8217-7803-X

First Printing: September 2006
10 9 8 7 6 5 4 3 2 1

Printed in the United States of America

To Beverly Moore.
You're smart, sweet, funny, beautiful,
and you fit right in.
I am so very glad that you found Jake,
and that he found you.
Love ya bunches!

Chapter 1

Trailing close behind in the rusted, rattling junk heap of a car, he watched her, plotting, planning . . . growing tense and hard and excited.

Between two jobs and school she scattered her routine, but he'd figure it out. Everyone fit a pattern eventually. People were sheep. Predictable. Easily overcome. Especially with his unique brand of tools.

She was the one to blame, the one who'd fucked up all his plans. She was the one directly responsible for ruining his life.

Before she caught on to him, before anyone could stop him, he'd have her. Then he'd have his much-deserved retribution.

She turned into the parking garage at the building where she worked the night shift. Slow and watchful, he drove on past the entrance. And he saw things he hadn't expected. He smiled with the discovery. Another way to twist the knife, to get his revenge.

The little bitch deserved no less for putting her nose where it didn't belong.

With building impatience and anticipation, Quinton Murphy leaned against the cinderblock wall and checked his watch for the tenth time. How pathetic for a grown man to go to such lengths to talk with a woman.

A woman who had refused him—*after* kissing him senseless.

He didn't leave. He *wouldn't* leave. Not until she showed up and he had a chance to set things right with her.

Loosening his tie and pulling at the collar of his dress shirt, he cursed the unseasonable warmth of the October night and the stifling stillness of the parking garage. He checked his watch yet again, and then, finally, her yellow Civic pulled through the entrance.

Headlights flashed around the gray, yawning space, now mostly empty except for his Porsche Carrera and the vehicles of the night shift workers. Her brakes sounded a little squeaky, and she parked with a jerk of the gears that shook the aged automobile.

Always in a hurry—that described Ashley Miles. At least from what little he'd seen of her. He had to wonder if she ever relaxed or took a day off to laze around.

As soon as her engine died and her headlights went dark, the driver's door swung open and she stepped out. Quinton soaked in the sight of her, letting his gaze meander along the length of her long legs, her trim midriff, and the understated curves of her small breasts before settling on her face.

Once again, he mulled over her startling effect on him—and wondered at it. At thirty-three he was hardly a monk. He'd had infatuations, relationships of convenience, and once he'd even been in love.

But something about Ashley, some indefinable nuance in her nature got to him in a most unusual way.

Pieces of her were perfect: her dark eyes, her long silky hair, and her mouth . . . God, he loved her mouth.

She smiled easily, had a sharp tongue, and said no far too often.

But she kissed with an enthusiasm and hunger that made her impossible to dismiss, almost as if she'd never kissed before and the sensation of it overwhelmed her. He wanted more. He wanted everything. Until he had her, he wouldn't be able to get her out of his thoughts.

Put all together, Ashley made a mostly average appearance. But when she spoke, all that sassy attitude came crashing out, and it made her seem appealing yet unattainable, brash yet vulnerable.

She said things he didn't expect, behaved in ways unfamiliar to him. She smiled, and he wanted to strip her naked.

Her car door slammed hard and she looked around the garage behind her, talking to herself in low mumbled words that reeked of irritation and disgust.

Unaware of his presence, she said, "For God's sake, Ashley, get a pair, why don't ya."

Never taking his gaze off her, Quinton pushed away from the wall. Patience, he told himself. He'd have her, and soon.

"A pair of what, Ashley?"

She screeched. The high-pitched yell of panic bounced around the cavernous garage in deafening force, causing Quinton to wince. "For God's sake, it's me."

Eyes wide, she whipped around, zeroed in on him, and went from startled to furious in a heartbeat. The change was something to see.

And she looked as desirable pissed as she did impatient.

After stomping across the concrete floor, she thrust her chin up close to his face. Since this was the second time he'd startled her in the garage, he felt a little guilty. Holding up his hands in concession, he said, "My apologies."

She didn't soften a bit. "You're making a habit of this, Murphy, and I don't like it."

Quinton gave in to a half smile, gently touched her hair, and lied through his teeth. "Not on purpose. I just finished some late business. Since I knew you were due in soon, I decided to wait to say hi before heading home." The last time he'd seen her, he'd been with a client. A sexy, blond, female client, and though he knew Ashley wouldn't admit it, she'd misinterpreted the situation.

Now he needed to make her understand his interest for her and her alone.

For a single suspended moment she stared at him, mostly at his mouth, her expression soft and giving . . . then with a frustrated growl she strode away from him.

Damned contrary woman. She wouldn't make this easy for him. But she did make it interesting.

Quinton propped his hands on his hips and watched her long-legged retreat, undecided on whether or not he should say anything more.

But after only three steps she halted. Her straight, stiffened back still to him, she snapped by way of explanation, "I usually don't scare so easy."

An olive branch? He gladly accepted it. "I gathered as much." He hadn't known Ashley long, but already he accepted that she wasn't a timid woman, definitely not a woman who jumped at shadows. In fact, he'd have described her as ballsy beyond belief. "So what's going on? Why are you so jumpy?"

"It's nothing."

She shut him out and he didn't like it. "Okay." He'd let that pass for now. Harking back to her earlier comment, he asked, "What do you need a pair of?"

Her shoulders relaxed and she turned to flash him a cheeky grin. "Balls."

"Well, good God, I hope not."

She shook her head. "I could use them in the figurative sense."

He chose to see her chattiness as an invitation and fell into step beside her. "Want to tell me why?"

Her shoulders lifted. "I've had the weird feeling that someone's watching me." She glanced up at him. "It's probably you giving me the willies."

"Me?"

She poked him in the chest. "Every time I turn a dark corner, you seem to be there."

Half under his breath, he muttered, "Not exactly the reaction I'd hoped for." The first time he'd met

her, she'd been running for the elevator and he
was stepping out. She'd ended up in his arms, and
from that point on, he'd been a goner.

He stepped ahead of her to open the door to
the building.

In her usual long-legged march, Ashley went in
past him. He had a feeling she'd keep walking until
she left him far behind.

On a sigh, he said, "Ashley, wait."

She paused and one slim brown eyebrow lifted.
"For what?"

She looked . . . well, adorable. Her disheveled
brown hair draped her shoulders, partially concealing the ridiculous long-sleeved T-shirt she wore.
Ashley had the oddest fashion sense he'd ever witnessed, but somehow it suited her spirit.

Tonight she wore a purple and pea green striped
T-shirt that would have made most women look
bloated. On Ashley it made a statement of individ-
uality. For certain, he'd never seen anything like it
on anyone else.

Droopy broken-in jeans hung low on her slim
hips, leaving a thin strip of pale, smooth belly to
tantalize him. Her slip-on sneakers clashed in a
glaring shade of pink with silver trim.

What was it about her?

She tried so hard to appear disinterested in him,
but when they kissed, her body language told him
otherwise. And thinking that . . .

Quinton narrowed his eyes. "If I kissed you right
now, what would you do?"

Expression arrested, she asked, "Scream again?"

"You aren't certain?" He stepped closer. She
didn't back away, but she did plant her feet as if

preparing for a confrontation. He didn't want to rush her or scare her off.

Without touching her, he suggested, "Maybe we should find out."

She stared at his mouth. Her lips parted on a shaky breath, then slowly curved in a sexy female smile that reeked of confidence. "Yeah," she whispered. Her gaze drifted to his. "I have a few minutes, so why not?"

Damn it, one little invitation from her and his heart pounded as if he'd been jogging up three flights of stairs. Not waiting for her to change her mind, Quinton tunneled his fingers into the cool weight of her hair, tipped up her chin, and sealed his mouth over hers.

Being so close to her rioted his senses.

He loved the feel of her hair against his palms, the warm scent of her skin, the way her heartbeat matched his. With only the touch of his tongue, her lips opened under his, so soft and sweet.

Just as he remembered, she intoxicated him.

They were in the building's basement, not exactly a place conducive to seduction.

She had to start work.

He needed to head home.

He knew all that—but at that moment, he didn't care.

Her hands on his shoulders, she snuggled into him, pelvis to pelvis, her breath coming fast and hard, her mouth moving with his.

Her breasts were small, but he could feel her stiffened nipples rasping against his chest and it made him nuts because he knew she was braless, that only a thin T-shirt kept her from him. Lost to the here and now, he ran his hand down her back all the way to her rounded bottom, spread his fingers wide over the softened, worn denim of her jeans, and pressed her tight against his erection.

With him every step of the way, she made a purring sound of excitement and dug her fingers hard into his shoulders. Her response pushed him over the edge and he started considering the possibility of taking her in the darkened hallway, against the wall, her long legs wrapped around his waist . . .

She freed her mouth. Breathing hard, her forehead to his chest, she half laughed, half moaned.

His own breathing was ragged. He felt primed, more than ready to strip off her jeans and sink into her. But he had enough sense not to press her. Instead, he rubbed his hands over her back, soothing her, enjoying the feel of her in his arms. "God almighty, woman."

"Yeah." Her fingers fisted in his dress shirt. She swallowed twice, let out a long breath. "And now you see why you have to leave me alone."

He stiffened from his hairline to his toes. "You must be joking." She *had* to be. He couldn't remember the last time a mere kiss had affected him so strongly. And she wasn't immune either. He could feel her trembling.

"Sorry, no joke." Her forehead pressed hard into his sternum and her voice lowered in near desperation. "You have to stop waiting for me—"

He forgot his lie about work and said, "I've only waited twice, damn it."

"—and you definitely have to stop kissing me."

Quinton caught her shoulders and held her back far enough to see her face. A pulse thrummed wildly in her throat. Her swollen and damp lips were open to accommodate her uneven breaths. Heat flushed her cheeks and lust shone in her big dark eyes.

She felt everything he felt.

Determined to understand her, he demanded quietly, "Tell me why."

Her long hair trailed over his wrists as she shook her head. "We both know you were waiting for me tonight because, for whatever reason, you've decided you want to take a turn in the sack with me."

"Take a . . ." The way she put things forever boggled his mind. He gently shook her shoulders. "I want to make love to you. We'd both enjoy it." Hell, he'd love it. "But I also like you." He was close to being obsessed with her.

"You barely know me." With shaking fingers she tucked her hair behind her ears, straightened her T-shirt, and moved back to put space between them.

His hands fell to his sides. "True enough. I don't know you as I want to." He managed a strained smile. "But I'm trying to correct that."

"Why bother? Our schedules conflict. We don't work the same hours."

"I'll manage." Given how badly he wanted her, he didn't sleep much anyway.

"We don't even work for the same company."

"But we do work in the same building." They'd met only by chance when he'd had to stop by his office late and she'd been leaving work early. Among other things, he was CEO of a consulting firm. Ashley cleaned the office building where he leased space. "Though it's a good thing we don't officially work together, given most company policies would forbid coworker dating."

Still refusing him, she shook her head. "We're not dating. It'd be a waste of time."

Did she deliberately insult him?

He scowled, but she shook her head and said, "I mean because we have nothing in common."

He touched her mouth with one fingertip. "Oh, I think we have a few things in common." He looked into her eyes and his lust ratcheted up to the max again. He wanted to devour her.

"Yeah, okay." She drew a quick breath. "It's a first for me, but I'll admit we've got the whole sexual chemistry thing going."

"Thank you," he said with dry humor.

"But," she continued, once again on the move, "I've got too much on my plate to be messing around with you right now."

Messing around with him? She made him sound like an inconvenience. Easily keeping pace with her on her path through the building to the locker room, Quinton asked, "So what's on your plate? Anything I can help with?"

"Nope." She kept her head down and her gait long.

She said that too fast, and with too much conviction. The take-charge part of his personality didn't like it. "I'm not without means, you know."

She stopped long enough to roll her eyes at him. "Yeah, I know. You have 'means' coming out the ying-yang. Thanks but no thanks."

On their first meeting, which also accounted for his first rejected invitation to her, he'd learned that Ashley had a spirited way of putting things. He liked it. As he said, he liked her.

He already knew that she attended college classes in addition to working the third-shift job. Busy, but not so busy that she couldn't fit in a date with him.

Unless something, or someone else, was keeping her away.

From two feet behind her, he asked, "Do you find me unattractive?"

"Oh please." She laughed without looking back at him. "As if."

Well . . . That was nice. At least he knew his appearance didn't repel. "So is it that you dislike men with 'means coming out the ying-yang'?"

"Your means don't matter to me one way or the other." Now she sounded irritated. "I'm sure you work hard for what you have."

"I do." But he'd also been born into money, not that he intended to say so with her being so prickly about it. "And now you have me working hard to figure you out."

"Might as well stop before you strain something." Finally they reached the locker she used to stow away her purse.

Again, Quinton tipped up her chin. "Tell me what's troubling you." Then he'd resolve it and get her focused on him instead of other things.

She crossed her arms over her chest, cocked out one hip, and eyed him up and down. "All right, fine. First and foremost on my mind is the wedding."

The *wedding*? Denial lumped in his guts. But a quick glance at her finger showed no engagement ring. He scowled at her for nearly stopping his heart.

"Yeah, my sentiments exactly." She wrinkled her nose. "But you should try it wearing pink taffeta." She turned, opened the padlock with deft movements, swung open the squeaky metal door, and shoved her purse onto the top shelf inside the locker. "Let me tell you, humiliation takes on new meaning." She slammed the locker shut with a little more force than necessary.

"Hold up." Quinton put a hand to her shoulder and turned her to face him. "You're not getting married?"

"No way." And with annoyance, "Where'd you get a dumb idea like that?"

Relief sank into him. "So who's the lucky bride?"

"My best friend."

"And she's getting married when?"

Her head dropped back against the locker with a clatter. "In a couple of days. And I've got all this crap to remember—"

"Crap?"

"Yeah, you know. Like how to do that idiotic walk on the rice paper, and to move her train out from behind her when she turns to go back down the aisle." She closed her eyes and huffed. "And to not say *crap* in front of the minister."

"Such a predicament," he teased.

"Yeah, well, for *me* it is." She screwed up her face. "I have a tendency to speak first and think later."

Without really considering all the repercussions, Quinton said, "This is where I can come in handy." Then he felt like cursing. He detested weddings almost as much as funerals. Still, he had the entire weekend free and if it'd get him that much closer to her . . . "As your escort, I'll assist you in minding your manners."

Ashley's eyes snapped open again. "Ho, no." She shook her head. "I'll pass, thank-you-very-much."

"Why?" He sidled closer, getting used to the idea. "Come on, Ashley. You know you don't want to do this alone. I'll make excellent backup."

"What makes you think I don't already have a date?"

Something cold, mean, and dark settled into his stomach. His humor fled in the face of jealousy. "Do you?"

She scoffed at his stern expression. "Don't go all caveman on me. My personal business is no concern of yours."

True—but at that moment it didn't seem to matter. "If you're dating someone else, why did you kiss me?"

"*You* kissed *me*."

"And you kissed me back."

"Let's don't split hairs." She grinned. "Besides, it doesn't matter because I'm not dating anyone else."

"You're sure?" He didn't entirely trust her attitude or her quick tongue.

"Well, I know I'm busy, but I think I'd notice a guy accompanying me around town."

After several seconds of contemplation he decided to believe her. The last thing he wanted was another contender in the picture, muddying things up. "So you planned to go to the wedding alone?"

"Unheard of, I know, but that's the way I roll. I'm the solo queen."

"I'm glad I don't have competition."

"Yeah, well, I could have a date if I wanted one."

The blustering of her pride had him smiling again. "That I don't doubt for a single second. After all, I just offered, right?" Ashley might be deliberately abrasive, but that didn't conceal her innate sensuality. It was a little earthy. Maybe even gritty. But it was there. Any man with eyes would see it. "So why don't you?"

She threw up her hands. "You really should pay attention. Like I said, I'm busy. Why should I waste my time on a guy who'd probably only get under my skin, then walk away?"

Interesting revelation. He pointed out the obvious. "I'm not walking away."

"Not yet." And though she tried to hide it, he glimpsed her vulnerability again. "But that's because you haven't gotten what you want, yet."

"Sex?"

"Bingo." And then, "Don't try to deny it."

The way she challenged him, her chin raised, her eyes narrowed, was both amusing and endearing. "We've already established that I want to make love to you. I'm a man. You're a very attractive woman."

"You're shoveling it on a little thick, aren't you?"

"You don't think you're attractive?" This had to qualify as one of the strangest conversations he'd ever had.

Again she rolled her eyes. "Why are we even talking about this?" She caught him by the collar. "My looks have nothing to do with it. It's because I'm not falling at your feet that you *think* you're interested."

"Ah, so that's what it is."

"Yeah. I figure a guy with your face, bod, and money probably has women chasing him all the time."

Deadpan, he said, "It can be so bothersome."

"You're used to having your pick of the babes. But here I am, a small-town Podunk, giving you the old heave-ho."

"I'm confident I can change your mind on that." Most of what she said now sounded like bluster, as if she felt she had to give lip service to her refusal before giving in.

"If I slept with you," she insisted, "you'd be over me like that." A snap of her fingers punctuated her statement.

As seriously as he could, Quinton suggested, "Let's test this theory." Her cheek was soft beneath the brush of his fingertips. "Make love with me today, right now, and I'll prove to you that I won't lose interest. I'll still escort you to the wedding."

Her lips twitched. "You want me to do the horizontal mambo here in the basement? Up against the lockers?"

"You have no idea how much." Gently he cupped her chin—and tried to win her over. "But Ashley, if you want to wait, I'll wait. I'm happy to spend time getting to know you better. You can trust me."

Her palms flattened on his chest, holding him at bay. "It's not about trust. It's about me having a limited amount of time right now."

"You can't tell me you never date."

"Wanna bet?"

"But . . ." She looked to be in her midtwenties. Maybe five or six years younger than he was, which made her far too young to sit home alone knitting or watching old black-and-white movies.

Ashley was the type of woman who exuded energy and determination. She would never be content with idle time alone.

Giving up, Quinton asked, "Why?"

"Men aren't on my list of priorities right now." With a shrug, she added, "Maybe after I get my degree and net a good job and can save up and get my own house—"

"So in, say, ten years, I should ask again?"

"Yeah." Her grin left a dimple in her cheek. "Maybe by then I can spare you a few hours. But right now I don't want any distractions from the big goal. And you, Quinton Murphy"—she patted the center of his chest—"would be a *big* distraction."

Quinton shook his head. The woman possessed a special knack for pushing him away while at the same time enflaming him. She spelled out her interest but claimed it didn't matter.

Her refreshing honesty frustrated the hell out of him. "So let's don't date." Who needed dinners out or movies or dancing? He'd gladly bypass it all. "We'll attend the wedding together and then see how it goes."

That suggestion made her laugh. "After that kiss, we both know exactly how it'd go." Her smile slipped. "Even though I come across as a sex-starved nympho, I'm not really that easy."

"Trust me, easy is not a word I'd use to describe you."

"It's just that you make me . . ."

"Hot?"

"More like scorching."

Somehow Quinton managed not to groan. "The feeling is mutual. So where's the problem?"

"*You're* the problem." She tweaked his chin. "I suspect you'd be addictive, and all my well-laid plans would go down the toilet." And with that she turned her back on him and walked away.

Again.

Incredible.

He'd need some careful maneuvering to win her over to his way of thinking. For whatever reason, Ashley had sworn off men, as if they had no place at all in her life. He'd have to give her good reason to accept him. "I'd like to offer a compromise."

Still walking, she clipped a CD player to the waistband of her jeans and connected a pair of soft headphones to it. "This ought to be good."

He caught up to her. "I'll protect you from yourself."

That stopped her in her tracks. "Come again?"

Pretending a nonchalance he didn't feel, Quinton said, "If you say you don't want intimacy with me, I'll ensure it."

"Uh-huh." She pursed her lips, considered him, then raised a brow. "And how will you do that?"

"My willpower is stronger than yours. I'll save you from yourself." He took a tiny step closer— and her attention moved to his mouth. Voice lowering, he whispered, "I'll still kiss you, and I'll still touch you."

Her eyes darkened. "Your plan is doomed to fail."

"But I won't let it go any further than that." He leaned a little closer to whisper, "Even if you beg."

Warm color shot into her cheeks. "Right. Dream on, big boy."

"Oh, I do. Dream. About you. But regardless, I won't let things go too far. You have my word that I'll accompany you to the wedding and return you safely home. Nothing more." He held out his hand. "Deal?"

She took a long time considering his proposition. A dozen emotions flashed over her face, but skepticism seemed most prevalent. And suspicion. She didn't yet trust in his integrity, but she would. He'd see to it.

And maybe, just maybe, she'd end up in the same desperate state of arousal that he was in.

Finally she nodded. "All right. Just to watch you squirm . . ." She took his hand and gave it a firm shake. "Deal."

When she started to retreat, Quinton held on, pulled her up to her tiptoes, and wrapped an arm around her waist. "Until then, Ashley . . ." He sealed their bargain with a kiss hot enough to leave her clinging to him. He used his lips, his tongue, his teeth . . . And she reciprocated every inch of the way.

He'd win this battle of wills one way or another. And judging by her small moan when he ended the kiss, it'd be sooner rather than later. "Give me your number," he whispered. "I'll call you."

Very slowly her eyes opened. "Wow."

Wow indeed. She had a knack for understatements, too. "Your number?"

"My phone is either in my locker or turned off when I'm working."

But he knew when she got off work. "If need be, I'll leave a message."

She licked her lips as if savoring his taste before nodding, then rattling off a phone number.

Quinton added it to the memory on his cell phone and then tucked his phone away again. "Thank you."

Composure restored, she said, "You'll probably regret this."

He just smiled. "You won't. I promise."

With one last stroke of her silky hair, he made his escape before he lost sight of the prize. But before he got too far away to hear, the prize started mumbling to herself.

And she didn't sound happy.

Too bad. The laws of nature, of man and woman, dictated he was bound to win. And that made him very, very happy.

Chapter 2

Whatever could go wrong, did.

Murphy's Law.

In her case it was more like Quinton Murphy's Law because when she got near him, she made mistakes left and right. One look at the man and she forgot common sense, self-restraint, and her touted goals for the future.

She knew how important goals were because her parents had never had any. They'd been more than content to scrape by on the generosity of others.

Being the charity case of the neighborhood didn't make life easy for a gangly, shy kid with overly strict parents. In fact, her life had bordered on hellish until she and May became best friends. Thanks to May, she'd learned to conquer insecurities, stand up to bullies, and separate herself from her parents' way of life.

At seventeen she'd escaped their suffocating environment of rigidity and poverty by disowning them and moving out on her own. For years it had been all she could do to make ends meet, and sometimes they hadn't. She'd done without food, without adequate clothes, occasionally without shelter—but she'd never taken charity.

She was nothing like her parents, who still took advantage of good people with big hearts.

Now, finally, she had enough money to attend college, to set herself up to be fully self-sufficient and plan for a proper future.

She prided herself on making it on her own. Someday she'd have everything she wanted—her dream home, a new car, money in the bank, a retirement fund . . . She'd have it all.

Involvement with Quinton would only distract her from her long-term goals.

But . . . she couldn't help thinking about it, about him. She wasn't an unhappy person, but around Quinton she felt almost . . . bubbly. So stupid. She had to stick to the plan of work, school, and savings.

Unfortunately Murphy's Law wasn't content with blowing her state of mind. She also had to contend with the air-conditioning going on the fritz, leaving the building stuffy and her body sheened with sweat. From that point, she broke both the industrial-sized vacuum and a foyer lamp after accidentally sucking up an extension cord. Then she dropped a bottle of cleaner, spilling it everywhere. She spent more time cleaning up her own messes than the building, when usually she prided herself on a job well done.

She blamed Quinton for her clumsiness. After that consuming kiss, no one could expect her to function properly. Her knees still shook, her heart still thumped, and a strange tingling in her midsection made concentration iffy at best.

A single glimpse of Quinton and she wanted to drag him off for some hanky-panky. He personified the term *stud* with his dark blond hair and fierce green eyes and that confident smile that proclaimed enough experience for ten men. For a corporate type he had an incredible body, tall and strong and roped with lean muscles.

Suits had never appealed to her. But the way Quinton wore a suit, with such relaxed ease, only amplified his masculinity.

Maybe if she'd expected to see him tonight, she might have been prepared. But after catching him with Zara Trilby in what had appeared to be a very intimate discussion, she'd overreacted big time. Luckily, not in front of Quinton, but she'd been eaten up with jealousy, proving she was in over her head. Even though she later discovered that Zara was a very nice lady and no more than a client for Quinton, she'd thought to avoid him.

She'd already resolved to ensure he'd left the office before entering to clean. The only reason she'd entered the first time was that she'd planned to ask him to the wedding. Big mistake.

One look at poised, refined, beautiful Zara, and she'd indulged in private comparisons that had her quickly chickening out. Pure fate had Zara at the rehearsal dinner as the best man's date. And to Ashley's surprise, the woman was actually nice. But even after Zara's assurances that she and Quinton were only business associates, Ashley had planned to forgo anything personal with him.

He was wealthy; she was poor.

He was drop-dead gorgeous and she was just plain funky in looks and demeanor.

He was CEO of a lucrative consulting firm while she still had college to finish.

Doing her best to keep him blocked from her mind had been easier than she'd expected with her thoughts bouncing between worry over the headlights that kept flashing in her rearview mirror, and the wedding that thrilled her, even as she dreaded it.

She loved May, and she loved seeing May so happy.

But . . . she'd never in her life dressed up. Her childhood wardrobe had consisted only of second-hand clothes. Many times what she wore had holes, stains, and didn't fit. Humiliation had become her constant companion. Whenever her parents got money, they indulged personal vanities that didn't involve their only child.

Naturally she'd avoided proms and other school formals. By the time she got her GED, she'd been on her own, completely estranged from her folks. Other than May, no one had really cared what she did or where she went.

Now she could afford finer things, but she had college loans, rent, and insurance. Whatever was left over went into saving for a house. She dressed for function, period. If it kept her warm and dry, that was a plus.

In the worst times of her life, May was her salvation—more so than May realized, and more so than Ashley could ever tell her. So for her, and only for her, would she wear a formal gown and dressy shoes and have her hair done and all the rest of the fuss that went with being a maid of honor.

But that didn't mean she'd enjoy it.

She had to admit to relief that Quinton would accompany her. But that brought out a completely new set of problems. He skewed her perspective on things. He toyed with her libido. Without even trying, he chipped away at the willpower necessary to see her dreams through.

Even when it didn't appear deliberate, Quinton got to her. All he had to do was stand there looking good, or smile in a way that made her feel special, or touch her so carefully, and she wanted to molest him.

Diabolical. That's what he was. Downright diabolical. Somehow he knew her weaknesses, and he used them against her.

Lost in conflicting thoughts, it wasn't until she left the building at four in the morning that she recalled her nervousness earlier. *Had* someone been following her? Or was she just overly nervous?

She reached the center of the silent, empty garage—and her cell phone rang. Expecting it to be May, who knew her schedule and often acted like a mother hen, Ashley retrieved the phone from the bottom of her purse. "What's up, toots?"

"Toots?" asked a now-familiar, masculine voice.

Oops. Not May. Ashley smiled as she strode to her car, no longer feeling so alone. "Hey, Quinton. You're up early. Or late. Or something."

"I have a question."

"Shoot."

"Are you really going to wear pink taffeta?"

Catching the phone between shoulder and ear, Ashley dug out her car keys. "It's four o'clock in the morning, and you're thinking about women's wedding attire?"

"I was thinking of you, actually, picturing you as you looked when I last saw you."

Meaning agog from a kiss, with wet noodles for knees? "Yeah, so?"

"I kept trying to align the image with pink taffeta, but it's not working. Or were you just pulling my leg?"

She unlocked her car and slid into the seat. For October the weather remained stifling and humid. It wasn't much cooler outside in the fresh air than it had been inside with broken air-conditioning. Her shirt stuck to her back, and her hair hung damp and limp on her shoulders.

"I don't even know what taffeta is, but the truth isn't much better." After starting the car, relocking the doors, and cranking up the air-conditioning, she asked, "You really want to hear about my dress right now?"

"Can you not hear the anticipation in my voice?"

Funny how talking to Quinton on the phone made all her exhaustion evaporate. Dangerous. "All right, then. You asked for it." She began backing out of her spot. "It really is pink, but a pale pink. Silk, not taffeta, but it's got some itchy lace on it. V-necked, floor length . . ."

His voice darkened. "Sounds lovely."

"Hey," Ashley teased, "is this turning into one of those perverted phone calls?"

"I'm just visualizing you in silk."

"Yeah, well, if you start breathing heavy, I'm hanging up."

Quinton laughed. "I promise to behave."

"Good. Because I've had a hard enough night."

She heard some rustling, as if he'd just settled back in bed to get comfortable. "How's that?"

"The air went off and Flint couldn't reach any-one from maintenance."

"Flint the security guard?"

"That's him." She carefully steered the car from the garage, and though her nervousness had dissi-pated, she still glanced around at all the shadows, looking for she didn't know what. She saw nothing but debris. No lurking madmen or threats of any kind. "The death of the air conditioner set the tone, and everything else went wrong, too. I'm sweaty, hungry, tired, and cranky."

"Now that's an image I can reconcile better than pink taffeta."

"Ha ha." But he was right. She couldn't see her-self all dressed up, either. She just knew she'd end up looking stupid. "Right now I'm aiming to eat, shower, and hit the sack, in that order. No time for phone sex, sorry."

"Another time then." In the middle of her laugh-ing, he added, "I haven't eaten yet, either. Breakfast sounds terrific. Where should I meet you?"

Her punching heartbeat ended the laughter. Butterflies started a brawl in her stomach. Her fin-gers hugged the steering wheel. "Who says you're invited?"

He gave an exaggerated sigh. "You tell me that you have no time to get to know me. Well, I'm up at this ungodly hour, and we're both hungry, so sharing breakfast is the perfect plan."

"If the hour seems ungodly to you, why are you up?"

Ashley could almost hear him thinking.

"I have some things to do today."

To her ears he sounded evasive. "Before dawn?"

"Soon. And no, I didn't get up just to shanghai

you for a meal. Actually, I assumed you'd be going straight home to bed. When I called, it was with the intent of hearing your voice, that's all."

Ridiculous how badly Ashley wanted to believe him. With the offer out there, going home to sleep no longer seemed so appealing.

So what would one meal hurt? A public restaurant would be a natural block to her explosive sexual urges. She'd have to keep it in check, and so would he.

"Besides," he said, intruding on her thoughts, "we should discuss the wedding. You haven't even told me what time to pick you up, or where we're going."

He had a point. Ashley glanced at the clock on her car console. "I was going to grab a bowl of cold cereal at home, but . . ." She decided to take a chance. "Know where the Squirrel is?"

"Up a tree, I'd assume."

Ashley couldn't help grinning. "The Squirrel is a little mom-and-pop diner in Stillbrooke, close to where I live." She gave him brief directions. "They serve a lot of truckers, so they're open now, and they make a mean ham and eggs breakfast. I'll meet you there if you're still interested."

She was sure he wouldn't be. She doubted Quinton had ever been in a greasy spoon, much less dined on their fare.

"I can be there in fifteen minutes."

Her jaw fell open. "No joke?"

"Don't back out on me now, Ashley."

"Wouldn't dream of it." New life entered her tired muscles. He was going above and beyond to see her. That had to count for something, right? "Fifteen minutes. Bye."

After she hung up, she found herself grinning. She wouldn't get much sleep before her classes started, but these days, sleep was an elusive commodity anyway.

She had work, school, a wedding . . . and once again the steady beams of headlights filled her rearview mirror.

Damn it, she *was* being followed. Now she had to decide what to do about it.

Quinton parked his Bentley a good distance from the entrance of the diner. The light of the moon reflected off Ashley's little Civic, situated among a variety of work vehicles. His Bentley wasn't the best choice for detouring to the Squirrel, but he'd made a promise he intended to keep.

Gravel crunched beneath his feet as he crossed the cluttered lot for the open door of the diner. A warm glow, accompanied by the sounds of laughter and conversation, spilled out into the otherwise quiet night. Leaning against a fence, a man and woman embraced. Standing alongside a rig, two truckers conversed quietly behind the red smolder of cigarettes. Quinton glanced around the rest of the area, enjoying the quaint atmosphere, the small-town familiarity.

That's when he felt it.

Someone watched him with ripening tension. Being rich hadn't made him an idiot, and he didn't ignore his instincts. He did a subtle perusal and spotted the junker parked across the street. A shadowed figure sat behind the wheel.

Reminded that Ashley had also had a feeling of

being watched, Quinton's temper slipped up several notches. A coincidence? He tried, but couldn't convince himself of that.

In his position of wealth, he was used to being followed, photographed, and sometimes stalked—and he had no problem ignoring it most of the time. But he'd be damned before he let anyone harass Ashley.

He started across the street with a purposeful stride.

Before he even reached the curb, the car burped and gurgled to life, then sped away on balding tires.

Damn it. He watched until the taillights disappeared around a corner before striding into the small restaurant. He located Ashley sitting in a booth toward the back. Turned sideways in the bench seat, her spine slumped against the wall and her legs stretched out, she looked to be half-asleep.

Quinton's frustration eased away, replaced by sexual awareness, tenderness, and an odd and inexplicable pleasure.

For long minutes he just looked at her. Even in repose her face seemed so expressive to him. Signs of exhaustion eased away the cockiness and defensiveness. He wished for some way to protect her from herself and her staunch determination for independence. He didn't yet know her background, but he had a feeling her life hadn't been an easy one. Unlike him, she most likely came from moderate means.

Why else would she just now be working her way through college?

When the waitress eyed him, Quinton smiled at her and unglued his feet from the entrance. Ashley didn't stir until he slid into the seat across from her. Then her head turned toward him, her eyes opened, and her lips curled in greeting.

"Tired?" he asked, needing to say something to break the spell of intimacy.

As her eyes adjusted, the automatic nod of agreement froze. While slowly looking him over from his gray sweatpants to the print on his Rolling Stones T-shirt, she straightened at the table.

Feeling a little self-conscious with her visual examination, Quinton ran a hand over his hair. "Have I grown a third eye that I'm unaware of?"

She shook her head while her gaze crawled all over him, as effective and stimulating as a touch, before finally coming to rest on his face. She licked her lips, but said nothing.

Quinton felt like he'd just been the recipient of sizzling foreplay. Every place she'd looked at him now tingled with awareness. He cleared his throat. "Cat got your tongue?"

"It's . . . shocking. That's all."

The way she reacted, you'd think he'd shown up naked. "Excuse me?"

"You look even better in sweats than you do in a suit. And I didn't think that was possible. I mean . . . you look *really* hot in suits."

Ah. She liked him in casual clothes. Too bad he wouldn't be comfortable wearing them to the office. "Thank you."

"Makes me wonder what you'd look like . . ." She whistled. "Never mind."

"No, please." He crossed his arms on top of the table and leaned toward her with a smile. "Say it."

Not one to let a challenge pass, she gave her

own cheeky grin. "All right. I'm wondering if you look as good in the buff."

"Want to find out?"

She shrugged, slid her gaze over him again, but said, "I'll pass."

"Chicken."

"Naw. It's just that I don't want you to get arrested for indecent exposure."

Laughing, Quinton indulged his own quick perusal, and couldn't resist reaching across the table to smooth her hair away from the side of her face. "You're a terrible tease. But you do indeed look sweaty. I hope they get the air fixed before I go in at noon."

Rather than be insulted, she chuckled and lounged back in her seat—out of his reach. "So what has you up and about so early, and dressed so comfy?"

He didn't intend to share his plans for the day. What he did in his spare time, well, it was personal and private, his alone, something he did because it made him feel good. He'd decided years ago that parts of his life would not be for public consumption, so he shrugged off her question.

"Personal business." To keep from expounding, he picked up a menu. "So what are we ordering?"

"Personal," she insisted, "as in intimate? With a female?"

That she pressed the issue when he'd made it clear he hoped to avoid it shouldn't have surprised him. Naturally, Ashley didn't bow under the pressure of good manners; he should have known that. And given the look on her face, she wouldn't give it up any time soon. Still, he tried a nonanswer to distract her. "When I get intimate, rest assured it's with a female."

She propped her chin on her fists. "Look, if you're seeing another woman, it's no skin off my nose. I didn't ask to—"

He took her hand and gently squeezed her fingers. "I haven't looked at, haven't even thought about another woman since I first met you."

She hesitated only a moment before jeering. "If you say so." Sarcasm dripped from her tone. She might as well have called him a liar outright.

He released her and dropped back with a scowl. "You have absolutely no idea what it's like to walk around with the start of an erection all day, do you?"

"Uh . . . no. Can't say as I do."

"Well let me tell you, it's not comfortable. But I can't seem to help it since every available second, I'm thinking of *you.* As to that, I'm spending all available seconds *chasing* you. I've done everything in my power to get to know you better. Do you honestly believe I react that way often?"

She gave an indolent roll of one shoulder—and his temper ignited with a growl. "Ashley—"

Her chuckling cut him off. "Hey now, don't get in a snit."

"I don't get in snits, damn it." He was insulted. And frustrated. And getting desperate. And he hated the way she zeroed in on his reactions. He *was* in a snit, blast her. But most women wouldn't have put it that way.

She flashed a grin. "I bet women never give you a hard time, do they?"

Not usually, but he wasn't about to admit it to

her. "There's been a challenge or two. But I have to admit you're the most difficult."

"I've been clear about my position."

"Absolutely." He tapped his fingers on the tabletop. "You compliment me, admit you want me, admit to thinking of me in very involved ways, but then tell me to get lost." His smile mocked her. "How could you be any clearer?"

Pretending to wince, she asked, "I was too honest?"

She toyed with him, but Quinton couldn't tell if it was a deliberate ploy for control or a cover for uncertainty.

That was the thing about Ashley—she was neither predictable nor common. Rules that applied to other women had no bearing on her. "You kiss me like you want to eat me alive."

She sighed. "Yeah, I know." Her gaze avoided his. "That's probably because I sort of do."

Shit. When she said things like that, his body just reacted. She made him insane with her push-pull rejections.

He sat forward to twine his fingers with hers. "One way or another, Ashley, we will get together. Then you can kiss me anywhere and everywhere you want." Before she could deny him, which she looked ready to do, he added, "But I meant it when I said I'd keep things platonic for now. I'm willing to give you as much time as you need. As long as you don't ever think I'm filling that time with another woman—because I'm not."

She tested his grip, trying to ease her hand away, but when he pretended not to notice, she relaxed again.

While he had her attention, he decided to clear up any notion she had of other women fulfilling the desire he had for her. "Understand, Ashley. You might see me with other women—"

Her gaze clashed with his.

"But only in a business sense." His thumb rubbed over her knuckles. "I have lunch and dinner with a lot of prospective clients. It's part of business."

"Whatever."

He shook his head. "No, don't act like it doesn't matter. I haven't forgotten how you reacted to Zara Trilby." She'd immediately jumped to the wrong conclusion, which had set him back on his courtship. Zara was known for flamboyance and lots of hugging and kissing. But she wasn't his type. "That particular client—"

"Don't worry about it. I know it didn't mean anything."

"Do you?"

"Yeah. She's dating a friend of mine now."

Further explanations died on his tongue. Zara Trilby was a beautiful, voluptuous, very demonstrative and outgoing businesswoman. But she was also rich as Midas, so it surprised him that she and Ashley might mingle socially. "You're serious?"

"Yeah. She seems nice enough." Ending that subject, she curled her fingers around his. "I'm just busting to know . . . what's the appeal?"

Lost to her meaning, he raised a brow. "Excuse me?"

Gesturing between them with her free hand, she said, "You, me, this little lust-fest you have going on. I'm not stacked. I'm not gorgeous. I haven't been all that nice. And other than a few unruly comments, I haven't led you on, not deliberately, anyway. So . . ." She lifted her shoulders. "Why me?"

"You're serious?"

She nodded. "Believe it or not, men aren't throwing themselves into my path. They don't chase me. For the most part they ignore me just as I ignore them."

"You didn't ignore me."

"I tried. You wouldn't let me."

She looked genuinely perplexed, prompting him to kiss her knuckles. He was used to women who knew their own allure and used it to the fullest. He'd dated women whose charm got them anything and everything they wanted. He enjoyed the feminine guile—but he appreciated Ashley's in-your-face attitude more.

"It's a lot of things."

"Like?"

"You're sexy."

She rolled her eyes. "You're into teen bras and skinny legs?"

"I love your fashion sense."

Laughing, she said, "Yeah, I can tell rummage-sale couture is your speed."

"You're unique and fun. And honest. I adore your hair. And your long legs. And your smiles. I see you, I hear your silliness, and I want to kiss you."

She tilted her head. "My silliness, huh?"

"That audacious way you have of talking." He'd seldom heard such imprudent bluster from grown men, much less a slip of a woman in outrageous clothing. "You're honest to a fault, uncaring of the consequences. You know what you want and what you don't want, and you spell it out."

She chewed her bottom lip before meeting his gaze. "Some would call me obnoxious."

"Maybe someone threatened by your confidence."

Her smile went crooked. "Is that how you see me? Confident?"

"You have a candid approach to life that I find very sexy. And I can't help wondering if you'll be that decisive in bed." He rubbed her knuckles again. "I hope so."

With an odd look on her face, she eased her hand away from him. "Uh, no, I wouldn't."

"I don't believe that. One feature of life always reflects another. You're assertive, a woman in control. A woman who spells it out without shyness. Experienced. Forceful."

She looked so dumbstruck by his observations that he thought to reassure her.

"I'm not criticizing, Ashley. I find your brazenness a real turn-on."

Her lips twitched before parting on a full-blown laugh. "This is too funny."

"It is?"

With a shake of her head, she said, "Sorry, Quinton. But you've based your attraction on some huge misconceptions."

Very softly, Quinton said, "No, I don't think so. I think I'm getting to know you pretty well." And the more he knew her, the more he liked her.

"Well, you missed something somewhere because I'm not what you think I am."

"In what way?"

"First off, I'm not so hot in the sack, so get that idea out of your head."

Quinton settled back, ready to be enlightened. And about damn time. He'd spent too long trying to get her to open up. If she'd had a bad experience with a man, that'd explain much. "You're saying a past lover failed to satisfy you?"

Her face went hot. "No."

He'd never thought to see Ashley blush. "I refuse to believe it was your fault. Men have it easy when it comes to sex. For a woman it's more complicated." His voice dropped. "Pleasure isn't something that can be rushed or taken for granted."

"*Okay* . . . This is *way* out of hand. I'm not going to talk about this." She snatched up the menu and stared blankly at it.

"Come on, Ash, don't do that. Don't shut me out. And don't judge me by other men."

Through her teeth, and with her gaze still glued to the plastic menu, she growled, "I'm *not*."

He caught the edge of the menu and lowered it so he could see her face. Her cheeks were pink, her gaze elusive. "If other men haven't encouraged your dynamic personality, especially in bed, then they're fools."

She groaned, covered her face, but then spread her fingers to glare at him. "There weren't any other men."

He heard the words but they didn't make sense. "Excuse me?"

"Jesus, Quinton. Hello!" Her palms slapped the booth. "Catch on, will you? There are no past lovers. No bad experiences and no good experiences. None. Nada. I'm a . . ." Her voice dropped like a stone off a cliff. Another groan, and she went back to hiding behind her hands.

Shock had a stranglehold on his throat. "You're a . . ." He had as difficult a time saying it as she had. Finally he rasped, *"Virgin?"*

Her bravado burst to life right before him. Her head snapped up; her lip curled. "Yeah, so?" She actually jutted her chin toward him in defiance. "Don't say it like it's a dirty word."

Quinton stared back. A virgin? With her mouthy comebacks and lack of discretion? Impossible.

Yet . . . In an absurd way, it sort of made sense. "You're not ribbing me?"

"Horrible, huh?" Affecting an indolent attitude of unconcern, she slouched back. "I hear there's an isolated island somewhere that houses other oddities like me."

Doing his best to reconcile what he knew with what he'd just learned, he shook his head and stared some more.

She snapped her fingers in front of him. "Come alive, Quinton. Now'd be a good time for you to scramble out of here."

"Scramble out?" He wished for something more intelligent to say, but he couldn't manage it. He kept thinking of initiating her, being her first. That image obliterated everything else.

"Yeah. Virgins are scary things. What's the stereotype? Oh yeah. Prudish and pining for marriage. You better get while the getting's good."

She was making verbal mincemeat out of him, and he was letting her. He gathered his wits. "No one would ever call you prudish, and I assume if you wanted to be married, you would be."

The smugness of her grin raked along his nerves. "Haven't you made enough assumptions to last a lifetime?"

A coffeepot-wielding waitress saved him from having to answer that. She apologized for the delay, and Quinton pulled himself together enough to accept the coffee and quickly peruse the menu.

Without looking at him, Ashley did the same. They both agreed on the "special" of ham, eggs, hashbrowns and toast. By the time the waitress departed with their orders, Quinton had himself back in full command of his senses.

Ashley still acted antagonistic, but now he didn't mind. Things were starting to come together, at least in bits and pieces. He sipped at his coffee, watched her, and waited.

After several tense moments, she slapped her hand on the table and glared up at him. "Well? Let's have it."

"It?"

"You know you're just dying to laugh."

He slowly shook his head. "Oh no. Trust me, I'm a long way from humor. But I will tell you that you've sealed your fate."

Her expression darkened. "What's that supposed to mean?"

"I'll be your first." He gave in to a smile. "And honey, I can hardly wait."

Chapter 3

Idiot, idiot, idiot. Quinton had been hot on her heels before, but now he looked ready to stand up and beat his chest in a primitive claiming. His reaction wouldn't matter—if she didn't want him just as much.

But she did.

She'd never survive this.

Through several minutes of silence, she all but squirmed in her seat. Quinton kept scrutinizing her, as if seeing her through new eyes. Or maybe he'd never seen a virgin before. From what she could tell, they were in short supply, especially in her age group.

She felt . . . naked. She felt defensive. But she didn't want to be the first to crack.

The waitress brought their food and departed with a friendly but curious smile. Quinton dug in. After several bites, he nodded. "You're right. It's delicious."

Her breakfast could have been unseasoned oatmeal for all that she tasted.

He took his gaze off her long enough to glance around the interior of the diner. "Very quaint atmosphere." His green eyes were bright with an unspoken dare. "I like the old black-and-white photos of the area."

Ashley laid down her fork and put her hands together.

"I've never eaten in a place like this." He opened a small packet of apple butter and spread it on his toast. "I like it that you can introduce me to . . . new things."

His inexhaustible good humor wore her down. "Okay, I can't take it."

"Yes, you can." He washed down the last of his toast with a drink of coffee.

Her hands were shaking! Her hands never shook, except maybe with exhaustion, but that didn't apply right now. No, she shook because she was totally out of her element.

"I mean it, Quinton." She looked up—and got caught in his mesmerizing gaze. "You're going to have to stay away from me."

He didn't smile. "The hell I will."

Strange how her heartbeat started racing at his refusal. "Look, Quinton, I'm not what you expected. You said so yourself."

"You're who I want. That's all that matters."

How in the world could he want a twenty-seven-year-old virgin? A virgin who antagonized almost everyone to avoid relationships, a virgin from the wrong side of the tracks. A virgin who, until meeting Quinton, had intended to stay a virgin. "You're nuts."

"That'd be your fault. I was perfectly sane before meeting you. An overdose of unrequited desire is what's pushing me toward the loony bin." He turned his wrist to see his watch, then laid his napkin on his empty plate. "When will you have some free time again?"

So she could show him new things? She lifted her chin. "I don't know that I will."

He groaned as if in pain, then half laughed. "All right, let's add another notch toward insanity."

"Quinton . . ." she warned.

"We can play it your way. But the day after the wedding, all bets are off."

"Fine, whatever." What *was* she saying? Her stomach knotted even as her heart started racing again. "But you agreed to mind your manners till then, and I'm holding you to it." She needed some time to get used to the idea of opening herself to anyone other than her best friend, May.

"I'm a man of my word. Your little disclosure won't change that." He looked at her mouth. "Let's talk about something else."

Thank God. She needed to get his mind—and her own—on safer ground. "Like?"

"How is it you've never had sex?"

Well hell, his mind hadn't traveled far at all. "I've come close." Even to her own ears, she sounded aggressive.

"How close?"

Not very. She shrugged. "The typical, I guess." *Oh, how lame.* She picked up her coffee cup and started to sip.

"Has any man given you a climax?"

The cup nearly fell out of her hands. She quickly thunked it down to the counter. "You want a blow-by-blow report? Well, forget it. I'm not going to sit here in a restaurant and spell things out for you. Get your jollies somewhere else."

"If you want privacy for this discussion, we could sit in my car."

"Hell, no." In private the topic would take on new proportions, she didn't doubt.

His smile appeared again. "All right. Don't get in a snit."

Ashley narrowed her eyes. "Are you mocking me?"

This time he actually chuckled aloud. "I'm trying to understand you and the choices you've made. That's all."

"It wasn't exactly a choice. More like something that just happened and I decided I didn't care enough to change the situation."

He gave her a chastising look. "Men are easy, honey. A glance, a smile—and they're ready. Especially for someone as attractive as you. You're definitely a virgin by choice. I just want to know why."

"You want the nitty-gritty, huh? Fine." She wasn't the type who opened up easily, but with Quinton, she wanted to. "It's tough to get laid when I've never even had a boyfriend."

His surprise lasted one heartbeat. "Another deliberate choice, I'm sure."

"Actually, it wasn't. You see, my family was poor. Not poor as in, new shoes were hard to come by. Poor as in, we relied on the church and neighbors for clothes and food. Mom and Dad could have worked, but they didn't. And whenever they did get money, they blew it on things that in no way changed our circumstances."

"They couldn't find jobs?"

Ashley toyed with her coffee cup. She hadn't seen her folks in ages. Sadly, she didn't miss them at all. "They could've if they'd wanted them, but they enjoyed their leisure time too much. I mean, what's better than sitting on the couch all day with a cold beer, a cigarette, and the soaps?" She laughed, remembering how, even as a little kid, she'd known they weren't good people. "Dad had been a truck driver, but after he got laid off, he spent all his time bitching about the company instead of looking for new work. He wanted everyone to feel sorry for him."

"How long was he off work?"

"From the time I was ten until I skipped out at seventeen. After that I don't know. I haven't been back."

"You left your home at seventeen?"

"Yeah. I was a real crusader, out to prove something. I've forgotten what." But she didn't want to talk about that. The memories sucked big-time, and rehashing them wouldn't change a thing. "Trust me, leaving was the best decision I ever made."

He grew very solemn. "Then home must have been pretty tough."

She mustered a heavy dose of sarcasm. "Mostly it was an embarrassment. I had a self-proclaimed 'stay at home' mom, who was determined that I'd be different. I wasn't allowed to do . . . anything— but that was mostly because anything I might have done would have required her involvement. Our house was a dump. Our yard was a jungle, housing a bad septic system that could be seen and smelled for blocks. It seemed everyone who looked at me did so with pity."

"Jesus." He reached for her hand, but she didn't

want sympathy any more now than she had as a child.

She slid into the corner of the booth and affected a casual slouch. "Yeah, well obviously if I'd *had* any friends, which I didn't, I wouldn't have brought them home with me. I didn't like being at my house, so subjecting anyone else to it was out of the question."

"You had no friends at all?"

She didn't tell him that other kids had ridiculed her. "They didn't want me around, and I didn't want to be around them."

"I'm sorry."

Through a haze of remembered humiliation and learned aggression, she saw the compassion in Quinton's eyes. It made her stomach churn. She considered making a run for it, but that felt too cowardly.

Instead, she resorted to more sarcasm. Staring him straight in his sexy green eyes, totally deadpan, she said, "And then my dog died."

So much horror filled his gaze that she half laughed and took pity on him. "Ah, buck up, Buttercup. I was just funnin' you."

"Funning me?"

"I didn't have a dog, Quinton. In fact, I've never had any pet. One kid was more trouble than my parents wanted. No way in hell would they have put up with an animal too."

Irritation overrode his earlier emotions. "It's hardly a joking matter."

"You were getting all sappy on me. I thought you were about to cry."

He grumbled under his breath, which only made her chuckle again. "It wasn't all that bad, seriously.

I made friends with May, and when you meet her, you'll see that one friend like May is worth a million others."

"A friend is not the same as family."

But in this case it was. She shook her head, not about to share that thought aloud. "If you knew my family, you'd know that May is much, much better."

He still appeared disgruntled with her, but he let it go to say, "I look forward to making her acquaintance."

"So." She spread her arms out, then let her hands drop onto the table. "You wanted to know why I hadn't gotten involved with anyone. Now I've told you. End of story."

While thinking through what she had told him, he toyed with his coffee cup. "That had to have been eight or nine years ago."

"Ten. I'm twenty-seven now."

His gaze swept up to capture hers. "A long time to hang on to your virginity." His eyes narrowed. "Are you telling me that in all that time, not a single guy has interested you?"

"I've had a date here and there over the years. But other things took precedence."

"Like?"

Survival. She shook her head, not about to share that with him. "I keep telling you, I've been too busy—"

"So there you are."

At the sound of that cantankerous voice, Ashley jerked around and found Denny Zip looming over her.

She groaned. "Great. Just freaking great." As an

ex-military man, ex-fighter and trainer, and overall bossy forty-seven-year-old hard-ass, Denny made a most impressive sight with impeccable timing. His appearance kept her from saying something maudlin that would make her feel foolish.

Tall, muscular, and with an air of complete control, Denny turned heads in the diner. He wore a snug tan T-shirt and brown trousers. Through his thinning brown hair, a mean tattoo showed.

But for Ashley he was a pussycat. A pseudo father, big brother, and knight in shining armor all rolled into one. His best friend, Jude, was marrying her best friend, May. She supposed that accounted for Denny's weird loyalty and mile-wide protective streak toward her.

But then Denny's protectiveness went beyond her. Despite the rough exterior, he was a genuinely nice guy who wanted to take care of anyone smaller, weaker, younger, or older than he was. Ashley adored him, but she'd never told him so. He enjoyed their antagonistic banter too much for her to steal his fun.

"Excuse me?" Quinton rose out of his seat, his tone courteous but his expression suspicious, bordering on hostile.

Ashley didn't know if he intended to challenge Denny, which would be a mistake, or introduce himself.

Denny defused the motive, whatever it might be, by waving Quinton back down. "Save it, boy. It's too early for a pissing contest." And then to her, "Scoot over, girl. I have a bone to pick with you."

Scrambling fast so he didn't end up on her lap, Ashley said, "Gee, Denny, why don't you join us?"

"I intend to." He took her coffee cup and drained it, then, with covetous intent, stared toward her mostly full plate. "You going to eat that?"

She shoved it toward him. "Help yourself."

"Thanks. I'm starving but haven't had time to eat."

Quinton cleared his throat, reminding Ashley that money wasn't the only thing she lacked. Social niceties had never been her forte, either.

"Now where have my manners gone?" she asked.

Around a bite of cold eggs, Denny snorted. "Like you ever had any?" He tipped an imaginary hat toward Quinton. "I'm Denny, a good friend, so don't let her tell you otherwise."

Sweetly, Ashley said, "Now, Denny, what else would I ever call you?"

His robust laugh showed off a silver tooth before he gave his attention back to a befuddled Quinton. "She calls me a lot of things, but I know she doesn't mean any of them. It's her way of showing affection."

"So you two are . . . affectionate?"

Ashley rolled her eyes. "What are you doing here, Denny?"

Pointing at Ashley with the fork, he frowned. "When you didn't show up at your apartment, I started to worry." To Quinton he added, "Believe me, I can worry with the best of the old biddies. Luckily, I know the places Ash frequents, and her yellow Civic is easy to spot."

An affronted breath stuck in Ashley's throat. "I *knew* I was being followed."

Denny's interest in the food disappeared, and his teasing fell silent beneath thick menace. Expression volatile, he laid the fork beside the plate and swiveled to face her. "Someone's been following you?"

Damn, she had a big mouth. "You," Ashley reminded him with hope.

"No." Food forgotten, he swiped the paper napkin over his mouth and shoved the plate out of his way. "I was at your apartment this morning because it's possible Elton Pascal was spotted in the area."

Oh shit. Elton Pascal. Her skin crawled with the possibilities of that bomb-crazed maniac on the loose. "I figured that nutcase was long gone."

Quinton asked, "Who is this?"

They both ignored him. "I figured he was, too. With the Feds onto him, as well as state and local officials, a smart fellow would've hightailed it outta town. But we already know Elton's not the brightest bulb around."

Quinton looked between them. "Who's Elton?"

"God." Ashley dropped her forehead into her hands. "May must be frantic."

"May is safe in Jude's house, which is where you should be if you weren't such a stubborn cuss. Besides, she was mostly fretting about you. I promised to make sure you're okay. But I never followed you. By the time I got the news, you were already gone from work."

Elton Pascal. Ashley closed her eyes for only a second, then snapped them open again. "It's nothing, Denny."

"Bullshit." Denny's graying brows bunched down over shrewd eyes. "You said you were followed."

"Only because I thought *you* were following me. I didn't actually see anyone."

Tired of having his presence discounted, Quinton lost his temper. "I have no idea who this Elton

Pascal person is, but Ashley was a little jumpy when she got to work last night, and she told me then that she felt like someone had been tailing her."

Of all the nerve! The last thing she needed was someone to fuel Denny's mothering instinct. "Stay out of this, Quinton."

His glare plainly said *not on your life.* "By the time I got here this morning, Ashley was already inside. As you said, her Civic is easy to spot. I started in, but I noticed a car across the street just watching the diner. It was an ancient Buick, white but covered in rust and dirt. When I started to approach, it pulled away."

With each word Quinton spoke, Denny seemed to get bigger. Ashley figured it was the bulging of muscle that gave that impression.

The fury built in his scarred visage. *"Why didn't you call me?"*

Alarmed at the outburst, Quinton again started to stand. Ashley shook her head at him. Denny didn't scare her, but the rest of the folks in the diner were getting nervous.

"Calm down, King Kong. You're making the natives restless."

Denny peered around, scowling at one and all, until his gaze landed on Quinton. With a roll of his eyes—but in a quieter voice—he said, "I respect the intent, son, but she doesn't need protection from me." Then to Ashley, his tone moderated, "You damn well should have called me right away."

"Don't come in here bossing me around, Denny. You might be known for bullying fighters into shape, but I'm not that easy. And don't you dare go upsetting May with any of this. This is her time, and God knows she deserves it. If someone *is* following me, which I doubt, there'd be absolutely no reason to assume it's Elton. He doesn't even know me so—"

Suddenly Quinton snapped to attention. "I *knew* I recognized you. You're Denny Zip, DZ, the legendary trainer of the SBC."

The smoke settled around Denny, and he actually preened. "That's right. You're familiar with the sport?"

"What red-blooded man isn't?"

Denny went from ignoring Quinton to admiring him. "When you approached that car, what did you plan to do if he hadn't driven away?"

He shrugged. "Whatever I had to. Something about it didn't feel right, and with Ashley inside, I wasn't going to take chances."

New respect brought a smile to Denny's face. "You'll do."

Quinton gave a droll, "Thank you."

Ashley stared at the ceiling. She had a feeling that with Denny's stamp of approval, Quinton would be in her life whether she wanted him there or not.

Crossing his arms on the table and leaning in, Denny said, "Hey, do you realize you're dating—"

"We're not dating," Ashley clarified. Not yet, anyway. "We're only sharing one breakfast."

"The future sister-in-law to Jude Jamison?"

"Damn it, Denny." She had really wanted to keep that to herself for a while longer. As a movie star and celebrated cage fighter, Jude's name was well known.

"No shit." Quinton blinked at Ashley. "*That's* the wedding we're going to tomorrow?"

Ashley twisted her mouth in disgust. Men. In so

many ways they were all the same. They shared an admiration for cars, boobs, and brutal sports. "Jude's marrying my friend May, but May and I . . ." She tripped over the words, then finally spit them out. "We *aren't* sisters, so I won't be Jude's sister-in-law."

Denny blustered a moment, his expression odd. "Yeah, well . . ." With palpable discomfort, he insisted, "You're just like sisters, anyway."

What they had was better than a blood bond, and that was what mattered most. Ashley nodded. "You've got me there."

Quinton again glanced at his watch. "I'm sorry, but I'll need to get going soon or I'll be late." He, too, leaned in to speak privately. "Can you quickly explain to me what's going on? Who's Elton Pascal and why would he bother Ashley?"

Denny gave a furtive glance around before divulging the details. "You know Jude was accused of murdering that young starlet?"

"I read about it, yes, but he was acquitted some time ago."

"Damn right he was, because Jude would never hurt a woman." Just talking about the accusation had Denny bristling with fury all over again. "Elton Pascal is the murderous bastard who killed both her and Jude's driver at the same time. The sick fuck has an affinity for homemade bombs."

Ashley reached for Denny's hand and gave it a squeeze. He could not be dispassionate when it came to this topic.

Denny calmed, saying in a more controlled tone, "Elton hates Jude and anyone who knows Jude. He had some of his goons work over May's brother, Tim, who I reckon you'll meet at the wedding."

"Lucky you," Ashley said.

Denny slanted her a look. "Tim's working on changing, girl, so cut him some slack."

Not likely. She didn't tell Denny that the last few times she'd seen Tim, he'd come on to her, and it really creeped her out. He was such a weasel. But again, for May, she tolerated him.

"Anyway," Denny continued, "Elton had thought to use Tim to get to Jude, but his plans backfired. They caught one of Elton's henchmen, who spilled his guts on Elton's involvement in the bombing, and now the cops from Hollywood, where it happened, the local police, and the ATF all want him for questioning."

"This is unbelievable," Quinton muttered, watching Ashley with growing concern.

"They should have had Elton by now, but he's disappeared, and it seems no one can find him. Until he's behind bars, our little hedgehog here needs to show more caution."

Ashley tried to slug Denny in the shoulder, but with hardly any movement at all, he dodged the blow and she ended up sprawled over his lap.

"Easy, now." Grinning like a loon, he dragged her upright again. "Was it the hedgehog remark?"

Mortified, she shrugged off his hands, smoothed her hair out of her face, and reseated herself. "Listen up, Gramps—"

He laughed, then pulled her into a bear hug that squeezed all the breath out of her lungs. In the next second, with Ashley still snuggled up to his side, his gaze pinned Quinton to the spot. "Ashley recognized Elton having dinner here in town. She called Jude, and like dominoes, it all fell apart for him."

"So I know how to use a phone," Ashley murmured. "You might as well call me Superwoman."

Quinton still watched her, now with purpose as well as amazement.

Denny put his elbows on the table and leaned in. "So. What's up between you two?"

It needed only this. "Back off, Denny." Again she took her own seat.

"I'm just lookin' out for you. For all you know, Elton could have hired him."

Such an active imagination. "Since he's as rich as Elton, that's not likely."

"Really?" Denny sized up Quinton in a long perusal. "What business are you in?"

"Consulting."

"On what?"

"Everything. I show businesses how to make more money by cutting out unnecessary expenses, maximizing for efficient human capital composition, and at the same time providing better benefits to employees."

Denny blinked. "Helluva mouthful."

"I've rehearsed it." Quinton's lazy smile showed loads of confidence. "Basically it means that my employees help clients to determine problem areas through employee interviews, computer analysis and projection, competitor comparisons, market research, and historical trend research."

"And you own this business?"

"With my uncle, but I'm the CEO and major stockholder. We have a couple hundred employees and multiple locations." With satisfaction, he added, "And I'm not working for Elton."

Denny's fingers tapped on the tabletop. "I might do a background check anyway."

Ashley groaned.

Quinton merely stared him down. "I might do the same." His eyes narrowed in what Ashley now recognized as determination. "For a mere friend, you're awfully involved in her welfare."

Denny's jaw tightened. "Now don't go speculating on things, boy. I won't like it."

"And I don't like being threatened."

Both men rose from their seats, but damn it, Ashley didn't want Quinton mauled before she could enjoy him.

She elbowed Denny in the ribs. "Don't even think it." He was so involved in his intimidation tactics that she caught him off guard and he stumbled.

"Brat," Denny complained, rubbing where her pointed elbow had landed.

"Bully," she countered right back.

Quinton looked from one to the other before coming to some private conclusion. "All right, children, play nice."

Denny huffed at him, but Quinton extended his hand as an olive branch. "I like Ashley," he admitted, and even though she'd already heard it, Ashley's heart fluttered. "I've asked her out but she keeps turning me down."

Denny took his hand. "Yep, that's our Ashley. Stubborn to the bone."

"I finally managed to finagle an invitation to the wedding as her escort, but I had no idea it was Jude Jamison's wedding. I'll understand if the security is tight and you'd rather no strangers be there."

Odd, how the idea that he might not accompany her deflated Ashley. She didn't want to go alone. "Denny," she said with cool insistence, "tell him that it's fine."

Denny grudgingly did just that. "If she vouches for you, then I'm sure you're okay. Ashley's no dummy. Just pigheaded and prickly and strong enough to carry around a mighty big chip on her shoulder."

"I noticed." Quinton turned to her while digging a business card out of his pocket. "Here's my number. Call anytime, okay?"

"I'll be busy."

He gave a sigh of annoyance. "Come on, Ash, you've worn that line out. How busy can one woman be?"

Denny opened his mouth, but Ashley slapped her hand over it. "Busy enough, okay?"

Quinton quirked a brow. "More secrets, huh?"

Denny, with his mouth still covered, managed a shrug.

Left-handed, Ashley tucked the card away in her back pocket. "Don't push your luck, Murphy."

Openly pleased with the exchange, Denny pried her hand away and said, "Don't worry. I'll see that she gets home safely."

Ashley's jaw dropped. He had to be kidding. She'd be on a busy road, headed to her busy apartment complex. No way would Elton try something out in the open. "I don't need—"

"Thank you." Quinton returned her feral expression with one of his own. "I agreed to your terms, now agree to mine."

Relationships sure were troublesome. She waved a hand at him. "Let's hear it."

"Promise you'll call me if anything even remotely suspicious happens or if anything spooks you."

Denny took exception to that. "She can call me."

In a magnanimous concession, Quinton nodded. "If you can't reach me, by all means, call Denny."

"Or Jude," Denny added.

"Call *someone*—but me first. Promise me, Ashley."

Denny started to object, and Ashley put the back of her hand to her forehead. "First no men, now two are fighting over me. How dramatic."

Quinton leaned across the table, caught her shoulders, and pulled her up. Ashley thought he was about to curl her toes again, but he only put an affectionate peck on her forehead. "Promise?"

"Yeah, sure. I'll put you on speed dial."

"Thank you." He kissed her once more. "Be very careful, and we'll talk soon."

With that, he left.

Slowly, Ashley sank back in her seat. "I need some ice water."

"All that growling give you a dry throat?"

"No. I think I have a fever."

Denny eyed her while switching over to Quinton's side of the booth. "So you like your new beau, huh?"

"He's not a beau."

"I think he'd tell it differently." Denny signaled the waitress in a request for coffee.

She hustled over, her smile too bright, her eyes dreamy. After she'd produced another cup and filled it, Denny thanked her with more affection than necessary, and she floated away on a sigh.

Another woman smitten. Amazing. Denny made the whole woman/man game look so easy. If only she didn't struggle so badly with it. "For an ornery old codger, you sure rack up the babes."

"It's my charm."

"It's something, all right." Ashley considered him, then asked, "So what about Zara?"

"What about her?"

"You still seeing her?"

"Here and there. She won't be at the wedding, if you're worried about Quinton running into her."

That made her laugh. "After seeing her with you, I haven't given it another thought. I figured you'd ruined her for all other men."

"I'm sure you're right."

Grinning, Ashley glanced at the clock on the wall. "I wonder where he's going so early."

"Who? Quinton?"

"He's dressed all casual when he usually wears suits, and it's too early for him to be going to the office."

"Want me to find out?" When she just stared at him, Denny said, "Well, I can, you know."

"Don't even think about actually checking up on him." Her order didn't faze Denny one bit. "I mean it, old man. He's driving me nuts, but—"

"He's bothering you?" And then in a growl, "Maybe I don't like him after all."

"Oh God, don't start cracking your knuckles. It's not like that." Quinton was a handful all on his own. She didn't need to juggle Denny now, too.

"Then how is it?"

"You've got gonads. Put it together."

"Ah." Denny's ears actually lifted, he smiled so big. "He's bothering you *that* way. I get it."

In that moment Denny seemed like a damn fine confidante. She didn't have anyone else to talk to except May, and May had an upcoming wedding to deal with. She was euphoric, and Ashley didn't want to bring her down with her petty concerns. "If you stop grinning like the village idiot, I'd like to get your thoughts on this mess."

"Mess?"

"Exactly." She propped her head in both hands. "Before meeting Quinton, I liked my life just fine."

"No, you didn't. You just accepted it."

Because she'd never envisioned anything different. "Maybe."

"So what's the problem? Quinton putting a kink in the works?"

"In a big way. Since meeting him, I feel half sick most of the time. I can't get him off my mind, which means I'm falling behind at work, and I can't study worth a damn, and—"

Very matter-of-factly, Denny said, "Hey, if you're feeling froggy, leap. It'll solve your problems, and then some."

Such a down-to-earth way of looking at all things sexual boggled her mind. "You think sex is a regular cure-all, huh?"

He saluted her with the coffee cup. "I guarantee it'll cure what ails you."

"Maybe, but it's not that simple."

"Seems simple enough to me. You're a grown, intelligent, independent woman."

"Well, hallelujah, you've finally admitted it."

"And he seems like a responsible guy." Denny shrugged. "Go for it."

"It'll complicate things."

"Baloney." He rubbed his jaw, scrutinizing her. "You're not an inhibited girl. You obviously want the man. I'm surprised you haven't used him up already."

"Do I look like a hoochie or something?"

He ignored that to ask, "What's really going on here, Ashley? Why all the hesitation?"

"We're as different as night and day."

"Since you're like the Tasmanian devil in neon, *no one* is like you. You might as well get used to it and not let it stand in the way of some fun."

Ashley wrinkled her nose at him. "That's not what I mean, smart-ass. He's filthy rich. Socially affluent. And so damned cultured."

"Ah. He scares you."

"Get outta here." Actually, it was her reaction to him that left her frightened.

Denny's gaze, filled with understanding, settled on her face. "You know, you don't have to be a hard case all the time. Everyone is entitled to be a chickenshit every now and then."

"Including you?"

"Sure." He fashioned a lofty look. "I'm secure enough to admit to my weaknesses."

Clutching her chest in melodrama, Ashley gasped. "You have weaknesses, Denny? Say it isn't so."

"I do." He nodded toward her. "And you're one of them."

Her heart expanded. She wasn't used to anyone being so open in his feelings. "If that's your excuse for bossing me around, you can forget it."

He flashed his silver-toothed grin. "As to differences, look at May and Jude. She didn't let a little thing like Jude being a wealthy, well-known fighter and movie star get in her way."

May had never let the opinions of others get in her way of being Ashley's friend, either. But in so many ways, May was stronger. "I'm not looking to marry the man, Denny."

"Start at step one and go from there."

Step one. She wrinkled her nose. "The thing is . . . I told him to keep his hands to himself until after the wedding."

One bushy brow lifted. "He'll need his hands to make you happy, girl."

Ashley shook her head at him. "God, Denny, you are so . . ."

"Earthy?"

"I was going to say full of it." She softened that insult with a smile but quickly grew serious again. "I've never talked about this stuff with anyone before."

"I'm honored." He reached for her hands and held them in his meaty fists. "I mean that. You're too much of a loner."

"Let's not turn this into a chick-flick moment, okay?"

He shook his head at her. "I know your daddy wasn't there for you when you needed him. Your mom, either. May has told me some things—"

"May's a snitch." But May had already spoken to Ashley about it, warning her that she'd shared some of their childhood with Denny and Jude. She didn't begrudge May that openness with her new family, but it still embarrassed her to think of anyone having intimate details of her very failed childhood.

"May loves you, and she figured if I understood you, I might not strangle you."

"As if." It was an odd feeling, but Ashley knew Denny cared for her. With no ulterior motives. Without coercion. And without pity. He had no blood tie to her, but he treated her more like a daughter than the people who'd raised her ever had. "Thanks, Denny. Really. I appreciate the advice."

"But?"

"I've been on my own an awfully long time." Not since she'd left home had she worried about making time for anyone other than May.

"Hey, even ballbusters have to take a day off every once in a while." His crooked smile encouraged her. "I'd like to see you happy, so go for it."

"But what if I do this, if I . . . let him in, and then he makes me unhappy?"

Denny mouth curled in a wicked grin—and he cracked his knuckles.

Chapter 4

He heard the whistling and knew it was Ashley. His uncle was in the middle of a diatribe about keeping up appearances, but Quinton didn't care. He strode out from behind his desk, leaving his uncle to gape at him, and opened his office door.

And there she stood. She didn't look up; the headphones on her ears kept her oblivious to his scrutiny. Tonight she wore her rich brown hair braided down her back. A double layering of teal and navy tank tops topped a long colorful gypsy skirt with bells sewn in at the waistband. Flat flip-flops finished the outfit.

Quinton found himself smiling. God, she was so adorable.

As she pushed the noisy vacuum along the hallway, her hips sashayed in time to the music, and he could barely detect the tinkling of the tiny bells on her skirt. He propped a shoulder against the door frame and watched her, waiting for her to get close enough to notice him.

She wouldn't expect to see him, but this time he had a legitimate reason for staying over. His uncle joined him in the doorway. "What are you—" He spotted Ashley and stared. "Who in the world is that?"

"An employee for the building. She cleans during night shift."

"She dresses like that to clean?"

"From what I've been able to deduce, she dresses any way that piques her fancy." Still grinning, Quinton looked over his shoulder at his uncle. "And she likes color."

"So I see."

Ashley started to sing along with the music, and Quinton laughed. She had a terrible voice, but she exhibited a lot of enthusiasm.

"Good God. Please don't tell me she interests you."

Quinton's humor disappeared. "She does, and I trust you'll keep your opinions on the matter to yourself."

"But she's—"

Quinton tuned him out. Ashley had just caught sight of them and she went mute. In very precise movements, she yanked off the headphones, turned off the vacuum, and slowly stomped toward him. The jingling of bells accompanied her every step.

When she was practically nose to nose with him, she stopped. "What," she demanded, "do you think you're doing?"

"Watching you dance." His mouth twitched with humor. "And listening to you sing."

Her eyes narrowed. "I won't blush."

Very softly, still amused, he said, "I know."

"You should have been gone already. The floor should be empty."

He held out his arms. "And yet, here I am." He grinned. "But acquit me of plotting. It just so happens I had legitimate business tonight that kept me over."

Her eyes slanted toward his uncle, and with a tip of her head in his direction, she asked, "Who's this?"

"Warren Murphy, my uncle." Quinton put his arm around her waist. "Uncle, this is Ashley Miles."

Ashley thrust out her hand. "How's it going?"

It infuriated Quinton that his uncle stared at her hand a moment before taking it. "It's going . . . well. Thank you. And how are you?"

"Behind schedule, actually—which is your nephew's fault."

"How am I to blame?" Quinton asked.

"I got almost no sleep, thanks to you."

Warren puckered up. "I'm sure I don't need to hear details. If you'll both excuse me . . ."

Ashley *did* blush then—but with annoyance, not embarrassment. "Oh, no, hey, get your mind out of the gutter. I didn't mean . . . that is, we had breakfast. After I finished my shift last night. Or rather this morning. But then I had classes so I didn't get much of a nap in between . . ." She halted in mid-sentence. "There wasn't any hanky-panky going on."

Because Warren looked more discomfited by the moment, Quinton pulled Ashley closer and said, "You might as well head on home, Uncle. I'd like to talk to Ashley for a few minutes."

"We have more to discuss."

"No, we don't. I told you I'm not interested."

Ashley tried to ease away, but he clamped her a little tighter. Forcing a smile, he said, "Tell Aunt Ivana I appreciate the invite, but I'll be otherwise engaged."

"She expects you there."

"She'll survive the disappointment."

Warren aimed a glare of exasperation toward Ashley.

She crossed her arms and started tapping her foot. With a too sugary smile, she said, "Quinton resembles you a lot, especially when he's in a snit like that."

Warren stiffened.

"But you're wasting that look on me. I'd be out of here if Quinton would turn me loose. He's the one keeping me here, so if you want privacy, you should be killing him with your glares, not me."

"She doesn't intimidate easily," Quinton told his uncle, who responded by giving them *both* a nasty look before disappearing back in the office.

"Ouch." Ashley clutched her stomach. "I think that last one was fatal."

Staring down at her hand, knotted just beneath her navel, Quinton said, "Hmmm. Want me to kiss it and make it better?"

She ducked out from under his arm. Bells jingled and Ashley laughed. "No." Her lashes swept down to hide her eyes. "At least, not here and not now."

Quinton went still, a dozen lascivious images flashing through his brain. He took a step toward Ashley—and his uncle reappeared, briefcase in hand.

"You're making a big mistake," Warren said one more time. "It'd be beneficial to all of us."

"I don't need those kinds of benefits."

"You are so damned stubborn."

Quinton saluted him. "A family trait, or so I'm told."

Warren visibly gave up. Good manners dictated that he nod in Ashley's direction, and a minute later, he was on the elevator and the doors had closed.

"Wow," Ashley said. "Look at the steam he left behind. What'd you do to make him so mad?"

"My aunt wants to play matchmaker. But I have a wedding to go to."

Predictably enough, Ashley went stiff as a poker. "Well, hey, don't let me stand in your way. By all means, make Auntie happy."

"I don't want to." He reached out to trail his fingers over her shoulder, down to her wrist. He captured her hand and tugged her forward. "I told you, you're the only woman I'm thinking about." Backstepping, Quinton drew her into his office.

"Your uncle doesn't like me."

"He doesn't know you. Don't worry about him." He nudged the door shut, then trapped her against it. "Now." He flattened a hand on either side of her head. "Let's talk about the wedding."

"The wedding? Really?" She started breathing a little faster. "What about it?"

Bending his elbows brought him in closer until only an inch separated them. "I still need some details." He brushed a featherlight kiss against her temple. "What time should I pick you up?"

"Is one o'clock okay? The wedding doesn't start until five, but May wants me there—"

He shushed her with a soft, lingering smooch.

"One is fine." While kissing a path to her throat, he said, "Jamison lives in Stillbrooke?"

"Yes." She tilted her head and closed her eyes. "It . . . it takes only about fifteen minutes to get there from my apartment."

"I'm going to need your address." He drew the soft flesh where her shoulder met her throat against his teeth, and she moaned.

"I don't know."

"You don't know what?"

"Where I live. I can't think when you're doing that."

"Can you think when I do this?" Holding her gaze with his, he pressed his hips inward until his fly nudged between her thighs.

"No." She grabbed his neck and smashed her mouth against his.

Chuckling, Quinton trailed one hand down her back to her bottom. Despite her protests to the contrary, she had a great body, all lean and tone but soft. Against her lips, he whispered, "Damn, you feel good."

"You do, too." She flexed her fingers into his shoulders, down to his chest. "Real good."

"Open your lips a little for me." As soon as she did, he teased with his tongue, being careful not to go too fast or too far.

She didn't show the same reserve. Just as he'd suspected, she took what she wanted. She sucked his tongue in deeper, then groaned and went on her tiptoes to better align their bodies.

He wanted to touch her everywhere, and doing so in his office assured that things wouldn't get out of hand, as per their agreement.

He paid very close attention to her every reaction, no matter how subtle, so he felt her stiffening as he brought his hand up her side, toward her breast. Anticipation? He certainly felt it. At that moment he wanted to explore her breasts more than anything.

But still he went slow, caressing her waist, tracing each rib, all the while kissing her, feasting off her mouth. And still, when he'd just curved his fingers over her breast, she pushed away.

The sudden distance rocked him. They stared at each other, both breathing deeply, she wary, he confused. He saw the excitement in her rosy, swollen lips, her dazed eyes, yet she'd stopped him. She looked incredible and hot and he didn't understand her sudden retreat.

Laboring for breath, he waited to see what she'd do. Her gaze took a quick trip over his body, then shot back to his groin, where she stared.

"What's wrong?"

She shook her head, then licked her lips. Her hand lifted toward him, as if reaching for his erection, and he held his breath. But then she dropped her hand back to her side and said, "I don't have any boobs."

"What?"

Fingers spread wide, her hands covered her chest, one over each breast. "Your fingers went wandering, but I don't have much here to tempt you."

One big step had him close enough to grip her shoulders. "That's nonsense, Ashley. You tempt me so damn much I'm a hair away from exploding."

She looked up into his eyes, still a little foggy.

"It's why I have an erection, damn it. I kiss you, and it's as effective as foreplay."

As if instructing him, her voice flat, she said, "Men like women who are busty."

"I like *you*." She still had her hands over herself, and it was making him nuts. "Every part of you."

Her gaze dipped to his mouth, and she leaned forward to give him an ultrasoft, lingering peck. Relieved, he thought they were back on track—until she smiled at him. "Thanks, but I'd rather you leave that part of me alone."

Quinton hesitated, trying to settle on how to proceed. Then he decided, to hell with it. He'd give her the truth and she could deal with it.

"That's not going to happen."

"What isn't?"

He cupped her face and kissed her quick and hard. "We're going to make love, and when we do, we'll both be naked and you can damn well be assured I'll look at, touch, and taste every part of you. No way in hell will I leave your breasts alone."

She tucked in her chin. "Taste?"

"Every. Part."

"Oh." She blinked fast, then quirked her mouth to one side. "That sounds . . ." She cleared her throat. "Well, for now, I'd rather you didn't. If I was built like May . . . That girl is stacked. But me . . . No, I'd rather wait before you start doing . . . any of that stuff. Touching or tasting. Or even looking."

She said so many things at one time, Quinton nearly got lost. "If you don't want me looking, then you should wear a bra."

"What for? I'm barely an A-cup. Sometimes A-cups are too big. Bras just get in my way. They're uncomfortable. I don't need a bra."

Quinton stared at her. How was it they kept ending up in the strangest discussions? "I can see your nipples, Ashley."

She snorted. "You can not." Then she looked down, realized her nipples were tightly puckered, pressing against the tank tops, and she slapped her hands over herself again. "That's your fault!"

"I know." God, but he enjoyed talking with her, even when the subject was absurd. He nodded at her breasts. "They want me to touch them."

Her mouth opened, then closed again and she laughed. "They do, huh? Well, I'm running this ship, not my unruly hormones, and I say no touching right now."

"All right." He snuggled her closer to kiss her cheek. "I'll wait. But not for too long."

"Okay then." Hands still cupping herself, she walked around him to his desk. Keeping her back to him, she tore a sheet of paper off a note pad and picked up his gold pen to do some fast writing. When she faced him again, she had one arm shielding herself. "Here's my address."

"Thank you."

She hesitated. "I need to get back to work, but . . ."

"Yes?"

"The stupid dress I have to wear."

"What about it?"

"May picked it out. I didn't. The thing is, it's made for someone like her, not someone like me."

After indulging a few odd conversations with her, he finally felt qualified to decipher her meanings. "For someone with a larger bust?"

"Yeah. It sort of goes along with her wedding gown. But it looks pretty lame on me."

"I'm sure you'll be beautiful."

She rolled her eyes. "You are *so* doomed for disappointment if you believe that. I just wanted to warn you." She started to head out of his office.

"Ashley?"

"Hmmm?" She looked over her shoulder at him.

"If you really dislike the dress so much, why didn't you just tell May?"

"Because she loved the design, and I didn't want to disappoint her."

"You say she's a good friend, so I'm sure she would have understood."

Ashley stared at him for a long moment, then shrugged. "One time, I think it was eighth grade, a class bully kept ridiculing me. He called me Patches, and Pigpen, and no matter how I tried to ignore him, he wouldn't stop. I was close to losing it. I mean, I was this close"—she held up a finger and thumb, a half inch apart—"to crying. And I'd have rather died than cry in front of him."

Something clenched in Quinton's chest, causing a pain he'd never felt before. Ashley was so brash, so seemingly confident in all situations, that he hated to think of her as a young needy girl, tormented by a bully.

"I hope you kicked him in the crotch."

She smiled and shook her head. "No. I didn't even need to. May jumped him."

"She chewed him out?"

"No, I mean she literally leaped onto his back like a monkey. She knotted her hands in his hair and damn near yanked him bald. They both fell to the ground and he got a broken wrist. By the time the teacher pulled May off him, he was the one in tears."

Quinton saw so much emotion in her eyes. He

hadn't yet met May, but he already liked her. A lot. "I'm glad she showed him the error of his ways."

"Yeah. May did that a lot, came to my defense and protected me, until I toughened up enough to defend myself. It was funny when she did it, because May has always been a very proper woman. She never curses or causes a scene. But for me, she'd do whatever it took. She's the most loyal person I know. I'd end up laughing, and she'd start laughing, and I've loved her *more* than a sister ever since."

And so she'd wear a dress she didn't like, a dress that made her uncomfortable, because in some small way, May had saved her back then. "I see."

"I figured you would." She shook off the excess sentiment and returned to her old self. "So no ogling me in the damn dress, and if you dare to laugh, I'll brain you."

"A warning I'll take to heart, I promise." Where Ashley was concerned, he took everything to heart. From that first time of meeting her, her impact was like the kick of a mule—always in his heart.

"Good." She gave a sharp nod. "Now get a move on. I need you to go home so I can get back to work without you bothering me."

Pleased that he *could* bother her, Quinton smiled. "All right." He picked up the papers he needed from his desk, turned out the lights, and followed Ashley out the door.

She walked him to the elevator and waited beside him until the doors opened and he'd stepped inside. Catching his tie, she pulled him down and gave him a sweet kiss. "Bye."

He brushed his knuckles over her cheek. "I'm looking forward to tomorrow."

She stepped out of the elevator. "Quinton, just so you know. I think I changed my mind."

Alarms bells rang out in his head. "About what?"

As the doors started to close, she tipped her head and smiled. "About waiting. I think the sooner we resolve these crazy sexual urges, the sooner I'll be able to regain some sanity."

"You mean—"

"Yeah. Let's go to your place after the reception. My place is the pits."

The doors shut before he could say anything more. He yanked out his cell phone, but in the elevator he didn't have any reception. When he finally reached the parking level, he dialed again, and Ashley answered on the first ring.

"If you get me fired—"

"That was mean-spirited timing. I hope you know I won't be able to sleep tonight."

"Good. Neither will I."

"But you'll be working."

"And thinking of you." She gave a long, exaggerated sigh. "You know, Murphy, I really hope you're worth all this trouble."

She hung up on him, and Quinton started laughing. A man of lesser ego would feel pressured by her expectations on performance, but he had enough experience to know they'd be good together. He just needed to get her over the hang-up on her breasts—which he thought were perfect.

Thinking of her and the coming wedding, reception, and following night, he smiled all through the parking lot—until he reached his Porsche. He must have run over broken glass and not realized it because both tires on the driver's side were flat. But deflated tires couldn't ruin his good mood.

Settling against the fender, he called for a cab. In the morning he'd have the car repaired. He could have gone back inside, but he truly didn't want to interfere with Ashley's work. He'd have her to himself soon enough.

With that in mind, a few flat tires were nothing more than a mere inconvenience.

Ashley paced her living room, alternately stewing and anxiously checking her watch. When the doorbell finally rang, she leaped forward and yanked the door open.

Quinton stood there in a very fine dark suit and tie with a snowy white shirt. Ashley looked him over, struck by how his presence made her feel as if the sun shone down on her head. She grabbed him around the neck, pulled him down, and kissed him silly. It was a ticklish kiss because Quinton kept smiling. His big hands settled on her waist and he lifted her enough that he could walk them both through the doorway.

She heard the door click shut, felt her back press against the wall, and Quinton had both hands on her bottom, lifting her up so that she just naturally wrapped her legs around his waist.

"Jesus, honey . . ." Groaning, he put his forehead to hers; then, as if he couldn't help himself, he took her mouth again. His tongue slid in, tasting her deeply, caressing her. He readjusted for the best fit, kissing her once again, before whispering around a ragged breath, "This is nuts."

"I know." She wanted to go on kissing him, but Quinton put his chin to the top of her head.

"You're not dressed, Ashley."

His throat looked so appealing that she took a small taste of him—and wanted more. "I'm supposed to do all that at Jude's." She tightened her legs and nipped at his chin. "He's got a whole blasted staff waiting to work me over and make me presentable."

"Staff?" Quinton tilted her back to see her face.

"Yeah. Make-up artist, hair stylist, manicurist, and so on and so on." She wrinkled her nose. "That's why I'm scrubbed clean with no makeup. I don't think Jude and May trusted me to do it right."

"No, I'm sure that's not it. You always look lovely. More likely, it's a treat, a way to thank you for taking part in their special day. It's not uncommon for the females in a wedding party."

Impressed, Ashley asked, "Do you just know everything about everything?"

"I don't know enough about you." Without straining, he balanced her against him with one hand curved under her bottom, and with the other, he smoothed her hair. "Will your parents be at the wedding? I'd like to meet them."

How naïve. She shook her head and said, "I don't have parents."

He gave her an indulgent look. "Nature decrees otherwise."

"Maybe once long ago I did. But I divorced myself from mine, remember? Far as I'm concerned, they've ceased to exist."

He appeared troubled by her sentiments, so she teased him, saying, "Besides, you wouldn't want to meet them. Trust me on this. Meeting May's parents will be enough of a trial."

"Why? What's wrong with her parents?"

Using one finger, she made a loop-de-loop in

the air. "They're insane. Not just a little goofy, but full-blown nuts. May's brother, Tim, is their golden child, the heir apparent who can do no wrong, regardless of the fact he's a weasel. Her mom's a mean, depressed drunk and a chain smoker. Her dad's a sleaze and a habitual cheater. And May is keeper of the loony bin, the one they all rely on to make sure they don't destroy themselves."

"Was she poor, like you?"

"No way. May's family owns a car dealership and they've always managed to stay afloat, despite a lot of extravagances, mostly thanks to May." Ashley ran her palm along his jaw. He'd shaved recently and his skin was smooth and warm. "Did I tell you that May owns an art gallery? That's how she and Jude met. They share a love for art. After their honeymoon, they're going to do some major traveling around the world, promoting the SBC now that Jude's bought into it as more than a fighter. May hopes to make some contacts with other artists and maybe pick up a few new pieces."

He put a tiny peck to the bridge of her nose. "You have very fascinating friends."

"Yeah. I'm going to miss them. But Denny will still be around. And speaking of Denny . . . Which of you ordered Flint to escort me to my car when I finished my shift?"

Rather than answer, Quinton softly kissed her cheekbone, her jaw, the corner of her mouth. He ran his tongue along her bottom lip before nibbling, and finally pressed his mouth firmly against hers.

As usual, Ashley melted. He tasted good and smelled even better and the careful, loving way he touched her made her stomach flutter.

"I did."

The soft admission broke the sensual spell. "Hey, you can't—" His mouth closed over hers again, smothering her rebuke. It was a rotten, macho-inspired tactic, and still she allowed herself to relax in his arms. She even went so far as to kiss him back.

But the second he lifted his head, she said, "Don't try to take over my life, Quinton. I mean it."

"I want you safe."

"And you think I don't?"

That bemused him. "I don't know. I didn't mean—"

"Let me tell you something. Elton Pascal is a certifiable maniac. A murderer, a villain, a conscience-less bastard. He's not only killed people, he beat May's brother to a pulp. And he threatened to get May and anyone else important to Jude. Trust me, I want nothing to do with him." Except that she did want to see him behind bars, where he couldn't further threaten May or the family May loved so much.

"Glad to hear it, but I didn't mean—"

"Did you know that he fancied himself in love with the woman he murdered? But the poor girl was infatuated with Jude, so Elton blew her up, along with Jude's driver, and deliberately framed Jude. When Jude managed a 'not guilty' verdict, Elton started dogging him, doing everything he could to make Jude miserable. That's how he ended up in Ohio. He pegged Tim for a pawn right away."

"I suppose he knew Tim was May's brother?"

"Yeah, and even though May didn't realize it, everyone else knew Jude wanted her. Elton made it easy for Tim to borrow fifty thousand dollars from him."

Quinton whistled.

"Right. And when Tim couldn't pay it back, Elton gave him the option of killing Jude for him, to even the debt."

"Jesus." Quinton looked more alarmed than ever. "Tim agreed to that?"

She shrugged. "It took a sound beating to motivate Tim to Elton's way of thinking." It amazed Ashley that Quinton made no move to set her down. He held her as if she weighed nothing, as if he enjoyed chatting with her in just such a position. "But Elton hadn't counted on the fact that Tim would go crying straight to May."

"Because Tim expects May to fix all his problems?"

"Yep. And May, not being a dummy, went straight to Jude."

Quinton broke into a grin. "I can only imagine how Jamison took it."

"I think he used it as an opportunity to get closer to May."

"That's what I would have done. But he would have wanted to protect her anyway."

"Of course."

"The way I want to protect you."

"You just ran that one full circle, didn't you?" He gave her an unashamed grin—which Ashley returned. "Well, genius, so did I. You see, I saw Elton's handiwork firsthand after he'd pulverized Tim. Trust me, I'm aware of just how ruthless he can be, which is why I went to Flint to ask him to walk me out."

"You did?"

"I keep telling you I'm not a dummy. I figured as night guard, Flint might as well earn his pay. But

that's when he told me he was going to see me to
my car anyway. He just wouldn't say why, or who
put him up to it."

To defuse her annoyance, Quinton brushed his
thumb over her cheek. "I'm glad you're being cautious."

"Why would you assume I wouldn't be? I don't
have a death wish. You have to trust me to take
care of myself, all right?"

He shrugged. "I'll promise to try, but that's the
best I can do."

"Quinton . . ."

His hand opened on the side of her face, and
his tone became guttural with some unnamed
emotion. "I can't bear the thought of anything
happening to you."

Wow. He looked . . . really serious and sincere,
and that was so far beyond what she was accustomed to, it unnerved her. Without even meaning
to, she resorted to the ingrained defenses of a
credible laugh and a hint of sarcasm.

"If that's how you feel, then maybe you better
put me down before your suit gets wrinkled and
we end up late to the show. Jude will strangle me
for sure if I mess up the big day. I've never seen a
man so anxious to get legal with a woman."

For the longest time Quinton looked at her, *into*
her, as if searching her soul. "Did I thank you for
the enthusiastic greeting?"

"No. But you have held me this whole time."

He nodded. "I like it." And with that, he cradled
her in close for a tender hug, kissed her ear, and
let her legs slide down to the floor.

A little wobbly in the knees, Ashley avoided his
gaze and scuttled out of his reach. The man was

just too potent for her own good. She gathered up her purse, slid her feet into flip-flops, and went out the door without a word.

This would be the longest day of her life.

But she had high hopes that the night would be worth the wait.

Chapter 5

Quinton stayed alert as he escorted Ashley to his Bentley at the curb in front of her apartment. After the garage told him that someone had deliberately slashed his tires, he'd made up his mind to hire protection for her.

Given her reaction to Flint's escort, she'd be really pissed to know she now had two bodyguards standing watch over her at all times. But damn it, he couldn't leave her at risk when he had the means to assist. Unlike his uncle, he'd never been obtuse to those around him. Sometimes, as his uncle suggested, he thought he felt and empathized too much.

With Ashley, he knew only that he needed her safety ensured.

Before picking her up, he'd driven through the lower-middle-class neighborhood where she lived. The older streets were in need of repair, but well shaded by tall oaks and elms, and lined with large houses converted into apartments.

A few miles down, he'd passed a trailer park. Farther up was a small strip mall and window factory. To the back of Ashley's apartment complex were some abandoned lots and a crumbling drive-in that had gone out of service a decade ago.

It wasn't a bad neighborhood by any stretch, but neither would he call it quiet. Youths hung out on every corner. He saw her neighbors on their porches, tossing back beer. Young kids, most of them barefoot and shirtless, played in the street and on the sidewalk. A few disreputable characters might have been drug dealers, and a young couple made out in a parked car.

In her loose jeans and tie-dyed baby doll T-shirt, Ashley fit in, while he and his suit stuck out like a sore thumb. "How long have you lived here?"

"A few years now."

She sounded funny, drawing his scrutiny away from the surrounding area to her.

Slack-jawed and wide-eyed, she stared at his car.

He would have brought the Porsche, but the garage hadn't yet replaced the tires. Arriving at a wedding in an Aston Martin V12 Vanquish didn't feel appropriate, so that left his Bentley.

"I'm a little enamored of vehicles," he admitted to her.

"It's . . . *awesome.*" She stepped away from him and dashed the last few feet to the car. Bending at the waist, she peered in the window without quite touching it. Her backside invited a pat, but Quinton restrained himself.

"Glad you like it." Pushing a button on the pocket remote unlocked the doors. Quinton opened the passenger side for her, then caught her arm before she could scramble inside. "Would you like to drive?"

"No way!" She swung around to face him. "You're pulling my leg."

In that moment, he wanted to *give* her the damn car, just to keep her so happy. "Sure. You're not reckless, are you?"

She bit her lip, turned to look at the car again. "God, you're a terrible tease. And no, I'm usually a terrific driver."

"Usually?"

She held out her hands, which trembled. "Jitters." Her fingers curled into fists. "I hate to admit it, but this whole wedding thing has me off-kilter. There won't be many people there, just May and Jude's immediate families, a photographer, and Denny. But . . . I've never met Jude's family, and the idea of being photographed makes my skin crawl."

Quinton sympathized. "Then perhaps after the reception you can take the wheel."

"I just might hold you to that." She climbed in and spent a little time running her hands along the leather before buckling her seat belt.

Amused, Quinton came around to the driver's side. He didn't see anyone suspicious on the streets or in the nearby houses, but then he didn't see the bodyguards either. He only knew they were there because he'd spoken with them before picking up Ashley.

After he turned the key and the engine purred, Ashley asked, "I'll bet weddings never make you nervous, do they?"

"I'm used to crowds. Right after graduating from college, I lost my parents in a boating accident and inherited the company. I've been dealing with large groups, socially and in business, ever since."

At the mention of his loss, she went very still. "I'm sorry. I guess I never even thought to ask you about your folks."

And he hadn't mentioned them because, unlike her, he'd always felt loved by both his mother and father. In comparison to her upbringing, he almost felt guilty. He'd had it all: wealth, love, security . . . while she'd had nothing.

"It was a long time ago. They were sailing and a bad storm blew in. The boat capsized. My mother drowned. They never recovered her body."

"Your father?"

"He had a head injury and didn't recover. After three weeks in the hospital, he passed away."

Ashley touched his arm, speaking in a soft, unfamiliar tone. "That must have been excruciating for you."

"It was, yes. Sometimes I still miss them, but Uncle Warren stepped in to finish my education with the firm. I've been in front of employees, prospective clients, and target groups enough times that I don't even think about it anymore. I just do it."

With the topic deliberately lightened, she gave way to her curiosity. "Do you have any brothers or sisters?"

"No. My parents tried, but they never conceived again after me."

"What about your uncle? Did he give you any fun cousins?"

"Two, both female, which my uncle claims is why he's so close to me. The son he never had and all that." As he spoke, he checked his rearview mirror for any cars that might trail him. He saw no one. "His daughters are both sharks, but they have their own interests. One is a clothing designer, the other a news correspondent. I only see them on the occasional holiday."

"Impressive family."

He shrugged. To some they might seem that way. To him they were just terrific relatives whom he enjoyed visiting.

"So you and your uncle get along?"

Her interest pleased Quinton. It was the first time she'd cared enough to ask him about his life, friends, and family. "Most of the time. He's different from my father. More formal and stiff. Dad was pretty laid-back and easy to be around. He was as happy throwing a football in the backyard with me, as he was running a fast-growing business. He and my mom were in love until the day they died. With Uncle Warren and Aunt Ivana, it sometimes seems like they're strangers in the same house."

"They have a bad marriage?"

"I wouldn't call it bad. It's as they want it, and they both seem content. But it's . . . cold."

"Your uncle seemed plenty annoyed with you last night."

"Warren doesn't like it when his plans are thwarted."

"His plans being a match between you and some socially acceptable female paragon?"

The way she sneered that showed shades of jealousy. Normally, any sign of possessiveness set him on edge. With Ashley, he chose to see it as strides in the right direction. "You're going to give yourself wrinkles, frowning like that."

"Frowning comes naturally to me."

"I noticed." He reached for her knee and gave it a squeeze. "But this time it's not warranted. I wouldn't have accepted the dinner date even if I hadn't made prior arrangements to attend the wedding with you."

"Why not? You don't like her?"

"I don't even know her, but I know her type. To get Warren's approval she'd be fresh out of Yale, a debutante with high aspirations for a career, two perfect children, and an adoring husband, in that order, acquired on a specific timetable. No, thanks."

"Marriage doesn't appeal to you?"

She didn't even flinch when asking that. In almost every circumstance, marriage was a touchy subject, one that both people tiptoed around until they knew they were both on the same page. Not Ashley. She blurted it out without a single hesitation.

Grinning, he glanced at her. "I don't know. Why? Are you planning to propose?"

She countered, saying, "Are you avoiding the topic?"

She probably didn't want a serious discussion, but what the hell? It wouldn't hurt for her to know more about him. If she wouldn't shy away from the M word, neither would he. "I want what my parents had—love, commitment, loyalty—not an arrangement and a scheduled family."

She went quiet, so he asked, "What about you?"

"I've never even thought about marriage." She traced a finger along the console's bur walnut veneer. "Dad married my mom because she got pregnant with me. It was a stupid thing to do, because they detested each other as much as they did me. More than once over the years, he said he didn't think I was his, and she wouldn't deny it. She'd just laugh in his face."

Every time he thought he'd heard the worst, she shocked him with another revelation. He'd never been able to reconcile such insensitivity toward a child. "Do you think your mother just wanted to hurt him?"

She shrugged. "Who knows? Mom must have slept around a lot before they married, because Dad brought it up every time they fought, and they fought a lot. But if I'm not his, it's no skin off my nose. Most times I wish I weren't hers either."

Her choice of words left him edgy. "You mean they argued?"

She puffed out a laugh. "Sure, they argued every day, about everything under the sun. Lots of times they argued about what I wasn't allowed to do—which was just about everything. But they also duked it out on a regular basis. Dad would slap Mom. She'd throw something at him, or pull his hair. And the battle would begin. I learned to get out of the range of fire." She made a face. "Luckily neither of them had Jude's skills as a fighter, or they'd have killed one another."

She crossed her arms and turned in the seat to face him. "You know, I guess I have thought about marriage a little. At least, I've thought of the reasons why I wouldn't marry."

"Enlighten me."

"Well, I'd never use a baby as an excuse. I don't plan on getting prego, but if I did, I'd be independent and able to take care of the kid on my own—without a man's interference. I'd never make a baby pay for my mistakes."

Because she'd been made to pay? Damn her

parents. Fury roiled inside him, and he said, "No child should have to live with that."

"Yeah, I know. That's why I bailed."

She was too matter-of-fact when he knew it still had to pain her. How could it not? Had she never been able to reconcile with her parents? Had they not come after her to make amends, to check on her and make sure she was okay?

Apparently not, given her attitude. Ten years, then. With new insight, he understood what her life must have been like.

Pressing a hand to her belly, she said, "Oh, God. We're here."

Quinton took in the sight of the impressive stone fence surrounding a generous proportion of acreage and a sizable mansion. "It's beautiful."

"Yeah, just wait till you see the inside. Or . . ." She frowned at him. "Is your house as big as his?"

Her lack of tact didn't insult him because he knew she hadn't asked out of prurient interest. Ashley wasn't a gold digger. In fact, she looked almost accusatory as she waited for him to answer.

On a groan, she said, "It is, isn't it?"

The idea obviously didn't please her. "How about you tell me, after I've taken you there tonight?"

The reminder of the evening to come had her straightening in her seat again. "Okay, I will." She looked out the windshield. "Pull up to the intercom and push the button to let them know we're here."

Quinton did as directed, and a second later the gate opened. A voice he recognized as Denny's said, "Nice car. Come on in, then. I'll walk out front to show you where to park."

Quinton accelerated through the tall gates,

which immediately clanked shut once the car was clear. All along the tree-shaded drive, monitors picked up activity. Jude Jamison's home had good security. He liked that.

Wide porches wrapped around a two-story brick and stone structure with a six-car garage. A sweeping cobblestone walkway led to double columns at the entrance. Fall colors bloomed in the landscaping around the house, grounds, and a large fountain.

Instead of Denny stepping out, as he'd said he would, Jude Jamison himself strode down the porch steps. As a fan of the SBC, Quinton was anxious to meet Jude. But as a man soon to be intimately involved with Ashley, he wanted to talk to Jude about threats, security, and any plans that might be in the works.

Leaving the car running, Quinton opened his door and stepped out. He couldn't help grinning as he extended his hand. "Jude Jamison. This is a pleasure."

Jude smiled, too, and accepted the handshake. "I can say the same. Never in a million years did I think to see Ashley with a date. How'd you do it?"

Ashley yelled out the window, "Just look at him, Jude. It should be obvious."

Jude laughed. "It's Quinton Murphy, right?"

"I take it Denny filled you in."

"He's a regular chatterbox." Jude nodded at the Bentley. "Mind if I take a look? I'm a bit of a car nut myself."

"Feel free."

Jude opened the door and slid behind the wheel. "I almost bought one of these, but since meeting May, cars haven't been the first thing on my mind." He flexed his hands on the wheel, then turned to Ashley. "May is anxious to see you. Why don't you go on in?"

"Oh, I get it." Lip curled, she opened the door and flounced out. "The boys wanna talk shop. By all means. I don't want to get in the way."

Jude rolled his eyes. As Ashley started past Quinton, he caught her arm, pulled her around, and gave her a sound kiss on her mulish mouth. A breeze caught her hair, and he tucked it back, then smoothed his hand over her cheek to her shoulder. "See you in a bit."

New color bloomed in her face. Her lashes fluttered and one side of her mouth tipped up. "Yeah. Sure. In a bit." She sighed, turned, and strode away in that long-legged, impatient way of hers.

Satisfied but also anxious, Quinton watched her go up the front steps and through the entry doors. He'd never tire of looking at her, just as he'd never tire of her mood swings.

"I see your interest in cars is about to wane, too."

Pulled from his introspection, Quinton grinned at Jude. "Convince Ashley of that if you can."

"She scares me, so you're on your own."

"Yeah, right." Quinton studied Jude through the open driver's door window. He was big and lean and muscled all over. "How's that promotion go? Jude Jamison is the most fearless man in the SBC?"

Jude dismissed that claim with a shrug. "Everyone has to have a slant."

"In your case, I believe it." He braced his feet apart and crossed his arms over his chest. "I was there in Colorado for your title fight with Sanchez. Biggest night the SBC ever saw. Those tickets were sold out months in advance."

Grinning, Jude propped one arm through the open window. "That was a hell of a night, wasn't it?"

"I got my money's worth. No one had ever beaten Sanchez, but you dominated the fight from jump. Sanchez spent all his time backing up, trying to avoid you."

"I like to push the fight."

"That's obvious. You always have the other fighter on the rebound. Ducking you did Sanchez no good. You knocked him out in the third round. Everyone was screaming so loud, my ears rang for days afterward."

Again, Jude shrugged. "Anyone who stays in it long enough is bound to lose."

"You've never been knocked out."

"I've been lucky. Hell, that night with Sanchez, he damn near had me a few times. Unfortunately for him, he didn't follow through on his submissions. He relied on a stand-up fight."

"And he ran out of gas."

"While my tank was still full." Jude grinned in pleasure. "Lack of preparation has brought down more than a few fighters."

"Speaking of lack of preparation . . ." Quinton walked around to the passenger side and got in. "Do you have a few minutes?"

"A couple of hours, actually. The ladies will be a while getting ready."

"Perfect." He patted the car's console. "Why don't you drive her to wherever you want her parked, and we can talk."

"I take it this has to do with Elton Pascal?"

"Denny told me some of it, and Ashley filled me in on the rest. I don't want to put a damper on your big day—"

"Anything that threatens May or Ashley takes precedence."

"I assumed as much." Quinton accepted that any man with honor would want all the facts. "I have some news to contribute."

Jude put the Bentley in gear and drove around to the back of the garage, toward a large tent erected specifically for parking. "Between my cars, Denny's, and May's, the garage is full."

"But you still want additional cars out of sight," Quinton guessed, seeing other vehicles had already taken residence inside the tent.

"So far, the press hasn't caught on to anything unusual. I snuck my family in during the middle of the night. May's family comes and goes so that's not news to anyone. I don't want my wedding to become front-page fodder for more speculation."

"I imagine the press can be a real pain in the ass for someone with your public profile."

"And my history." He squeezed the steering wheel. "Elton's done his best to make my life hell with his fucking accusations. I'll be so glad to put this business behind me." He visibly relaxed his shoulders. "But in the meantime, I promised Ed Burton an exclusive on the wedding. He's a reporter and photographer for the local papers, but he's also become a friend. He'll take our wedding photos."

Jude pulled into an empty space and turned the car off. When he handed the keys to Quinton, his face showed the strain he was under. "Every second I have to guard against paparazzi and intruders and now Elton. I'll be leaving with May tonight, as soon as I can get her away from the reception."

"That'll be here also?"

"Yeah. With Elton still lurking around, I wasn't about to risk taking May anywhere else. I want her out of the country where I know she'll be safe."

Quinton nodded his complete understanding. "Denny told you that Ashley felt like someone had been watching her?"

"He told me."

"Last night, while I was at work with her, someone slashed two of my tires."

Jude's expression hardened. "You think someone saw the two of you together?"

"I think it's probable enough that I hired two bodyguards to keep an eye on Ashley. She doesn't know, and I'd just as soon keep it that way. She's . . ." Unwilling to insult her, Quinton searched for the right word.

"Prickly to the point of drawing blood? I know. But she's also family to me now, so you don't have to watch what you say around me. May loves her, so I love her." He shrugged. "It's as simple as that."

"Glad to hear it." If Ashley's own family wouldn't step up to the plate, at least she had solid support from the next best thing.

"The bodyguards are reliable?"

"I've used them before. They're the best."

"I take it with a quarter-million-dollar Bentley, you can handle it on your own?"

"I can and I will." Even with a man about to get married, Quinton felt territorial. "I won't let anything happen to her."

"Good." Jude opened his door. As he was stepping out, he said, "Then I guess I better call off my guys before they all run into each other and start a riot."

It took Quinton a second before he burst out laughing. He too left the car, grinning at Jude over the roof as he pocketed the keys. "How long have they been watching over her?"

"The night of our rehearsal dinner, we learned that Elton had slipped under the cops' radar. Denny put men on her then and there. Before she'd even gotten home, they were tailing her."

"I'm relieved to hear it."

Jude looked out over the land surrounding his home, came to some inner decision, and gave Quinton an incomprehensible nod. "Wait until you see May and Ash together. They have a special bond that goes deeper than even they realize."

Whatever Jude tried to tell him, Quinton didn't get it. "Meaning?"

Jude just shook his head. "I love May, so I'm not about to let anything hurt her. That means protecting Ashley, too."

That rubbed Quinton the wrong way, and he slowly straightened. "You can relax on that score, because from now on, I'll be taking care of her."

Of course, Jude didn't back down an inch. "Denny won't like it."

"He'll get over it."

"Ash might not like it, either," he warned.

"I'm working on her. She'll come around."

With a laugh, Jude started them on the path to the back of the house. "So. Have you had any training?" he asked. "You have the cockiness of a fighter."

"Actually, I have. Mostly for exercise and just because I enjoy it. I'm nowhere near the league of the SBC guys, but I can hold my own."

Jude clapped him on the back. "Good. With a woman like Ashley, you're going to need every advantage you can get."

Stiff in the pink gown that showed too much of what she didn't really have to show and made her feel like confection, Ashley paced around the spacious bedroom. The wall fountains didn't catch her interest any more than the incredible artwork on every wall.

Except for the hairdresser who still toyed with May's hair, everyone had left. Ashley was now coifed, painted, buffed, and polished. In some ways she felt uniquely feminine.

In others she felt like an utter fraud.

What would Quinton think when he saw her?

And damn it, since when did she care so much what anyone else thought?

Across the room, her cell phone rang inside her purse. Was Quinton calling her? Like an anxious schoolgirl, she dashed across the thick carpeting and dug out her phone. Breathless, stupidly excited, she smiled and said, "Hey."

"You think you're a real tough girl, don't you?"

Icy cold dread washed over her, then sank into her belly like lead. She swallowed, but couldn't say a single word.

"You're still just a girl, and all girls need a man around to keep them in line. I'll show you. When I have you, you'll be punished for what you did."

Through the doorway to the enormous bathroom, Ashley could just see May. She wore a huge smile, carefree and glowing with happiness. Keeping May in her sights gave Ashley courage; this was May's big day, and she wouldn't let some scum-ball coward mess it up.

In a whisper, she asked, "Where are you hiding, Elton? What snake hole did you crawl into? You might as well give yourself up, you know. Eventually, the police will find you. They'll—"

"You can run, little girl, but you can't hide. Not from me. Hire a hundred men to protect you if it makes you feel better, but it won't be enough. I'll still get to you. Count on it."

"Why don't you just die and save everyone a lot of trouble?" With that parting shot, Ashley disconnected the phone and dropped it on the bed.

She stared at it, then snatched it back and clicked onto her received calls file. Private name, private number. That figured. Elton was insane, but not stupid enough to leave a number. She turned off the phone so there wouldn't be a repeat call, and stuffed it back into her purse.

"All right, out with it."

Guilty, Ashley jumped away from the bed. "What?"

The soon-to-be May Jamison shook out the skirts of her extraordinary gown, strode across the room with a concerned frown, and took Ashley's hands. "I've known you too long, Ash. Something's wrong. Spill it."

Ashley glanced behind her to the hair designer. Smiling, the woman excused herself and slipped quietly out the door.

Joy blossomed in May's eyes and flushed her cheeks. She looked stunning. Wildly in love. And now worried.

If anyone deserved a "happy ever after," May did. She was head over heels in love with her famous fiancé.

Despite Elton's threats, Ashley felt confident that Jude would never let anything happen to May. Knowing that brought Ashley a measure of peace.

Later, she'd tell Jude and Denny about the call. But no way in hell would she worry May on the day of her wedding.

"It's nothing."

"Uh-huh. That's why you won't look at me. That's why you're clenching your jaw and blinking and doing all those things I know you do when you're really, really anxious about something."

Oh, God. Why did May have to be so astute? She quickly racked her brain for a legitimate excuse and came up with the perfect scapegoat.

Crossing her arms and stiffening her shoulders, she said, "It's Quinton."

May did her own share of blinking. "Quinton Murphy? That guy you have the hots for?"

"Do not." At least, not that she'd admit to May. "I like him a little, that's all."

"That guy you *kissed*," May teased, drawing the last word out in a singsong taunt.

"He kissed me," Ashley defended. Several times, in fact.

"You let him. And liked it. You said it damn near melted your bones."

Thrilled to have May on a different track, Ashley shook her head. "I should never confide in you. You enjoy it too much."

"You should *always* confide in me. Just like I confide in you." May made a big production of going to the door, closing, and locking it. Then, careful not to wrinkle her gown, she perched at the end of the bed. "I know I haven't had much time to talk the last few days, but . . ."

She said it like an awful confession, making Ashley laugh. "You've been a wee bit busy, toots."

"I'm never too busy for you. You know that."

Emotion lumped in Ashley's throat. What had she ever done to deserve such a wonderful friend? "You're getting married, May." Never mind Elton's ill-timed threat; Ashley's heart swelled with happiness. "Today. In about five minutes, in fact. We can save the catch-up chitchat for when you get back from Japan."

"Oh, no, you don't. I can tell something's going on, and no way am I going to wait a month to find out what it is." She folded her newly manicured hands over her lap and started tapping her silk slipper. "So fess up. What's Quinton done now?"

They did have a few minutes to spare, so what the hell? Deciding to tease, Ashley said, "Well, he kissed me again."

"Really?"

"Several times." She peeked at May, saw her rapt expression, and fought a grin. "I kissed him back."

May's eyebrows shot up, and a smile curled her mouth. "Tell me more."

"He's asked me out, too."

"And you finally accepted?"

Ashley nodded her head toward the floor-to-ceiling windows that faced the backyard. "Actually, he's here with me today."

May's mouth fell open, then she whispered, "You're kidding?"

"Denny didn't tell you I was bringing him?"

"That rat never tells me anything." May rose from the bed and headed for the window, saying on a whisper, "I've been dying to see the man who has you all tied up in knots."

Ashley trotted as fast as a woman could trot in pink high-heeled satin sandals and put herself in May's path. "Oh, no, you don't. Jude might see you. Isn't it bad luck or something for the groom to see the bride before the wedding?"

"That's what they say." May frowned, but gave up. "I suppose I can wait a few more minutes." She studied Ashley, half pleased, half concerned. "I'll give him points for determination. He stuck with it until he wore you down."

"Yeah, well, the man's nothing if not stubborn. But he's gorgeous, too. And smart. And funny. And he's an indescribable kisser . . ."

With dawning awareness, May said, "You sound half in love, Ash."

Ashley's heart dropped into her stomach. She went cold, and then hot. As if she'd just stumbled onto some great discovery, May all but clapped her hands.

"You are! You're falling for him."

Ashley tried to laugh, but ended up choking. "Bite your tongue."

May's expression softened with sympathy. "Come on, hon. Would falling in love really be so bad?"

It'd be catastrophic. But rather than say so, Ashley smiled. "If he turned out to be half as wonderful as Jude, then no. But how many guys like Jude can there be? Surely they broke the mold after that one?"

Sudden tears filled May's eyes. "Oh, Ash, he really is wonderful."

Uh-oh. *"Don't,"* Ashley warned, laughing as she turned her back on May. "If you cry, I'll cry. That's how it's always been and you know it."

On a watery gulp, May said, "I know, I know."

"We are such a sorry pair." Ashley thought fast. She needed to get May laughing so she could laugh, too. "Do you remember that time in biology when you started crying over that stupid dead frog?"

"You were going to cry, too," May accused.

"But instead I started snickering at you. Mostly out of nervousness. But then you started snickering, and we ended up laughing so hard, we got hiccups and both got sent to the principal's office."

"And instead of going straight home, we went to the creek."

Ashley's mouth twitched with the memory. "And we saw frogs everywhere," she said around a giggle.

"And within minutes, I was sobbing just from remembering that poor dead frog."

"And that got me sobbing." Ashley turned to face her. "Which is why you absolutely can *not* get weepy on me now."

May flapped her hands in front of her face, laughing and breathing fast to stop the tide of tears. "I'm sorry. It's just that I feel so lucky to have him."

"I know." Ashley fetched a tissue from the dressing table and dabbed at the trail of tears beneath May's eyes. "But he's a lucky cuss, too."

"Jude's been so busy with a million things. Not only did he organize the entire wedding *and* the honeymoon, he ran interference with my family.

And he had to appease his agent over that movie deal he turned down. And the SBC has been on the line with him a dozen times a day, setting up deals and cementing plans. And still . . ."

"He's found plenty of time to coddle you."

More tears fell as May nodded. "Denny hasn't done too badly either. Between the two of them, I feel like a princess."

"And why not?" Ashley asked. "You look like a princess today."

"Damn right," Denny stated from behind them.

They both turned to see him lounging in the doorway, shamelessly eavesdropping. Never mind that they'd locked the door. Denny wasn't a man hampered by a mere lock or social graces or, when you came right down to it, anything as subtle as discretion.

He looked resplendent in a dashing tuxedo that did nothing to diminish his hard-edged capability, especially when he flashed his patented wolf's smile.

Ashley frowned at him. "You were listening in to very private girl talk."

He shrugged. "More like girl whining, from what I heard. You two watering pots will have everyone thinking it's a forced marriage, instead of a match made in heaven."

Ashley made a face. "What do you want, Denny?"

"I came by to fetch you. Your beau is pacing a hole in the lawn. But after finding out more about him, I'm not surprised."

Annoyance snapped her spine straight and brought down her brows. "What are you talking about?"

"Calm down, baby girl—"

Already on edge, Ashley took exception to infantile terms. "Woman," she corrected through her teeth.

He shrugged. "Calm down, woman."

That made her growl and had Denny laughing. Ash wanted to smack him. "Have you been down there grilling Quinton all this time?"

"Of course not."

She started to relax.

"That's not the best way to get to the truth. People can lie. Records rarely do."

Worse and worse. "You checked him out?"

"Yeah. Did a whole background on him. He's clean as a whistle. Unlike Jude, he was born to money, but that hasn't made him a slacker, and from what I could tell, he doesn't abuse his position of wealth."

Slapping her hands over her ears, Ashley said, "I do not want to hear this." It was bad enough that Denny had invaded Quinton's privacy. She wouldn't add to that intrusion by listening to his findings.

May freaked on her, saying, "Ashley, your hair!"

"Oh yeah." Her hair was coifed in the same loose, casual high twist as May's. They even wore matching jewelry, thanks to Jude, except that May had white pearls and Ashley had pink. "Sorry."

"You both look exceptionally fine," Denny noted with the fond affection of a favored uncle. "The men will drop their eyeballs."

When Ashley scowled at him, he carefully cupped her face. "I'm sorry you disapprove of my concern, but—"

"But you're not sorry enough to butt out of my business?"

Now he scowled, too. "Kill a man for caring, but

I thought you'd be happy to know Quinton's wealthy and generous and—"

"I already knew all that, thank you very much." She crossed her arms to match his stance. "It doesn't matter to me."

Through his teeth, Denny said, "It should."

She threw up her hands in disgust. "Why? Is Quinton supposed to pick up my bills now? You expect me to be a kept woman?"

"No! I never said that."

"Then why should I care how much money he has?"

Nose to nose with Ashley, he growled, "At least he can provide you with some free entertainment, damn it."

May started laughing. When both Ashley and Denny swung around to look at her, she laughed harder. "You two kill me. You're both so much alike." She plucked another tissue from the dresser and again dabbed at her eyes. "Now knock it off before I ruin my makeup. And Denny, isn't that the music I hear starting?"

His graying eyebrows shot up to his hairline. "Well, shit. It is." And after that uncouth epitaph, he struck a gallant pose and held out his arm. "Ladies?"

Ashley rolled her eyes. Time to get the show on the road. At least the argument with Denny had helped to quell her nervousness and restore her bravado.

She picked up her flower arrangement, handed the bridal bouquet to May, and sashayed out the door.

Chapter 6

Stuart was waiting when they entered the yard moments later. Wearing his tux and a charming smile, May's father looked every inch the proud papa.

Ashley wasn't fooled.

Better than most, she knew that he was a self-centered, wasteful, and irresponsible womanizer who had never put his family first. He blamed others for his own shortcomings, and he'd raised Tim to be in his image. When things fell apart, he expected May to put the pieces back together again.

For a lot of reasons, Ashley detested him.

But May was a better person than she'd ever be. May hadn't walked out on her family. She stood behind them and did what she could to help them. And now they were all gathered together for the wedding, while Ashley hadn't seen her folks in years. But she didn't care. She didn't want to see them. She didn't want to live with their lies.

As far as Ashley was concerned, they should set May up for sainthood.

Standing in the yard waiting for her cue, Ashley took note of the clear blue sky, the fragrance of flowers in the air, and the murmuring of family and a few friends. Near the pond stood a large white gazebo adorned with orange blossoms and trailing ribbons that fluttered in the breeze, reminding Ashley of the beauty of a fairy tale.

"Knock 'em dead," Denny whispered near Ashley's ear. He patted her hand for reassurance and strolled off to take his place near Jude and the minister.

It was time.

Knowing everyone watched her, Ashley's heartbeat tripped and her palms felt sweaty, but she slowly made her way down the path. She never missed a step and she kept her chin up, her eyes straight ahead.

With relief, she finally reached the gazebo and took up her rehearsed position.

Too handsome for words, Jude's expression was hard and filled with anticipation as he watched Stuart walk May down the petal-strewn path to the beat of the wedding march. When she reached him, Jude's eyes glittered with possessiveness, and the corners of his mouth relaxed.

Stuart took his seat with May's family.

May's snowy white dress was in the same style as Ashley's pink gown, but layered in lace and pearls, and fuller in the skirt. Unlike Ashley, May filled out the bodice to overflowing. She really did look like a princess—a lush, sexy, over-the-moon-in-love princess.

A sigh lifted from the intimate audience when Jude took May's hand. Together they faced the minister, and the ceremony began.

Seeing their love made Ashley feel weepy again. She knew if she started crying, she wouldn't be able to stop. She needed a diversion, and bad.

While everyone watched the bride and groom, Ashley subtly looked around. Denny stood to the side of Jude, and damned if he didn't look ready to weep, too. He kept nodding, smiling, sighing. Only a true badass would be secure enough to put on such an emotional display in front of others.

Ashley wished she could be as secure in her feelings.

Then again, Denny didn't have to worry about mascara running down his face.

Off to the side, Ed Burton took his exclusive photos as prearranged with Jude. The sun was bright enough that no flash intruded. There was only the quiet click of the camera, barely discernible over the minister's deep voice.

Tim fidgeted in his seat, trying to get Ashley's attention. Unwilling to encourage him, she glanced right past him.

Beside Tim sat Olympia. May's mother, as ill-mannered as ever, drew on a cigarette while looking bored. Ashley briefly shut her eyes, saying a quick prayer that Olympia wouldn't do anything to cause a scene.

Next, Ashley looked at Stuart, and caught him eyeballing the women in Jude's family. Hadn't that bastard done enough damage with his unfaithful ways? Would he never learn? Or did he even know of the repercussions of his adultery?

Luckily, Jude's family was too enraptured by the ceremony to pay Stuart any mind. They remained unaware of his lecherous scrutiny.

She liked Jude's family a lot. They'd been thrilled to meet May and, by extension, Ashley. They were polite and kind, smiling with genuine pride and happiness. They were, in fact, the total opposite of May's family, and so far from her own folks that Ashley felt immediate respect for them.

Quinton sat off by himself, and the second her gaze found him, she was snared. He watched Ashley, or more precisely, devoured her with his eyes. A warm flush washed over her, making her almost lightheaded. He was openly admiring, making no pretense about liking what he saw.

The dress *was* beautiful, but it had taken a sturdy push-up bra for her to fill out the bodice and keep it in place. The seamstress had altered it as much as possible without ruining the lines of the dress. With the bra, everything fit just right—except that it left her at risk of falling out.

And wouldn't that just put a damper on the festivities?

Ashley had known both Jude and May wanted a very simple service, but before she even realized it, the wedding had ended, and the minister pronounced them husband and wife.

The air filled with cheers.

Startled, Ashley realized that she hadn't heard a single word. Her very best friend in the whole world was now a married woman.

The tears came, and there wasn't a damn thing she could do about it. Jude scooped May into his arms and kissed her silly. That negated Ashley's need to adjust May's train, and she laughed, celebrating with everyone else.

Denny's voice rose above the others. "Hang around, everyone. The reception's right here. Food will be out in a minute and the band will get things started."

Ashley followed Jude and May off the dais, and everyone surged forward with congratulations. Suddenly Quinton was at her side.

While the others laughed and talked, Quinton's long, hard fingers wrapped around Ashley's bare upper arm, and his warm breath teased her ear. "You look beautiful."

Shivers ran up and down her spine. She turned her face up to his, and he pulled her into his arms.

"Quinton," she whispered, trying to juggle both bouquets. "What are you doing?"

"Doing?" His gaze went from her contrived cleavage to her mouth, and finally to her eyes. "I suppose I'm doing this."

And to Ashley's bemusement, he kissed her right there in front of the wedding guests.

"Well, this is rude."

Ashley freed herself with a laugh. Tim stood over them, close to enraged and ready to challenge. The twit. She smiled at Quinton, thrust the bouquet into his hands, and said, "Excuse us a moment, please."

Startled, Quinton could do no more than graciously agree.

Ashley caught Tim's sleeve and dragged him off to the side.

* * *

Pleased for an opportunity to have Ashley's isolated attention, Tim went along willingly. He'd tried forever to get closer to her, but she always pushed him away.

Unfortunately, now was no different. Ash only hauled him a few feet before turning on him.

Trying to be slick, he bent to steal a kiss and got her palm smashed into his face instead. "Oof."

"Knock it off, Casanova."

Tim was so captivated by her appearance, he barely heard her. He'd seldom seen her in a dress, never a formal, and never in everything that matched. She was actually pretty. And her slim figure had turned miraculously feminine. "You look awesome."

"Oh, for crying out loud." She crossed her arms beneath her breasts and thrust out a hip in a typical *I'm-going-to-kick-your-ass* pose. "I don't even like you, Tim. Why can't you get that?"

He tried not to be hurt. "What's not to like?" he asked, hoping for a joking tone. "I'm a decent-looking guy."

She took his question literally. "You're not stone ugly, no. I'd even call you handsome. But it doesn't make any difference when inside you're spoiled and whiny and selfish. You're a user, Tim, weak and dishonorable and—"

"Jesus, Ash." Her vehemence stunned him, and he laughed nervously. "Cut my throat, why don't you?"

"There've been times I wanted to. The way you've always treated May . . ."

"But I'm changing that."

For a single second, he thought she might regret her remarks. Then her scowl darkened. "Look,

Tim, get it through your thick—" She stopped on a snarl and smacked him upside the head, making his ears ring. "Look at my *face*, Tim, not my chest."

"Sorry." He rubbed at his temple but couldn't quite pull his gaze from her body. "Till today, I didn't know you had a chest."

Another snarl, but at least she didn't slug him again. "Denny tells me you're working really hard to get in shape for an SBC competition. I think you're nuts, but hey, more power to you. I wish you a lot of luck. But we'll get along better if you just focus on that and keep me entirely out of your thoughts."

He started to tell her he couldn't when he noticed Denny approaching, dark as a thundercloud and twice as menacing. He did not want to tangle with Denny when he was in one of his moods, and around Ashley, he always seemed in a mood of one sort or another. "Shit. Gotta run, Ash. See ya around."

He heard Denny call his name, but he didn't slow down. He heard Ashley laugh but didn't care. At a fast clip, he left the crowd far behind. Maybe flirting with Ashley wasn't such a great idea. Denny was real prickly about that, warning him off in every other breath. Why, Tim didn't know for sure. Probably Denny figured Ash was too good for him.

But as he'd said, he was changing that. Following Denny's example, he was ready to take responsibility for himself. He'd make his own way. He'd be a man they could be proud of.

He'd just rounded the side of Jude's house where no one could see him, searching for a place to disappear for a few minutes. He spotted the tents for the cars and started in that direction, but

Denny's foot hooked his leg and sent him sprawling face-first into the grass.

As he'd been taught, he immediately rolled to his back in a less defenseless position. With the sun gilding his aggressive stance, Denny resembled an enraged deity. He stood over Tim, and he looked primed for violence.

"Hey, Denny," Tim brazened, pretty certain that Denny wouldn't actually hurt him. "What's up?"

"My foot in your ass if you don't stop hassling Ashley."

"I didn't!" Tim pushed to a sitting position. "I was just telling her how nice she looked. That's all." And then, feeling emboldened, he added, "Why do you care, anyway?"

Denny knelt down, causing Tim to scuttle back a few cautious feet. No, he didn't think Denny would maim him, but he wasn't above rattling his brains a little.

"She's not for you, Tim. Do you understand me? She won't ever be for you. Keep your beady eyes off her body. Hell, don't even think about her. Do I make myself clear?"

"I don't see—"

Denny caught him by the front of his suit. "We can go inside and discuss this right now if that's how you want it."

"No!"

"Then swear to me you'll stay away from her."

Denny seemed so insistent that Tim got curious as to why. Knowing Denny, he had to have a good reason to lay down the law like that. "Yeah, sure, no problem. I'll look right through her. I swear." Tim watched Denny, trying to read his thoughts.

"But . . . um, we're at a wedding. Won't it seem rude if I ignore her completely?"

Denny considered that. "Fine. If you have to talk to her . . ." He worked his jaw, looked up to the sky for guidance, and turned back to Tim with a tightened fist and the wrath of God in his eyes. "Treat her like a sister."

A sister! Well, yeah . . . he supposed he could. God knew she and May looked enough like each other to be sisters. And they acted closer than that. If he thought of Ashley in that way, he sure as hell wouldn't be noticing her cleavage. "Right. Got it. Sister Ashley. No problem."

"It better not be." As if the whole altercation hadn't happened, Denny stood and offered Tim a hand. After hauling him up, he dusted him off, straightened his tie, and said, "Looking good, Tim. Now go mingle and make your sister proud."

"Sure thing." Tim left with alacrity, but he couldn't help seeking Ashley out with his eyes. Yeah, she could be his sister. She and May had the same color hair, the same eyes . . . they even smiled the same.

Weird. Why had he never noticed it before?

Quinton stood still at the side of the house, watching as Denny rubbed his forehead with a curse before pasting on a smile and turning back to the guests.

Interesting exchange they'd had. Quinton didn't like Tim, but Denny seemed to be fond of him. So why so vehement that he stay clear of Ashley?

As usual, just thinking of Ashley had him seeking her out with his gaze. She stood beside May, both of them of a similar height, and at the moment, wearing almost identical expressions. He felt that familiar tightening in his pants, along with a kick to his heart.

Suspicions were a ghastly thing, so until he had more to go on, he'd leave it alone. But if it became necessary, if there was any risk of association, he'd have a man-to-man chat with Denny.

He wasn't about to let anyone, or anything, hurt Ashley.

Something May said must have tickled her because she threw back her head on a robust laugh, uncaring of the hazard to her careful hairdo. She'd broken down during the wedding, leaving makeup smudged beneath her eyes.

And still she looked so precious to him that waiting for the reception to end would be slow torture.

He stared at her long enough that she felt it and looked up to snag his gaze with her own. Her mouth curled and she used one finger to beckon him forward.

She'd sent Tim packing, but called him forward.

He felt pretty good about that.

"Don't you look fine," she teased when he reached her, "all decked out and holding flowers?" Her laugh teased along his nerve endings, inflaming everything he felt for her. "I forgot all about them. I'm sorry."

"No problem." He bent to steal a quick kiss off her smiling mouth. "My machismo can take the hit. But is there someplace to put them?"

"I'm supposed to stow them in the fridge while we wait for the right time for May to throw the bouquet." Her head tilted to one side, again threatening to tumble her hair. "You want to come with me?"

"Lead the way."

One hand curved around his biceps, Ashley darted around caterers and guests, tables and chairs until they entered the house from the rear. After leading him past an indoor pool, a theater room, and down a hall, she went behind a bar and tucked the flowers into a medium-sized refrigerator.

Quinton noticed several rooms that would afford a little privacy, so once Ashley finished, he couldn't help but detour her into one of them.

She laughed as the door closed behind her. "Now, Quinton, whatever are you planning?"

Other than filtered sunlight coming through drawn drapes, the room was dark.

"This." Quinton cupped her face in both hands and kissed her. He felt like a starving man, like he needed her more than his next breath.

Her arms went around his neck and she held on tight. He turned his head to the side and sank his tongue past her parted lips, tasting her deeply. He couldn't *not* touch her, and he ran his hand over her back, down to her waist, and onto her very sexy tush.

She arched forward, making him groan.

"God, Ashley," he whispered, "I'm going crazy wanting you."

Eyes slumberous and dark, she stared up at him. "Mmmm." Her fingers played in his hair, her forearms resting on his shoulders. "What brought this on?"

"I missed you." He started to kiss her again but she dodged him.

"It's the dress, isn't it?"

"The dress is nice." But it was the woman in the dress who was fast capturing his heart.

She laughed a little too loud. "Yeah, well, don't let your eyeballs fall out. Most of that isn't real."

His hand contracted on her bottom. Sure felt real to him. "What isn't?"

"The boobs. It's all push-up and padding and stuff."

Quinton looked down at her cleavage, and felt his stomach drop to his knees. Her raised arms had all but freed one small breast from the dress. He could see her right nipple, pale pink and puckered. His nostrils flared. Without even realizing it, he made a raw sound of hunger.

Ashley followed his gaze and gasped. She started to adjust herself, but he caught her arms at the elbows, restraining her, keeping them around his neck.

Very slowly, he leaned forward and kissed her temple. Featherlight. Barely there.

Next, he kissed her jaw. Then her chin. And the delicate skin of her throat.

Aware of his intent, she moaned and dropped her head back.

Going as slow as he could manage, Quinton kissed the top of her chest, the slope of her small, firm breast.

A slight trembling invaded her narrow frame. Her chest rose and fell with shallow gasps. Torturing himself, Quinton used his tongue to trace just above her nipple.

Her fingers clenched in his hair on a groan.

"Beautiful," he breathed . . . and sucked her into the heat of his mouth.

Her reaction was electric and immediate. She cried out and arched into him, holding him to her breast, giving him as much as he wanted.

He locked one arm around her waist and with the other, freed her other breast.

Small, yes, but so perfect, so sweet . . . He felt ready to burst his pants. He had to stop now, or he wouldn't be able to stop at all.

"Ashley, honey . . ."

She squeezed him tight. "I can't wait to have sex with you."

God, did she always have to say things that turned him inside out? He half laughed, half groaned. "I'm trying to be noble, but you aren't making it easy."

"Yeah, I know. Me, too. This isn't exactly the best place to be swept away, is it?"

"With you, I can't seem to distinguish until it's almost too late."

"We'll go back out." She nuzzled her nose into his throat. "In just a second."

"All right." He smoothed his hand over her shoulder, trying to soothe her. "I need a minute anyway."

"Because of this, right?"

Her hand cupped over his cock and Quinton squeezed his eyes shut, fighting off the rush of sensation.

"Dangerous, Ash." He caught her wrist and drew her hand away, then to be safe, he put some space between them. But damn it, her breasts were still bared, plumped up in a tempting offering by the shape of her dress and the support bra. He had a raging boner, and propriety just didn't seem to matter all that much.

She sighed significantly, turned her back on him, and tucked herself away. "This is so embarrassing."

"Why?" The single word sounded like a croak as he struggled with himself. He did not want her covering back up. Hell, he wanted to strip the dress off her and—

"This stupid push-up bra has all but pushed me right out of the dress. I don't have all that much to push—as you now know."

"Far as I'm concerned," he said, his voice hoarse with lust, "you're perfect."

Over her bare shoulder, she looked at him. "Really?"

He shook his head in wonder. "How can you not know that when I keep losing my head over you?"

He glimpsed her smile before she gave him her back again. "Well, same here. I'm still trying to decide if I like the way you mess with my head."

He didn't like the way she put that. "Ash—"

Arms out to her sides, she turned back around. "Okay?" Anxiety, and a vulnerability so sharp that it hurt him, shone in her makeup-smudged eyes.

"You're presentable." He reached out to finger one long curl that had escaped her pins. "Hardly anyone will know what we were doing."

That had her laughing. "*Hardly* anyone? I don't want a single soul to know."

"Then we'd best readjust your hair." One by one, he pulled out her pins until her heavy fall of hair hung free. With his fingers, he combed through it, straightened her part, and brushed it all behind her shoulders. "You are stunning, Ashley Miles."

"Mascara smears and all, huh?"

"Apparently mascara smears turn me on." He briefly kissed her bottom lip, then forced himself to slide his arm around her waist and draw her out of the room. "All right, woman, no more teasing me. Let's go before we're missed."

Where was she?

Elton hadn't eaten or slept for too long to count. His head pounded and he felt weak, but he couldn't relax, not now, not while she eluded him.

She wasn't at home, wasn't at work, and she'd turned off her cell phone.

Exhaustion, hunger, and rage all combined to sharpen his desire for revenge. But he fought it. He wanted to do this cold, with a clear head. She deserved everything he could give her, every excruciating second of his punishment.

Just as Jude Jamison had been deserving.

He'd wanted Jude rotting in jail, but the bastard was so golden, he'd even slipped out of a guilty verdict. Still, it had given him pleasure knowing that most of the world reviled him, that most considered him a murderer.

Now, thanks to her, it was one big cluster fuck. Jude was free and happy, no longer under suspicion, and, without the world as his backup, Elton couldn't touch him.

Denny was so smug, strutting around, just begging for Elton to make a grab at him. But he wasn't an idiot. Denny was as off-limits now as were Tim and his idiot sister, May Price. Elton took some satisfaction in knowing the lengths Jude had taken to protect them all, because it showed his fear.

Jude knew what he was capable of. Jude knew

what he could do to innocent little girls who turned on him.

Too bad Ashley Miles hadn't taken that into account before butting in.

His laugh sounded rusty and weak. That bitch had stolen his life. Thanks to her, he couldn't access his funds, couldn't contact his friends or visit his establishments. Luckily, he'd emptied one of his accounts before the cops could freeze it. Everyone assumed he'd used the money to skip town.

But he wouldn't leave yet, not before making her pay.

Trying to organize his scattered, churning thoughts, Elton paced across the tiny living room in the rusted, abandoned trailer. Dust rose in his wake and cockroaches scuttled across his shoes.

He curled his lip in revulsion. He used to be so fastidious, dining on the finest food, wearing the best designer clothes. Now he had to wash his hands with water from a jug and sustain himself on packaged cheese crackers and cold canned ham.

He'd once been every bit as polished as her . . .

Her boyfriend.

Ah. If Ashley wasn't at home, then she'd probably gone with her new lover. He snickered, remembering the satisfaction he'd felt in slashing the expensive tires. A cheap thrill, but these days, he took it where he could find it.

Discovering the man's identity and address had proved to be a piece of cake. Course, he was used to others doing the grunt work for him, but now, he found he enjoyed meting out the punishment himself. In the past, he hadn't had the stomach for it. But now, thanks to *her*, a ruined life gave him new strength.

She'd pay. And soon.

Only then could he get on with his life.

When the bouquet came flying her way—on purpose, Ashley didn't doubt—she sidestepped it, and it landed in the arms of Jude's sister. It was just dumb luck that she happened to catch Quinton's gaze a second later. He didn't smile, didn't mock her or look away. He stared at her, so long and deep and serious that her heart thumped against her breastbone and oxygen seemed in short supply.

The sounds of cheering and laughter and music faded away as he started toward her. Half an hour ago, she'd taken off her sandals and now her toes curled into the lush, cool lawn. Someone bumped her, but she paid no attention. All her focus was on Quinton and the anticipation that built with each step he took.

When he stood only a few feet away, he reached out a hand. "The bride and groom are leaving soon. I assume you want to see them off."

"Oh." What a dunce. "Right." Had she really expected him to rush her behind the nearest bush? She had sex on the brain in a bad way.

A little disappointed, she took his hand and together, they followed the small crowd to the front of the house.

Rather than depart in a limo, Jude had purchased a luxurious RV that already held their luggage. It'd take them to the airport to start their thirteen-hour trip to Japan. Jude had plenty of security lined up so no one had reason to worry.

As usual, good-byes took forever, but before she

left, May came to Ashley and hugged her for a very long time, her grip almost bruising. Over May's shoulder, Ashley could see Jude, Denny, and Quinton wearing tolerant grins, their expressions identical. Men.

But something about the way they watched the two of them brought out Ashley's suspicions. It almost appeared they had a well-kept secret among them.

When May released her, Ashley saw that she was shaking and new tears tracked down her cheeks. For a bride, she looked pretty rumpled and tear-stained, but content in a way Ashley had never before observed.

May swallowed hard. "Thank you for being here with me today."

"And where else would I be?" Then, giving in to her own overload of sentiment, Ashley said, "You're like my better half, May." Her vision went blurry and she sniffed. "Have fun on your honeymoon. Don't you dare worry about a thing, but know that I'll miss you like crazy every single second that you're gone."

May's voice broke on a sob, then she wailed, "*Me, too,*" and suddenly Jude was there, still smiling like a superior male as he pried the women apart and turned May into his chest.

She clung to him, her shoulders shaking, her sniffles audible. He kissed her forehead. "Sweetheart, we need to go so we won't miss our flight."

May nodded, blindly reached out a hand to Ashley, which she squeezed, then she turned and rushed up the small steps of the RV.

Jude cupped Ashley's face. "Listen to Denny, and be very, very careful."

"Hey, I don't want you worrying, either. We'll all be fine. You just concentrate on keeping May the most ecstatic woman in the world."

Just then, through the open window of the RV, everyone heard May's sobbing.

Jude looked toward the RV, shook his head and laughed. "You can count on it." His hand lingered on Ashley's cheek. "You're more special to her than you know."

After that cryptic comment, he kissed her forehead and bounded up the steps. With a final wave, he closed the door, and the driver started the engine. A black car holding two guards pulled away first, then the RV, then another car.

Strong arms wrapped around Ashley from behind. "You okay, honey?"

Another novelty—having someone to lean on, someone who gently cared. "I'm fine." Ashley covered Quinton's hands with her own, put her head back on his shoulder and watched the small caravan until it had left the private drive and turned onto the main street.

She twisted around to face Quinton. Keeping her gaze on his tie, she said, "I suppose it's time for us to go?"

"Unless you'd rather stay a while longer. It's early yet and Denny is happy to keep the party going. Jude's family will spend another night—"

Ashley shook off her shyness and put a finger to his lips. "I want to go."

New heat shone in his eyes. "All right."

She quelled a smile and teased, "You're so easy."

"You two are embarrassing me," Denny interjected with complaint. "Why don't you take this someplace private?"

Much aggrieved, Quinton rolled his eyes, but Ashley knew she had to tell them about the phone call.

A furtive look around the area ensured no one else was around to hear. "We need to talk first." Both men stared at her. Best to get it over with, she decided. "And I suppose I should call the cops, too."

Denny nearly popped the buttons on his dress shirt. "What's happened?"

"Elton called." She winced, knowing how they'd react. "He sort of . . . threatened me."

Chapter 7

The words no sooner left her mouth than Quinton had her arm, escorting her around the corner with alacrity. The second they were out of sight of the other guests, Denny caught her other arm and turned her to face him. "When? How?"

"For crying out loud." She dusted off their hands with more energy than necessary. "Take it easy, why don't you?"

Nostrils flared, Denny towered over her. "I'll kill that son of a bitch."

"When did this happen, Ash?"

Quinton seemed to be the calmer of the two, so she concentrated on him. "Right before the ceremony." And before Denny could self-combust, as he appeared ready to do, she added, "I planned to tell you all along, but I had to wait until May and Jude left."

"Jesus, Joseph and Mary. *Why?*"

"I didn't want to ruin their ceremony."

"But we could have—"

"What? The number he called from was anonymous. He wasn't on there that long, didn't identify himself by name, and said nothing that would clue me in to where he is." She held her arms out to her sides. "There's nothing we can do."

"You're sure it was him?" Denny asked.

She nodded. "I'm sure."

Quinton slashed a hand through the air. "What did he say to you?"

"You know," Ashley told him, eyeing his inflexible stance alongside Denny, "you're starting to look and sound a lot like old DZ here."

"God forbid." Quinton relaxed his posture but not his attitude. "I understand why you wouldn't want to say anything that might've ruined the wedding. But what about the hours since then? You've had ample opportunity to share something so important."

She nodded toward Denny. "Look at him. He's about to boil over. Even his ears are red. And Jude knows him real well, including all his moods. You really think Denny could have fooled him?"

"Now wait a minute," Denny protested. "How did this become my fault?"

"She's right," Quinton said, surprising Ashley with his support. "But that's water under the bridge. Tell me what he said, word for word."

This was the tricky part. She didn't want either man to blow a gasket and cause a scene, but she'd have to alert the authorities, which meant she'd have to tell Quinton and Denny first. "He took me by surprise, so I don't remember exactly. He said something along the lines of while I might pretend to be tough, I'm still just a girl and all girls need a man."

They both appeared boggled by that disclosure. Ashley gave it up. "Then he said he'd punish me."

"Son of a bitch."

Quinton, who watched her closely, ignored Denny's outburst. "So we can assume he hasn't left the area, not if he says he's around to punish you. What else?"

"He said all the guards in the world wouldn't protect me." Ashley looked from one man to the other. "So who put guards on me?"

Quinton took a step closer to her. He cradled her cheek in his big hand and nodded. "I did, and they're staying."

Surprised, Denny tucked in his chin. "So did Jude."

"I know." Quinton spoke without releasing Ashley from the force of his attention. "He and I discussed it first thing."

Ashley crossed her arms under her breasts. "You two cozied up real quick."

"We both have your best interests at heart."

"And the guards are staying." Denny agreed with Quinton.

"Mine are." Quinton's eyes narrowed at Denny. "But Jude's men aren't necessary."

Denny took that on the chin. "The hell you say! They're staying."

"I have it under control."

He jutted his face toward Quinton. "Yeah, well so do I."

"She doesn't need an army to protect her." Quinton turned to face Denny. "That'll just draw attention and put her at added risk. With too many unknowns hanging around, distinguishing the good guys from the bad guys gets tough."

"I handpicked those men." Denny nosed in closer, staring Quinton down. "I know them. I trust them."

Quinton didn't give an inch. "I don't care if half of them are related by blood. They're not—"

Refusing to be sandwiched between male one-upmanship, Ashley turned and walked away. Idiots.

"*Ashley.*"

She sent Quinton a dismissive wave and kept walking. They meant well, but their techniques could use some finesse.

Masculine grumbling erupted behind her, but what the heck, if they killed each other, it'd save her the trouble.

She located her sandals under a linen-covered table by a shade tree. Making use of one of the many chairs still scattered about, she dropped into the seat, then bent to slide the sandals onto her feet.

Just as she straightened again, a long shadow settled around her. "Uh . . . you okay, Ash?"

Tim. She swallowed her groan, pushed her hair behind her shoulders, and looked up at him. A gentle breeze rustled the leaves overhead. Dappled sunlight glinted on Tim's dark hair and in his wary eyes. "Just dandy. How about you?"

Propping one shoulder against the tree, Tim stared toward his parents and shrugged. "I'm okay."

Oh, great. Drama time. "You sound a little drunk."

He rubbed his face. "Yeah. Maybe a little. I tried to steer clear of the stuff, I swear I did, but Mom kept refilling my glass." Sheepish, he said, "I don't think May was too pleased to see her with a flask."

A flask? At her daughter's wedding? Good grief.

Because of her parents' drinking problem, May had a real aversion to alcohol. She and Jude had chosen to serve wine at the reception, but nothing stronger. "Olympia shouldn't have brought it against May's wishes."

"I know. I told her so."

"You did?" Astonished, Ashley dropped back in her seat. "Well, good for you, Tim."

Hands shoved deep in his pockets, his head hanging, he dug the toe of his black dress shoe into the soft earth around the tree. "May seemed happy, didn't she?"

Was Tim actually concerned for his sister? Chalk one up for Denny's good influence. "I'd say she's blissful."

"Yeah." He looked up with a smile, and Ashley thought he wasn't a bad-looking guy. If only his character weren't so weak. Then again, as he claimed, he'd been working on that, too.

After a moment of strained silence, Tim asked, "Do you mind if I sit?"

"The chairs are free."

"Yeah, I know, but . . . I don't want to run you off again."

Was she so transparent? She glanced toward Denny and Quinton. Quinton was on his cell phone, probably with the cops, while Denny paced a circle around him.

Tim's consideration seemed genuine, so she shrugged. "I'm not going anywhere." Waving her hand toward a chair, she said, "Take a load off."

"Thanks." Tim sat, but he in no way looked relaxed. "You know I've been training with Denny in my spare time, right?"

Tim was like a kid right before Christmas; he

talked of little else besides his current involvement in preparations for cage fighting. Ashley didn't think he stood a chance, but then, she wasn't the expert, and Denny had turned more than one guy into a champion.

Rather than converse, Ashley made a sound of agreement. She laid her head back and closed her eyes. The day felt so very peaceful, despite the low drone of Quinton on the phone, the laughter and chitchat of other guests, and the very real threat of a maniac who apparently had switched his hatred from Jude to her.

"So far I've spent only a few hours each day with him. Mostly learning the basics. I've wanted to do more, but any intense training takes six or more hours a day. I can't work and do both. A man doesn't take handouts, so I have to save up some cash first."

Ashley's eyes popped open. Since when did Tim refuse a handout? Hell, he'd always expected the regular handout and hand up and any old helping hand he could get from any source available.

She said cautiously, "I see," when really, she didn't see a thing.

Tugging at his ear, Tim cleared his throat and said, "I'll go on working, but I won't be able to run the car dealership for Dad anymore."

"And I bet good old Stuart isn't too happy about that?" Stuart Price cared about little other than those things that affected his fun. He didn't want to run the dealership himself anymore because it'd bite into the time he spent carousing.

Like a defeated pup, Tim dropped his head down. "He blames May."

Ashley looked toward Stuart Price and felt bone-deep loathing. "I just bet he does."

"Because she married Jude and Denny works for Jude, and Denny's the one encouraging me—"

"I know how it works, Tim. Whatever the path, it always leads back to May." Ashley's gaze transferred to May's mother. Olympia Price sucked on her cigarette like a nicotine-starved junkie. Ashley had gotten used to seeing the red glow of the cigarette in her right hand, a loaded drink in her left. "I've watched your folks dole out the blame for years."

Tim's shoulders went back in an uncommon display of backbone. "I want you to know . . . I told them they're wrong."

"Gave it some lip service, did you?" Far as Ashley was concerned, actions went a whole lot further than words.

"I had to. If it weren't for May, I'd be dead right now."

Well, hell, the shock of hearing Tim admit the truth damn near stopped her heart. Ashley narrowed her eyes in consternation. "Come again?"

"Elton wanted me dead. I was too stupid to handle things the right way. If it hadn't been for May, and how she dealt with it, I wouldn't have met Jude and Denny, and Elton would have probably beaten me to death, then left me in a ditch. You know he tried."

"He busted you up a little," Ashley said with a deliberate lack of concern in her tone, "but he didn't do any real damage."

Tim stared at her a long time, but rather than whine about things as he usually did, he gave her a lopsided grin. "It sure felt like real damage."

Ashley snickered. "Yeah, I can imagine."

He reached for her hand, and suddenly, he

seemed more like a man than ever before. "I was a coward. I *am* a coward."

She couldn't exactly debate that point, so she said nothing.

"But you aren't."

Praise from Tim? Not a come-on, but an honest compliment on her character? "What are you talking about?"

"I just . . . I wanted you to know that I appreciate everything you did for May. And everything you did for me. I know you don't like me much, and I don't blame you. It's okay. But I hope, all things considered, we can be friends."

All things considered. What the hell did that mean? "You want us to be friends?"

"Yeah." He gnawed at his upper lip, shook his head. "You're practically . . . family." His face turned red when he said that. "I know it won't be easy, because of the past and everything, but I'd like us to get along."

It was odd, but in that moment, Ashley felt connected to Tim. He was still a weasel because weasels didn't change overnight, but he *was* trying, and that counted for something. A lot, actually. Everyone deserved a chance to correct mistakes and make a better life.

She gave Tim's hand a squeeze.

In the next second, a shiver ran up her spine, and she twisted around. Both Quinton and Denny stood on the other side of the table, and neither of them looked pleased.

Denny zeroed in on their locked hands, and Tim quickly shook her off.

Quinton looked less concerned with the familiar touch, but definitely rankled. "What did she do?"

Tim and Ashley said in unison, "What?"

"You're thanking her for all she did. What'd she do?"

"Oh." Tim looked to Ashley for permission, but apparently decided he didn't need it. "She recognized Elton and his cronies having dinner at the restaurant. And even knowing who he was and how dangerous he could be, she listened to his conversation and heard enough to link Elton to the goons who beat me up. She called Jude, and he was able to confront Elton in the parking lot."

Ashley watched Quinton, but he wasn't an easy man to read, not when he wanted his thoughts hidden.

"That's why he hates you?" He looked at her so intently that she could barely find her tongue. "That's why he called you?"

"He's a lunatic. How should I know what motivates him?" Hopefully she sounded more cavalier than she felt. "I don't think he ever knew about me. I mean, I sure as hell didn't tell him I squealed. It's possible he might've just confused me with May. Except for a difference in body shape, which has been noticeable the last couple of years, she and I do look alike. From a distance we can still fool people when we wear the same clothes."

There was something, some deep understanding in Quinton's tone when he said gently, "I know."

She frowned, ready to question him on that, but Denny smacked a fist into his palm. "One thing I don't understand. How the hell did Elton get your cell phone number? It's private."

Tim's face contorted in rage, surprising Ashley. "*Elton* called you?"

"Yeah, it sounded like him. But when you hear from Jude or May, don't you say a word to them about it, understand? I won't have their honeymoon ruined."

Affronted that she'd suggest otherwise, Tim puckered up with indignation. "I wouldn't do that."

"Good." To let him know she meant it, she gave him a long stern look and then turned back to Quinton. "I have no idea how he got my phone number—"

"I got it from where you work," Tim volunteered.

Ashley swung back around to face him. "The hell you did."

"And why," Denny asked with constraint, "were you getting her number?"

One newly muscular shoulder rolled. "I was going to call her. You know, just to hang out. But," Tim said, forestalling Denny's tirade, "now I know we have a heavy workout schedule set up, so I guess I won't be doing that after all."

"Damn right you won't." It wasn't easy for Ashley to fit Quinton into her schedule. She sure as hell wouldn't go without sleep just for Tim.

"The thing is," Tim said with a frown, "I went in there to see her. She wasn't around that night, but the reservation desk posts a list of phone numbers, I guess in case they need to call anyone in. The numbers are sort of under a ledge, but all I had to do was lean over a little and peek inside the desk . . ."

When Tim realized everyone was glowering at him, he defended himself. "What? That's how I did it. And if I can do it, anyone can, including Elton."

"Reservation desk?" Quinton asked. "What are you talking about? There's no—"

Ashley diverted the conversation real quick. "Stop heaving, Denny. You look like a bull ready to charge, but no one here wants to be trampled by you."

"I'm heaving because you should have told me about the call first thing, as soon as it happened. I can be discreet, damn it."

"Says the man with fire coming out his ears."

"You should have told *me*." Quinton still had no real inflection in his tone. He looked to be in ultimate control. "And even though he's leaving the area, Jude would have wanted to know."

"I'll be calling Jude," Denny said, and he glared at Ashley, "regardless of what Ms. Smarty-pants says about it."

"Good." Quinton nodded. "He can handle it with May however he chooses."

Okay, Ashley thought, so Quinton sounded the same, but something in those piercing green eyes of his gave away the ferocity of his rage. She cleared her throat. "Like I said before you two started bickering—"

"Men don't bicker, brat."

She ignored Denny. "I didn't see any reason to tell Jude, since he'd already arranged protection for himself and May."

"It's his right," Quinton said. "And now you know that protection was arranged for you, as well."

"That wasn't news to me." At Quinton's bemused frown, she laughed. "What? You thought they could pull one over on me? Not likely."

"You're saying you knew all along?"

"From the moment Denny told me Elton was

suspected of still being in town, I figured he and Jude had called out the watchdogs."

Denny examined his nails. "Even before that, brat. A woman alone isn't safe."

"There, you see?" Ashley shook her head. "It probably wasn't Elton following me, but Denny's security people."

"No way in hell did you pick up on any of my guys following you. They're too good for that."

Ashley rolled her eyes. "God, you alpha types are arrogant."

"Maybe." Quinton crossed his arms. "But you know you can't lump me in with the infamous DZ."

His low, sexy voice sank into Ashley's bones and muddled her thoughts. She had to concentrate to keep up the banter. "Why not?" Flipping back her hair, she met his gaze squarely. "You might not have Denny's . . . flair, but you're still two peas in a pod."

Tim snickered.

Denny fried him with one glance. "She can get by with it, Tim. You can't."

Tim pretended to zip his lip.

"But you know something, Quinton?" Ashley couldn't look away from Quinton's mesmerizing smile. "It still surprised me that you'd . . . acted so quickly. I mean, at least Denny has the excuse of lumping me in as extended family, since May and I are close. You, on the other hand, barely know me."

That gibe turned his smile into something altogether different. It brought him around the table and behind her chair. He said nothing, but his movements seemed so predatory that Ashley stiffened in alarm.

All he did was settle his hands on her shoulders and begin massaging her neck. "We're officially involved, Ash. Isn't that right?"

With Denny and Tim watching in interest, she felt on display. "We've had one date, Murphy. That hardly makes us an item."

"Is that all there's been?" His thumbs moved to her nape, easing away her tension. "I seem to remember . . . more."

Smug indulgence oozed off Denny. The rat liked seeing her on the spot. Tim watched the scene with fascination. And Quinton, he just kept touching her with magic fingers, making it very easy to give in.

"Okay." Her eyelids felt heavy. "We're, uh, maybe getting involved."

Curving under her chin, his fingers tilted her face up and back. She had no choice but to look at him. "Under those circumstances," he murmured, "naturally I'd want to do what I can to ensure your safety."

"Right. Naturally."

He frowned. "As any man would."

"If you say so."

Quinton wasn't buying it. His hands stopped caressing to rest heavily on her shoulders. "You're actually going to be reasonable about this?"

"Reasonable?" She shrugged off his hold and pushed out of the chair. "Tell me this, Quinton. Would it do me any good to insist you let me handle it myself?"

"I would always take your feelings into consideration, but—"

"But you'll feel better knowing the guards are there?" He didn't have to answer; his expression told her how stubborn he'd be. "Do whatever you want. It's no skin off my nose. But I better not end up tripping over any of your goons."

Actually, she was so relieved not to be on her own that she wanted to throw herself against both men and hold them tight.

"Whatever I want, huh?"

Quinton's suggestive, husky whisper stroked over her, nearly devastating her senses. Her gaze clashed with his and he smiled.

"Thank you, Ashley. That has real possibilities."

Her hands clenched in reaction and her pulse sped into overdrive. Damn it, she always reacted that way to him—which was why she'd wanted to avoid him in the first place. "Stop it."

He shook his head. "Never."

Denny threw up his hands. "Here we go again." He slung an arm around Tim. "Come on, son. Let's get out of here before we're brought to a blush."

"Wait." Despite the image she often portrayed, Ashley wasn't cold or emotionless, and today of all days, she felt she owed Denny. She took her time reaching him, gathering her thoughts along the way.

Denny released Tim and propped his hands on his hips with a lot of bluster. "What is it now?"

When she hesitated, Quinton moved to stand behind her, and she had the awful suspicion that even when she barely knew herself, he understood exactly what she wanted and why. And damn it, his presence helped, in some indefinable way giving her courage and strength.

"Listen, Pops," she told Denny, trying for errant humor to lighten the mood, "I don't do this often, so don't think too much about it, but . . ."

Confusion lifted his brows clear up to his hairline. "Do what?"

She nibbled her lips, then just went with her heart. Sliding her arms around his trim waist and putting her cheek to his muscular chest, she hugged him tight. "Thanks."

After a couple of seconds, Denny returned the embrace with gusto, even lifting her off her feet.

With his head close to hers, his voice now filled with worry, he whispered, "What'd I do to deserve this?"

Ashley leaned back in his arms, smiling from ear to ear, feeling good inside and out. "Hey, it was a beautiful wedding, the sun is still shining, and you . . . care about me." It sounded so dumb now that she tried to verbalize it, but she didn't care. She even laughed while blushing.

Denny did care, and that meant so much to her. Unconditional caring wasn't something she would ever take for granted.

"Indeed I do." There was no smile, no softening of his expression as he smoothed back her hair. "Don't ever forget it."

She was just as serious. "So long as you know, it goes both ways."

Sunlight glinted off his silver tooth when he finally grinned. "Glad to hear it." He tweaked her chin, gave Quinton a nod, and beckoned to Tim. "Let's go see if the guests need anything else."

"Right." Tim gave Quinton a firm handshake and then put a quick peck on Ashley's cheek. "Be careful."

Left alone with Quinton, Ashley ducked her head. It struck her that touching other men— Denny, Tim, Jude—didn't set her nerves jangling or her heart popping the way it did when Quinton touched her. Just knowing he stood so close behind her had her pulse thrumming wildly.

"I already talked with the police." He spoke matter-of-factly, as if he hadn't just witnessed a monumental moment in her life. "They're aware of the phone call, but without proof that it was Elton . . ."

Ashley nodded. "There's not much they can do, I know. Even if they knew for a fact it was him, they don't know where to find him or they already would have hauled him in for questioning."

"That's about it." He caught a lock of hair that a breeze carried across her face. "They suggested you get a new cell phone."

"I'd already planned on it."

"They also said you shouldn't be alone, and I assured them you wouldn't be." Warm breath touched her ear. "I'm going to speak with the night guards in the office building to make sure they understand the seriousness of what's going on."

Why did he insist on dismissing her abilities? "I have a mouth, Quinton. I have brains. I can put together a coherent sentence, and I know them better than you do. I think I can handle alerting them to the situation."

"We'll both do it," he told her. Then he added, "I'm sorry if I seem overbearing. I only want to protect you. The thought of anyone scaring you or hurting you . . ." He trailed off, but she heard the forcefulness, the intensity of his feelings in what he said—and damn it, she liked it that he cared so much.

Because she cared too. Things were happening way too fast between them, but she had no idea how to slow them down.

She realized she was breathing too hard, that she'd fisted her hands and curled her toes inside her sandals. Urgency squeezed her lungs and made her knees tremble. Quinton was as controlling as Denny and Jude, but without the swagger. He was more . . . suave. Yeah, she liked that word applied to him.

To help conceal the mishmash of her emotions, she pasted on a cocky smile, started forward, and said, "Party's over, Murphy. Let's go."

Clouds rolled in during the drive to his home. Quinton knew it'd rain, but he didn't mention it, and neither did she. Small talk about the weather didn't interest either of them.

In the quiet confines of his car, Ashley sat stiff and silent, her hands pressed flat to the leather seat at either side of her hips—probably so she wouldn't visibly tense them again. The pulse in her throat maintained a fluttering beat. With every breath, her nostrils flared.

Desire or nervousness? He hoped she felt the same anticipation that rode him, but if not, he'd deal with it. He could be patient and slow and understanding. He *would* make this good for her.

The first spattering of raindrops hit the windshield, prompting him to turn on the wipers. From one mile to the next, the storm built, sealing in the heated passion, amplifying the things he felt, the things she made him feel.

Oddly enough, lust wasn't in the forefront. He wanted her bad, no two ways about that. But he kept recalling the way she'd hugged Denny—and thanked him for caring.

More often than not, Ashley trampled his heart just by revealing herself. Yeah, she tried hard to keep that rough-edged, no-holds-barred persona in place, but every so often it cracked, and the woman beneath was so damn sweet, so unguarded, she made him ache with unfamiliar urges.

As the fury of the storm expanded, so did the chill in the air. Quinton turned on the heat, then stroked a finger down her bare arm.

She jumped, and gooseflesh rose in the wake of his touch. He could hear her breathing and smell her scent.

"What are you thinking, Ash?" Maybe talking would help her to relax.

"You. Sex." She answered fast, then swallowed audibly. "How it'll go and what we'll do and how we get from the car to the bed and naked and all that."

Jesus. He had a boner on her second word. The rest of it left him edgy and hot. And protective. "It can go however you want."

"I don't know what I want." She damn near shouted that concern. Unsettled and panicky, she coiled toward him. "That's just it. I don't like not knowing."

Quinton slowed the car to accommodate the weather. Keeping his gaze on the road, he made a magnanimous offer—considering he'd never wanted anything as much as he wanted her just then. "We don't have to do this, honey. If you'd rather wait—"

"Are you nuts?"

"Uh . . . no." Now she appeared ready to smack him.

She leaned closer and nodded toward his lap.

"You're hard." Her tone dared him to deny it. "I know you want me."

Crazy Ashley. He shook his head, glanced at her, and smiled. Endearing, adorable, *sexy* Ashley. "Of course I want you."

"Then instead of trying to back out, why not just tell me what to expect?"

"I was not trying to back out." He flexed his fingers on the steering wheel. "It's just that there's no set pattern." She stared at him, all ears, eager to learn. He wasn't an idiot, so he wouldn't explain that it was different with every woman. Far as he was concerned, at that moment, no other women existed. "A lot will depend on you."

"Oh, great." She flopped back in her seat. "So if it all goes to hell in a handbasket, I'm to blame?"

Humor worked its way through his blinding lust. "No, honey, trust me. If things aren't right, it'll be my fault. And that's possible, because I want you so much right now, I might not be able to wait as long as I should."

"I don't want to wait." She sounded defiant and insistent. "Far as I'm concerned, tonight's the night."

"Glad to hear it, but that's not what I meant." He should start compiling all the weird conversations he had with Ashley Miles. Maybe when they were fifty, they could pull them out and laugh.

Then again, what made him think he'd even know her that many years from now?

He shook his head, glad for the storm that required his attention and kept him from having to look at her through this bizarre topic.

Trying to be pragmatic instead of seductive, he explained, "Women react differently than men."

"Liberated women would disagree."

So she wanted him to spell it out? Fine. "Right now, you could make me come with little effort."

She went still, then perked up in interest. "Really? How?"

Apparently, Ashley harbored some insane notion that he could comfortably discuss this when, to him, it felt like prolonged foreplay—making it far from comfortable. "Just being near you, smelling you, puts me more than halfway there."

"*Smelling* me?"

God help him. At her tone of affront, his smile went crooked. "You smell nice. Like a woman should."

Cautiously, she dipped her nose near her shoulder and sniffed. "I think you're nuts."

"No, I'm a man." He shifted his position, hoping to ease the restriction in his pants. "A few strokes with your hand, one thrust inside you, and I'd be a goner."

She said not a single word, but her rapt attention nearly made his muscles cramp. He could almost hear the wheels turning in her head, knew she was visualizing what he'd said, and that she'd love to see him lose control.

It was in Ashley's nature to push things, to be the aggressor—which was probably why she worried now. She didn't want to be out of control, with no idea of how things would progress.

"Climaxing is not so easy for women."

His plain speaking caused her to stiffen, but she kept her attention glued to him.

"They require more attention than men. And since I want you to enjoy yourself as much as possible, I'll need to take my time."

"I don't want to be a burden, Murphy."

So prickly. He shook his head and smiled. "Kissing you, touching you and tasting you, making love to you, will never be a hardship. Foreplay, yes. Torment, you bet. But that's part of what makes it so sweet."

"Sweet, huh?" She folded her arms beneath her breasts and gave her attention to the darkening sky. "It doesn't look sweet. I mean in movies and stuff. It looks sweaty and hot and . . ."

"Fun?"

She rolled a shoulder. "I guess."

Even in the shadows of the car, Quinton could see the flush of heat coloring her skin. "In a few more minutes we'll be at my place. I'll park in the garage, and we'll enter through the kitchen. Not a bad place for making love, but this first time for you, I think, should be in my bedroom. Don't you?"

"I'm not picky."

But she was a temptress without even trying. "Are you hungry?"

She gave him a look filled with incredulity.

"Good. Then we'll skip that and go straight to my bedroom. Once we're there, I'll close the door and kiss you."

"And then?"

Nothing showed on his face, but he smiled to himself, knowing he had her. "I'll go on kissing you until you want more. Not just your mouth, but your throat and your ears and your shoulders."

"Then we get naked?"

God, she could take the upper hand so easily. "If that's what you want."

"I'd like to see you naked."

He damn near wrecked the car. "Not a problem. I'll be happy to oblige."

"No modesty?"

"Not a speck, sorry."

"You look that good?"

Jesus. He turned the heat off and even considered opening a window. "I have no idea if you'll think so, but I'm not dissatisfied with myself. What about you?"

She shrugged. "I'm lacking in the upper works, but you don't seem to mind. Other than that, I'm okay."

Better than okay. She made him salivate.

"I'm in shape and trim," she added. "My legs are kind of long. So no, I won't mind losing the dress. I'm not real comfortable in it anyway. And I'll be thrilled to get rid of the stupid bra. It's suffocating. I'm not used to it."

"Comfortable or not, you look incredible. You always look good. Sexy and casual at the same time."

She shifted and somehow, even though she still wore her seat belt, she was closer to him. "The whole sex thing is more spontaneous in the movies. Not so orchestrated."

"They just make it look that way."

"No wild abandon or evaporating clothes?" she teased.

"Responsible men behave responsibly. They don't risk a woman's reputation through indiscretion. They don't risk her future by forgoing protection."

"Rubbers?"

"Exactly. No child deserves to be brought into

the world by accident, maybe unloved or unwanted."
As she had been. Never would he do that to a child.

"Not all accidental births are unwanted. Some
are happy surprises."

"Too many aren't. There are enough abandoned
children awaiting love and attention already."

Her brows knitted in confusion and curiosity.
Damn, but he'd sounded too fervent. Much more
of that and he'd be giving himself away.

"So you've never lost your head with a woman?"

More moderate, he stated, "I've never been so
overcome with lust that I couldn't think clearly about
consequences. I've made mistakes. I'm human.
But lust wasn't the cause."

Sounding less than reassured, she said, "Hmmm."

He looked at her and caught her staring at his
tie in deep contemplation. "Once we've ensured
privacy and taken care of birth control, feel free to
be as abandoned as you want."

She gave him a sweet smile that should have
warned him. "Thanks. And ya know, I think we
should start the undressing right now."

He laughed. "If you show any more, I'll wreck
the car."

"We can't have that." She slid her fingers around
his tie and pulled it loose. "Aren't you choking in
this shirt?" Under her deft fingers, one button
opened, then another and another . . . Her hand,
soft and curious, slid inside his shirt to rub over his
left pectoral muscle. Her delicate fingers felt cool
against his heated skin.

"I don't know if this is a good idea."

She paid no mind to his warning. In a whisper,
she asked, "Are you this hairy all over?"

Quinton shook his head, but it was more a loss of voice than an answer. Her fingertips grazed his left nipple, and he thought he'd split his pants.

Thank God, the lighted entry to his circular drive came into view. "We're here."

His announcement stilled her sensual exploration. "Where?"

"My home."

Her hands slid off him and she craned her head to see, then gave a soft, "Ohhh. Very nice. How big is it?"

At the indelicate query, Quinton regained some aplomb. Leave it to Ashley to ask what others wouldn't. "Around seven thousand square feet, give or take. Probably smaller than Jude's home, if that's what you're wondering."

"Ah well, you're not a movie star." She patted his chest, then settled back in her own seat, looking all around as he drove up the drive. "I promise not to hold it against you."

Her facetiousness, especially given that her dark eyes were wide with fascination, gave him a smile. "Thank you."

"It's really nice. Different. I'm not familiar with the style, though."

"It's called Tuscan, but I bought it for the acreage, not so much the design of the house. I like my privacy."

"Jude likes water. And bathrooms. I swear I could live in one of his bathrooms, they're so posh."

He and Jude had that in common, then. But rather than tell her so, he'd like to show her his newest toy in the bathroom—a spigot in the ceiling that filled the tub with the effect of a waterfall. He'd thought many times what a nice accompaniment his playground-sized tub, with subtle lighting and an invisible sound system, would be to romance. Until now, he hadn't brought a woman to his home to test that theory. He had a feeling Ashley would enjoy it as much as he did.

With the push of a button, one of four garage doors opened and Quinton drove inside.

"God," she whispered, her nose practically glued to the door window. "It's like a giant cave."

"The entire house has very high ceilings." He put the car in park and turned off the engine. "My security isn't quite as technical as Jude's. I don't have monitors in every room. But a highly recommended and reliable private company installed and runs the alarm system and specialty locks. It'll serve its purpose. I don't want you to worry."

Sparing him an impatient peek, she unhooked her seat belt. "Trust me. Elton and his idiotic revenge is the last thing on my mind right now." She had her door open before he could get out and do the gentlemanly deed for her. "Now get a move on, Murphy. Time's a-wasting."

Chapter 8

Ashley got as far as the kitchen and stalled. Not as big as Jude's? Somehow she doubted that. From what she could see, Quinton's home was immense, going on forever in all directions. He had an open, sprawling floor plan and mile-high ceilings. Marble floors gleamed, and leaded glass doors and windows sparkled with raindrops.

Looking around at a mammoth kitchen with a breakfast area and sunroom, across to a formal dining room with fluted columns, and finally toward a two-story foyer, she whistled in wonder. If it weren't for Jude and getting comfortable in his house, she'd be pretty damned intimidated right now.

"Rich people amaze me." She eyed the unique reverse tray ceiling over the polished mahogany dining table. "I had no idea there were so many ways to spend money."

"I didn't build the house, Ash."

Turning to Quinton, she said, "No, but you . . ."

Whatever thoughts she'd had dwindled into nothingness at the sight of him. He'd pulled his tie free and slipped off his suit coat. With his unbuttoned and untucked dress shirt, she got a great view of his chest, and man, oh man, he had a fine chest indeed.

Warmth blossomed out from her belly to her limbs and settled low, making her lock her legs together. She whistled again, this time at him. "Just hairy enough," she said in answer to her earlier question.

"I reset the alarms." The awareness in his fascinating eyes intensified while the corners of his mouth lifted. Her appreciation of his body pleased him. "This way."

He indicated she should precede him down the hall, and like a zombie, she did so. The touch of his hand burned on the small of her back as he silently guided her past the foyer and through a private vestibule to a lavish master bedroom. The room was bigger than her whole apartment.

Tiered, vaulted ceilings held small windows to let in moonlight. Oriental rugs warmed a porcelain tile floor. Dark mahogany bedroom furniture, a stuffed couch and two chairs, a gas fireplace, and floor-to-ceiling windows complemented the size of the room. Opposite the bed, glass doors led to an enclosed porch.

"Do you like it?"

"It's . . . I've never seen anything like it." She started to look again at the tray ceiling complemented with roped and recessed lighting, but Quinton caught her shoulders, turned her toward him, and took her mouth.

It was a slow, gentle kiss, lingering and sweet

and damp. She parted her lips and felt his tongue touch hers. Just that, nothing more, but it shot her temperature up a couple of degrees. She slipped her arms around him, then spread her hands beneath his open shirt to relish the feel of him.

His skin was so warm and taut, his scent delicious. With every breath he took, she experienced the shifting of his muscles. So much leashed power. The thin material of her dress felt like less than air when she cuddled against him.

She breathed deeper just to inhale him. His hand cradled the back of her head and he deepened the kiss, slowly sinking his tongue past her teeth while drawing her body into complete contact with his. She went on tiptoe to help him, clutching his back, trying to get as close as possible.

The press of his thick erection between her thighs both startled and stirred her. Urgency thrummed through her veins. She'd never felt like this and she didn't want it to go away. It was too exciting, too molten and exhilarating.

She freed her mouth from his. In a broken rasp she barely recognized as her own, she whispered, "Let's get rid of some of our clothes." She wanted to feel him everywhere. Right now.

Quinton stood there watching her in what appeared to be astonishment.

Was she moving too fast for him? Should she be more subtle? She looked at him, at his exposed chest, now-rumpled hair, and concentrated expression, and she didn't care about subtlety. He'd just have to deal with her eagerness. But as a concession, she said, "Don't worry. I can handle this part on my own."

Lifting first one of his heavy wrists, then the

other, she quickly opened his cuff links and went to a granite-topped nightstand to set them down. When she turned back around, Quinton still stood where she'd left him. His arms hung loose at his sides, his feet braced apart, his head slightly turned to watch her every move.

She felt like a kid in a candy store.

Hurrying back to him, she pushed the shirt off his shoulders and down his arms until it dropped to the floor. Then she just took her time looking at him.

He might not be a fighter like Jude, but he had an incredible physique, far different than she'd expected from a business exec. She knew he spent forty-plus hours at a desk, yet he looked like he spent an equal amount of time in physical exertion.

Instead of being bulky, lean muscles roped his shoulders, his pecs, and down his abdomen for an impressive six-pack. Dark blond chest hair drew her fingers, and she stroked over him, very aware of his stillness, the heightened anticipation in his every breath.

That enticing body hair trailed downward over his midsection, around his navel, then disappeared into his slacks. With one finger she traced that sexy line of hair to his belt. He inhaled sharply.

Anxious, she gripped his belt buckle—and he closed his hands over hers.

Lifting one fist to kiss her knuckles, he said, "This isn't a race, honey."

How could he be so calm and controlled? "If it was, I'd sure as hell win." The room hung heavy with growing shadows, brightened only by the occasional flash of lightning. "You got a light switch in here anywhere?"

Several seconds ticked by before a small sound of amusement escaped him. "Damn, but you please me, Ashley."

"You look confused, not pleased."

"Let's say pleasantly surprised." He smiled at her. "So you want light?" He went back to the nightstand and turned on a lamp. It sent a gentle glow throughout the room, not intrusive, but illuminating so that she could better see him. "Good enough?"

She'd prefer him under a spotlight, where she could really check out his goods, but she didn't want to push her luck. "It'll do."

He strode across the room to the window and with the press of a button, heavy curtains came together.

Ashley admired his broad back and the play of muscles in his shoulders. "Privacy?"

"There aren't any neighbors close by, but I don't like to take chances." Now on the other side of the bed, he faced her—and reached for his belt. With deft fingers he opened the buckle, gave a tug, and it slid free of his slacks with a quiet hiss.

Her heart popped into her throat, then dropped fast and hard to her stomach. "I need to sit down for this."

She slipped off her sandals, hiked her dress up to her thighs, and crawled up onto his massive bed to sit yoga-style. The plush, down-filled white comforter billowed around her.

With a steadying sigh, she folded her hands into her lap. "Okay, I'm ready. Go on."

Even with her fascinated concentration, he wasn't the least bit discomfited or uncertain. He just looked sexy as hell.

He toed off first one shoe, then the other. "I've never deliberately stripped for a woman before." Holding her gaze, he unzipped his slacks and pushed them down his hips. He bent to take them the rest of the way off and removed his socks at the same time.

When he straightened, he wore only snug black boxers that in no way concealed an impressive erection. He tossed the pants aside and stood there in a loose-limbed, in-control way, giving her plenty of time to look him over.

In a croak, she said, "You should do it more often. You'd make a fortune."

"I already have a fortune."

Ashley shook her head. He took her breath away. "Okay, damn, I wish I'd worn sexy underwear, too."

His half smile didn't soften the lust in his face. He came to her on the bed, knelt in front of her, and with one finger, toyed with the strap of her gown. "Now you."

"See, the thing is . . ." But she didn't really know what to say.

He stared at her while dragging the left strap down, down until the material drooped and he could play one finger across the top of her left breast, pushed up by the specialty bra.

She swallowed. "Never mind."

He teased his finger across her tingling skin again, gently nudging the bra down, and her nipple popped free.

His smiled faded. His eyes darkened. With a sharp inhalation, he caught her under the arms and lifted her.

Startled, she said, "Hey, wait—*oh shit.*" His mouth latched onto her nipple and he sucked softly, and God Almighty, she felt it everywhere: the stroke of his tongue, the pull as he suckled, and the flash fire of heat . . .

To balance herself, she sank her fingers into his bare shoulders and dropped her head back.

How could that feel *so* good? If she'd known, she'd have figured out a way to try all this a lot sooner. "Quinton?"

Her shaky whisper got her lowered flat to the bed, but he didn't release her nipple. He used one hand to plump up her breast and continued to draw on her, running his tongue over and around her, nipping with his teeth, tugging and pulling.

She moaned and writhed, but that only seemed to encourage him. His hands started caressing everywhere, down her sides to her hips, along her thighs.

"The bra's in the way," she complained.

He kissed his way up her chest to her throat and then to her mouth. His hand dipped into the bra cup and covered her breast. His thumb rolled over her now-wet nipple.

The press of his heavy body atop hers only exacerbated already sizzling nerves. She turned her head, gasping for air. "Oh God, wait."

Panting, he levered himself up on stiffened arms, giving her some space. As he surveyed her body, he looked more out of it than in charge.

Ashley touched his jaw. "I want to get out of my bra and dress."

His jaw locked. "Roll over."

That sounded pretty coarse and somewhat unnerving. "Yeah, uh . . . why?"

His head dropped forward and he groaned. "Although it's not an altogether unpleasant idea, I'm not planning to attack you from the rear."

"Quinton . . ."

"You have a zipper on the back of your dress. I prefer using it to ripping this thing off you like a barbarian."

"Oh. Right. My zipper." Feeling like an unschooled virgin idiot, Ashley rolled to her stomach and stacked her arms under her cheek. Then she waited. And waited some more.

Quinton didn't move, didn't make a sound.

After a few seconds she wiggled one foot. "Hello? You still awake, Murphy?"

His hand settled heavily on her bottom. "Then again," he rasped, "the rear view of you is awfully tempting."

Ashley deliberately wiggled. "Concentrate, Quinton. Zip-per."

"In a minute." His long fingers clasped her ankle.

Uh-oh. She froze in expectation, barely breathing as she waited to see what he planned to do.

His hand slid up her calf, then paused at her knee. Using just his fingertips, he stroked her there, trailing back and forth.

She stuck her face in the mattress and, trying not to be too blatant, opened her legs a little.

He took the hint and climbed his fingers higher again, along the inside of her thigh, up and up, until he slid over her satiny panties to cup her bottom. "You have a great ass, Ashley."

Her muffled, "Thank you," sounded absurd even to her own ears.

His thumb slid along the cleft of her bottom, not low enough to touch her where she really wanted to be touched, but enough to make her heart pound painfully. "Open your legs more."

Oh, God. She swallowed, and still with her face pressed in the mattress, said, "The dress is too tight."

"I'll help." He shoved up the skirt until her bottom was uncovered. Material bunched around her waist, while cool air drifted over her skin. A little hoarse, Quinton said, "There you go."

Right. Now he wanted her to . . . open her legs. She gulped—and parted her thighs.

Immediately, his hand slid over the crotch of her panties. In a seductive whisper, he said, "You're burning up, Ash."

No kidding. To prompt him, she wiggled a little.

One finger dipped between her legs, sliding along the slippery material of her panties and shooting sensation all through her. She tightened her shoulders and held her breath, and still a moan escaped.

"I think," he murmured, bending down to kiss her shoulder, "that virgins are more fun than I ever realized."

Ashley drew a deep breath and rose up to her elbows. "Right now I'm more interested in putting that virgin status behind me." She looked at him over her shoulder, and their gazes locked. "You wanna get on with it?"

His mouth quirked, but his eyes were molten. "No, actually I don't." His fingers searched over her panties, prodding carefully, and then he was touching her in a place that electrified. "I'd rather watch you come first. And incredible as it seems, I think you're almost there."

She wanted to protest, she really did. But words wouldn't come. Her eyes sank closed, her fingers knotted in his bedding, and she dropped her head forward.

Quinton began kissing her shoulder again, licking her skin, taking soft, sumptuous love bites that made her tingle all the way down to her toes. And all the while his fingers remained between her legs, teasing her, drawing her, until she felt herself trembling uncontrollably.

Without interrupting the rhythm of his fingers, he scooted closer to her. He kissed her nape, and then her ear, gently nibbling on her earlobe. His erection pressed against her thigh, and that tantalized, too, reminding her that this turned him on, that he enjoyed touching her almost as much as she liked being touched.

Something, some insidious, sweet sensation, coiled inside her, tighter and tighter until it became unbearable. She gasped for air. The muscles in her thighs tensed. And before she even realized what would happen, she broke, arching her back and moaning and pressing into the mattress in an embarrassing, uninhibited way.

Quinton groaned too, closing his teeth on the soft muscle of her shoulder and staying with her until the climax began to recede.

Her whole body went lax while a little buzz filled her head. "Man." That one word cost her and she had to suck air for a few seconds before she could clarify. "That was . . . awesome."

Quinton didn't appear to be listening. He was

too busy kissing her everywhere, and at the same time, sliding down her zipper. The back clasp of her bra opened with one small flick of his fingers. He went to his knees, pulled down the narrow straps of her gown, and then rolled her to her back.

With one arm, he scooped up her legs and tugged the dress past her hips. He tossed it and her bra over the footboard of the bed. An instant later, his fingers hooked in the waistband of her panties and peeled them down her legs.

So relaxed she felt like dozing off, Ashley watched him look her over, and she smiled at the hunger in his eyes.

"Your turn, Quinton?"

Without taking his gaze off her body, he rose from the bed. "And yours. You'll come again, honey, I swear it."

That sounded interesting. But she doubted the possibility of it. "I think I'm shot."

"I'll rejuvenate you," he said, and shucked off his boxers.

Eyes wide, Ashley turned to her side and propped herself on one elbow. She patted the mattress. "Come back to bed."

"You can count on it." He went to his dresser and opened the top middle drawer to draw out a box of condoms.

"You sure are taking your time."

That made him laugh. "I'm gathering my control so I don't ravage you."

"Ravaging sounds nice."

"You only say that because you've never been ravaged. Give me a minute, and I promise to make it worth your while."

Shrugging, Ashley sat up and looked around at

the bedding. "Should we fold down this comforter or something?"

"No." He moved to the side of the bed and set the box on the nightstand. Ashley eyed it and realized it was nearly full. "I like seeing you there, just like that."

She snagged a pillow and put it under her head. "Well, I'm starting to feel more than a little exposed, so come join me."

"All right." After opening a condom packet with his teeth, he rolled on the rubber and stretched out alongside her. Drifting his fingers through her hair, he said, "You're beautiful."

"I think I'm a little sweaty."

He didn't smile. He dipped his face into her neck and nuzzled her skin. "I think you're delicious."

Ashley pushed him to his back. "Now that you've locked all that iron control into place, I want to look at you and touch you a little. Okay?"

He closed his eyes, groaned, and said, "I'll try."

He sounded pained, but that didn't deter her. She sat up next to him and tried to decide where to start. "I've never before seen a naked guy up close and personal."

Quinton eyed her, took her wrist, and flattened her hand on his chest. His heartbeat thumped madly against her palm. "I told you, men are easy. From the time you agreed to come home with me, I've been ready. But that doesn't mean I want to rush things. At seventeen I rushed. Hell, at twenty I rushed. But I'm thirty-three and wiser and I want to savor this. I want to savor you."

Her heart felt too big for her chest. "You are such a sweet talker, without sounding corny." She trailed her hand down his chest to his stomach—

which went rock hard—and then down to his sex. "Now, hush."

Before she even really touched him, he groaned again. She watched him flex, then put her hand around him and felt it. Fascinated, she stroked along his length, then down, to cup his testicles. So much heat. Expecting his eyes to be closed, she glanced at Quinton.

His eyelids were heavy, but still open. He wasn't looking at her face; he watched her breasts and belly and he looked savage with lust.

As he'd promised, she felt revived. More than revived, she craved him. She wanted it all this time, him inside her, his own pleasure, everything.

Stretching out over him, cupping his face, she said, "This is so damned exciting, isn't it?" And then she kissed him and his hands were all over her, squeezing her behind, parting her thighs so that she straddled him, his clever fingers seeking her out again, and this time there wasn't any underwear to blunt the sensation.

She hummed with the pleasure of it—until he pushed one finger inside her. With a gasp, she reared up.

Quinton's hand curved around her neck, drawing her close again so that he could continue kissing her. He held her secure, not hurting her, but she couldn't shy away from his touches.

Not that she really wanted to. She'd lurched with the unfamiliar invasion, but only out of surprise. Truthfully, the feeling of helplessness amplified her arousal. She pressed down, trying to increase the pressure. Quinton obliged her by insinuating a second finger into her. He had large hands, and she felt stretched, deliciously so.

Her moan reverberated against his mouth, and he gave her a growl in return.

"So wet," he murmured against her lips, while working his fingers in and out. "God, I can't wait to get inside you."

Ashley wanted to be flippant and say, *Then don't wait*, but he didn't give her the chance. In one quick movement he twisted, and she was on her back with him between her opened thighs.

He reared up, his expression intent and dark. He reached between their bodies and she gasped to feel him touching her, opening her.

"Put your legs around me."

It was hard to move with him stroking her, spreading her moisture, rasping over her clitoris again and again. But as he looked patient enough to wait all day, she lifted her legs and twined them around his waist. She shivered in anticipation and a touch of nervousness.

As if he sensed her uncertainty, he whispered, "Okay?"

She nodded and braced herself. But he only smiled at her and gently nudged his erection in close to her while sinking down onto her. He laced his fingers with hers and raised her arms above her head.

Hands locked together, gazing into her eyes, he began pushing into her.

She hadn't expected any discomfort. After all, she wasn't a kid. But as he entered her, it did hurt a little, and try as she might, she couldn't keep the gasp quiet, or stop herself from turning her head away, her eyes squeezed shut.

Quinton didn't seem to mind. He licked the pulse in her throat, nuzzled her ear, and whispered hotly, "You're so snug and so wet. You feel like heaven." He slipped in another inch. "Damn. Just try to relax with me, honey. Open up and let me in."

Her hands gripped his, and she tried to concentrate on loosening up, but the damp heat of his mouth distracted her.

"That's it, Ash. A little more." His tongue touched her ear, sending a quiver down her spine. While his hips flexed and his shoulders bunched, he drew on her earlobe, teasing her with new sensations, until suddenly he was all the way in her and she was so full, so surrounded by him, she couldn't draw breath.

He released her hands to hold her face and kiss her with naked hunger. He didn't thrust, didn't even move. He just stayed buried inside her while kissing her and within moments, her body adjusted and even clamped around him.

"I'm sorry," he rasped, and he stiffened his arms to rise above her, driving into her in a fast, deep rhythm.

Pulled into the pleasure, Ashley cried out and automatically tightened her thighs, holding him as an anchor.

"Move with me," he urged darkly. "Move, honey. Like this." His hand slid beneath her bottom and he brought her into his rhythm so that she countered his every thrust. "Yeah, just like that. Perfect."

His fingers sank into her buttocks, but she barely noticed. That incredible mix of pressure and pleasure began to build again, rising quicker this time, hotter, more consuming.

"*Oh, God.*" She struggled against him, reaching for her own release. "Quinton . . ."

He stiffened, brows down, jaw clenched. *"Damn."* He groaned harsh and low, flooding her in heat, then thrusting hard, deep, his movements static.

Ashley watched him through a haze of acute pleasure. She was so excited to see him come that, combined with his continued thrusts, she found her own release. It took her by surprise, and it wasn't until Quinton sank against her, spent, that she realized her nails were digging into his shoulders and her heels were pressed into the small of his back.

Sweat dampened her skin and she couldn't yet speak, but she dropped her arms away from him, let her legs slide down to sprawl beneath him. "Sorry," she gasped around her panting breaths.

He said nothing, just continued to relax atop her, his own breathing jagged.

She stared at his ceiling and concentrated on regaining her wits. A minute later, Quinton kissed her shoulder, lifted himself away, and then drew her in close to his side.

"Sorry for what?" Sounding lethargic but pleased, he stroked her hair away from her face and pressed another kiss to her forehead.

Still on her back, she dropped an arm over her eyes. Even after everything they'd just done, his intimate scrutiny shook her composure. "I didn't mean to hurt you."

"You didn't."

She forced herself up enough to see his shoulder. Deep half moons marred his skin and contradicted his assurances. In apology, she touched him gently. "That was a little more intense than I'd figured on." She plopped to her back and sighed. "Pretty powerful stuff."

"I'm sorry I hurt you, too."

She shrugged that off. "It was necessary, me being a stupid virgin and all."

"There's nothing stupid about you." She could hear the smile in his tone and felt his tenderness in the way he continued to touch her. "Being your first gave me more pleasure than you'll ever know."

She slanted him a look. "More of that alpha male stuff?"

"Please refrain from comparing me to Denny."

She laughed. "I wasn't, not really."

He tipped her face up to his. "You're beautiful, Ashley."

Sex talk, she figured. She was passably pretty on good days, and right now, she had to be sweaty on top of having tangled hair and ruined makeup. "Whatever you say."

Instead of debating with her, he gave an indulgent shake of his head. "I need to go clean up. Stay put and I'll be right back."

After indulging in a massive yawn and stretching, she said, "Yeah, you do that." She rolled to her side, snuggled her head into a downy pillow, and closed her eyes. She had so many unanswered questions, but at least now, she understood how two people got from point A to point B.

And spontaneous or not, it was well worth the effort.

By the time Quinton returned from the bathroom, Ashley was half asleep. He stood beside the bed a moment, just looking at her, then he lay down behind her and drew her into the curve of his body.

She was curious about him, about the ease with which he treated the circumstances, the things he'd done to her and what he might have done with other women. Obviously he had some skills in the sack. Thinking of the things he'd said and how he'd anticipated her reactions, she sighed. Now she knew what she'd been missing, but she was glad she'd waited for Quinton.

That thought led to another, and since it wasn't in her nature to hold back her thoughts, she said, "Hey, Quinton?"

"Hmm?"

She twisted to face him. His eyes were closed, his face utterly relaxed.

She propped herself up on an elbow and asked, "Have you ever been in love?"

Chapter 9

Keeping his eyes shut, Quinton hoped to hide his shock. Love? Dear God, what woman brought up such a subject only seconds after sex? And not just sex, but extremely satisfying, mind-blowing sex?

When he said nothing, she huffed. "Bad question?"

Like the village idiot, he said, "Uhhh . . ."

She poked him in the chest. "You're suddenly as tense as a live wire. I didn't propose, Murphy. No reason to freak out."

"Ashley." Aggrieved, he opened his eyes and met her puzzled frown. "Do you realize you call me Murphy whenever you're irate with me?"

"I bet I call you that a lot, then. Especially when you're trying to avoid one subject by starting another."

He shook his head. "I'm not avoiding it." But he knew he was. "You took me by surprise, that's all."

"Asking you that was bad form, huh? Well, how

am I to know? If you don't want to talk about it, just say so."

An actual reprieve? Great. "I don't want to—"

"Because I'm only curious." She pushed out of his arms and sat up in a sulk, slapping the pillow into her lap to shield her body. "I mean, you're pretty good at this whole sex thing."

A compliment or an accusation? With Ashley he couldn't be sure. "Ah . . . thank you. I think." She looked adorable sitting there in the buff, cross-legged, a mulish scowl on her face. Her dark hair was tangled and hanging over her shoulders, her dark eyes circled by ruined makeup.

And damn, he wanted her again.

"So you had to have learned by practice, right?"

Seeing no hope for it, Quinton gathered his thoughts while propping himself against the headboard. He crossed his ankles, laced his hands over his abdomen, and got comfortable.

Ashley watched him with blatant suspicion.

Starting with the obvious, he said, "You already knew I wasn't a monk, honey."

She jumped on that. "But there's a difference in being proficient at something, and excelling."

Masculine pride lifted his eyebrows. "I excelled?"

She snorted. "Don't go fishing for compliments."

Unrepentant, he grinned. "I'm sorry."

"So have you ever been in love?"

He pondered the odds of snatching that pillow away from her, getting her on her back and turning her thoughts onto better things, but knowing Ashley, she'd probably brain him if he tried it.

Watching for her reaction, he shrugged and admitted, "Once."

"Really?" Her back went straight. "Did you marry her?"

"No."

"Well, why not?"

He put a fist to his forehead. "Ashley . . . you do realize that most women, especially a woman naked in bed with a man with whom she's just been intimate, don't want to hear about *other* women from the man's past?"

She swatted him in the arm. "I don't want graphic details on your bedroom antics. I'm not a perv. I just want to know more about you."

God, how did he tell the long and short of it without going into extended details? He looked at her expectant expression and settled on the truth. "She didn't love me back. She loved having sex with me, and she loved my wealth and my business. She loved some of what I represent, but not the whole of who I am."

"Just what the heck is that supposed to mean?"

He searched for the right words. "Not everyone is exactly who they appear to be on the surface. People have passions and disappointments, goals and failures. Not many women understand the things for which I feel most . . . committed."

She nodded and asked the obvious. "What things?"

Although he had a gut feeling that Ashley would understand and support him in his efforts, he wasn't ready to open himself up yet. "Not on a first date, after our first sexual experience."

"Secrets." She bobbed her eyebrows. "Now you've got me really curious."

"Then we're even because I'm very curious about you, too."

She deflected that easily, saying, "That lady you loved?"

"Yes, what about her?"

"I'm sorry, but she must've been a complete dope." Wearing a wolfish smile, Ashley ran her fingers up his biceps and over to his chest. "No matter what secret passions you have, you're still a catch. Gorgeous, funny, and kind."

"Not to mention rich?"

She went very serious on him. "Think what you want, but coming from my background, rich isn't as important as hardworking and honorable."

He believed her, but she appeared so somber, he had to tease a little. "So if I lived in a shack, you'd still be interested?"

"If you were working to change your circumstances, maybe. But I wouldn't live in that shack with you."

Deep-rooted wounds shone through her expression, making his chest constrict. He flattened his hand over hers, keeping her palm against his heart. "You've already done your time in a shack?"

"That's right. But I've spent my entire adult life working hard to change things. I don't need wealth, but I do need money in the bank, respectability, and security."

Thinking of her goals, he nodded. "Those things are really important to you, aren't they?"

"I'll do whatever I have to do to get them."

Whatever I have to do. Those words echoed in his head like a bass drum. "That sounds rather ominous."

"It's the truth." She didn't shy away from his gaze. "No matter how hard I have to work, or what I have to sacrifice."

Meaning she'd sacrifice her time with him? He never doubted it. On that much, she'd always been up-front and honest. But knowing it only made him want her that much more. "What if you fall in love?"

A devilish grin appeared. "C'mon, Murphy. You're the only guy I'm seeing. You're good, but not that good."

He laughed to cover his unease. "You wound me, woman."

She grew serious again, toying with his chest hair and effectively driving him nuts. "So what about other women? You've only been serious that one time?"

"I've had relationships that could have gone further and didn't for a number of reasons. I've had casual women friends—"

"Who you slept with?"

"Yes." She wanted to know, so he'd be straight with her. "Sex for the sake of sex is different, though."

"How?"

He struggled for the words to explain it. "It's . . . colder. Emotionally, I mean. It quells an urge. Feeds a hunger. Everyone comes and all that. But that's all there is."

She considered that before saying, "This felt like more."

He couldn't deny it. "Yes."

Tilting her head, she chewed her bottom lip in deep thought. Her expression gave her away, and he knew what she'd say before she said it. Snatching the pillow away from her, he caught her hand and tugged her into his arms. "Don't look so worried, Ashley. It *was* more, but you don't have to go skittish on me. I'm not in love with you." *Not yet, anyway.*

"Good. Don't fall in love with me." She cupped a hand to his face, smiling cheekily. "I know it'll be tough, but try to resist. I'm not ready to be in love with anyone, and I don't want to see you hurt."

Quinton laughed, but he needed her to know. "Fair enough, as long as you understand that this is more than sex for me, and you're more than a casual fling."

She put her thigh over his, her arm around his waist, and settled her cheek on his shoulder. "That's nice to know. Thank you." She went silent and stayed that way so long that Quinton thought she might be dozing off.

Incredulous, he peered down at her peaceful smile and closed eyes. She *did* look ready to nod off. Of all the . . . He swatted her behind with his open palm.

"Hey!" Bolting upright, she stared at her cheek, then glared at him. "I didn't sign up for any kinky spanking stuff, so get that out of your head right now."

Quinton rolled his eyes. "I realize you're hardly versed in situations involving men and lovemaking and after-sex conversations, but a little reciprocal assurance would be nice."

Expression arrested, she blinked at him, then grinned. "Ah, poor baby. You wanna know that I care, is that it?"

He made a grab for her and with a squeal, she darted away and scrambled off the bed, giving him a titillating shot of her naked behind before ducking around the footboard.

Grinning, she shook her finger at him. "How soon they forget." She braced her hands on the footboard and leaned in toward him. "Does the word *virgin* ring a bell? No experience on my end, remember, so I can't really do any comparisons—or assurances. For me, this was sex."

When he started to rise, she held up her hands, laughing. "Breathtaking sex. With a really remarkable guy. A guy I like and admire."

Satisfied, Quinton rested back against the pillows. "That's better. You're learning."

She waited until he was settled to say, "But no, I'm not in love with you—and don't you dare frown at me like that. You just said that you don't love me, either!"

But that was only a half truth. She fascinated him. Mesmerized him. And turned him inside out. He knew it was only a matter of time before he went ass over end for her. Until that happened, he'd do his best to win her over completely.

No way in hell was he going to fall in love alone.

"As long as this is about sex, I say we should get to it."

Her smile turned adoring. "Now you're talking." She backed up. "But I need a shower first." Her nose wrinkled. "I'm sticky. And sweaty. And . . ."

Quinton left the bed to stalk toward her. "And what?"

"A little sore."

She made that admission as if it were a sign of weakness. There were so many things to admire about Ashley. Her forthright manner, her loyalty to her friends. And her strengths. She'd be a very easy woman to love. "I have a cure." He lurched toward her, and before she could escape him, he scooped her up. "Just relax and leave it to me."

She laughed and put her arms around his neck. "How gallant is this? I feel pampered."

"Good." After carrying her into his opulent bathroom, he waited, and when her mouth dropped open, he grinned at her. "You like it?"

"Good God. It's . . . unreal."

"Wait." He set her on a plush padded bench in front of floor-to-ceiling mirrors and went to the enormous tub. After closing the drain, he said, "Look up."

She did, and he turned on the brass and enamel spigot, releasing the water from the ceiling in a sparkling cascade that quickly began filling the tub.

"Holy shit. That's amazing." She left the seat in a daze, watching the waterfall with wide eyes. "I've never seen anything like it."

"It's a fairly new design." He held out a hand, and when she took it, he stepped into the tub with her.

"It's not even splashing."

"Of course not. Wouldn't be much fun if it made a mess." He sat in a corner of the tub and drew her down onto his lap. "Once it's full, I'll turn on the jets. We'll soak awhile. That'll make you feel better."

She put an arm on the granite-tiled shelf around the tub, then did a double take. "Is it my imagination, or is this rock warm?"

"It's heated from underneath, as is the floor. It's computerized to adjust itself to the weather. I rarely have to adjust it."

"Incredible." Scooting around to get comfortable, she rested her head back on his shoulder and watched the waterfall. "I think I've changed my mind."

Still a little addled from the way her bottom twisted around on his lap, Quinton only half heard her. He'd just had phenomenal sex, but already he grew hard again. Over her slender shoulder, he could see her delicate breasts, her rosy nipples. Unable to resist, he reached around her and cupped her in his hands. "About what?"

"If I could bathe like this every day, rich would be nice."

He thumbed her puckered nipples gently, nibbled on her shoulder, and growled, "I think we can arrange regular visitations to my tub." Softly pinching, he added, "But it'll cost you."

Her eyes sank shut and her lips parted to facilitate her faster breaths.

Quinton kissed her throat, nibbled her earlobe, and teased with his tongue, all the while enjoying her breasts.

"I . . . I've changed my mind about something else, too."

Sliding one hand down her narrow torso to her belly, he whispered, "Let's hear it."

"I'm not that sore after all." In the next second she'd shifted around to face him, her long legs sliding around his hips, her mouth on his, kissing and nipping and licking.

Quinton blindly reached out to turn off the water.

Maybe through sex, he'd be able to become a priority in her life. He'd certainly do his best.

* * *

Ashley woke early the next morning, cocooned in Quinton's warmth. Before she even had her eyes opened, she smiled. Who knew sleeping with a bed hog could be so pleasant? Thank God his bed was specially made, even bigger than a king.

It seemed no matter where she'd curled up, Quinton had found her through the night. He tended to sprawl, and whenever he "bumped" her, he snuggled her in tight. At one point she'd actually been sleeping atop him, her head under his chin, their heartbeats aligned, and his hands over her bottom holding her secure.

She lifted her head enough to see the clock. Five-thirty A.M. Time for her to drag her lazy butt out of the bed. She had studying to do before class on Monday, and she had to work tonight. Lethargy pulled at her, but she forced herself to slip out from under Quinton's heavy arm. He barely stirred.

Naked beside the bed, she stared down at him. Despite what she'd told him—and herself—she knew she was falling hard. Just looking at him made her heart ache for things she knew she couldn't have.

Just sex, she reminded herself, and really, that should be enough. He'd made love to her three times, and each time had been better than the time before, when it had started off pretty mind-blowing. The last time, she'd actually screamed with the sharp pleasure of it. She'd cried afterward, too, though she didn't think Quinton had noticed. She hoped not. He knew too much about her already.

The muscles in her thighs ached, her breasts

were sore, and deep inside her, between her legs, she burned.

But if he woke up right now and reached for her, she knew she'd willingly climb back into the bed.

Dangerous. To her goals, her peace of mind, and her heart.

Silently, she turned her back on the bed and searched for something to wear. If she rooted through his closets, she might wake him, and she didn't want to do that. Not only did she not want to disturb him, but she wasn't ready to face him yet. She needed some time to get her defenses back into place. After the excess of the long night, she felt stripped emotionally, vulnerable, and more than a little scared.

She spied her gown on the floor, but no way could she put it back on. Lying in a bunched-up ball had wrinkled it beyond decency. Besides, she'd need to put the awful bra back on to wear it, and she refused to do that.

His dress shirt, however, looked none the worse for their adventure, so she slipped it on. The sleeves hung past the middle of her thighs, and the hem reached her knees.

She pulled the collar together and inhaled his scent, all man and hot sensuality. Her stomach went taut in delight, and that insidious twinge of need came to life again.

Buttoning the shirt as she walked, she left the room to search out coffee. Quinton hadn't shown her much of his house yet. They'd made a beeline for the bedroom and then hadn't left it, except to use the adjoined bathroom. But she remembered the direction to the kitchen.

Once there, she had a hard time finding things. He was immaculate in the extreme, everything put in a specific, orderly place, not a speck of dirt or clutter to be found.

No regular coffee for Quinton Murphy, CEO. Nope. He had only special blends, but luckily, he did have a coffeemaker beside the espresso machine.

Ashley measured up a strong pot and then, while waiting for the machine to finish brewing, she wandered his house. Everywhere she looked, she saw signs of his wealth. A leisure room included a wall of windows, a cast stone mantel, and a fireplace surrounded with built-in cabinetry. Plush, comfortable furniture in soft shades of cream, white, and tan gave the room a monochromatic color scheme.

As she moseyed from room to room, she counted the baths. Including the master bath that she'd used last night, he had five. Some were smaller than others, but six bathrooms for one man? Indulgent.

His office included not only a colossal desk, but a wet bar, snack bar, built-in microwave, wall oven and refrigerator. Specialty cabinets hid most of the office equipment. Two leather couches flanked a tall fireplace.

How could he possibly use all this space?

She knew the coffee would be done by now, but curiosity drove her downstairs to the lower level. She found a fifth bedroom with two sets of bunk beds, another bathroom—which made six total—an exercise room, theater room, and what appeared to be a play area, complete with foosball, air hockey, basketball nets, pinball machines, and shelves filled with puzzles and games.

Confused, she noticed subdued light flickering against the double glass doors. She crossed the room and pressed her hands to the glass to peer out. Landscape lights, mostly hidden by lush greenery, reflected off a koi pond stirred by large golden fish. Beyond that, a lagoon-style pool with waterslide, rock bridge, and diving board glistened with blue lights.

Amazing. Was there anything he didn't have? She reached for the door handle, anxious to examine the pool further, and a noise sounded behind her.

She jerked around and found Quinton propping a shoulder against the door frame—gloriously naked.

"Looking for something?" he asked.

Chapter 10

For only a moment, he thought Ashley looked guilty, then not a speck of remorse shone in her beautiful brown eyes.

She even smiled as she turned back to the door. "Your yard is gorgeous. I had no idea you were hiding all that out back."

She hadn't answered his question, and that sharpened his irritation. Resolute, Quinton strode across the room and took her shoulders. "You should have awakened me if you wanted a tour."

"Why?" With a mixture of hurt and defiance, she turned her face up to his. "Your house is big, but I don't think I'd get lost." She tried a half grin and teasingly put her fingertips against his sternum. "Besides, you were sound asleep, and after all that energy you expended last night, I figured you could use the rest."

When he didn't grin with her, her smile faded.

But damn it, if she'd gone outside, she'd have seen things he didn't want to explain. As it was, she stood in the middle of the activity room. That room alone was enough to rouse a million questions he didn't want to answer.

Putting his hand at her back, he urged her out of the room. She went grudgingly, and with each step a frown became more pronounced. "Where are we going?"

"The kitchen, where I assume you helped yourself."

Her shoulders stiffened. "I made coffee, if that's what you mean."

"I smelled it. That's what woke me." And the second he saw her missing from the bed, a knot had formed in his gut.

"I see. So you were in such a rush for a cup that you didn't bother putting on pants?"

She more or less stomped up the stairs ahead of him, and the angry swish of her derrière beneath his shirt drew his hand. He was annoyed with her, feeling suspicious, and still he couldn't help cuddling her naked buttocks. "You're not wearing pants, either."

She stepped a little quicker, trying to move out of his reach. "At least I covered up."

Safe upstairs, well away from telltale evidence, he snagged her elbow, backed her into the wall, and plastered himself against her. Annoyed or not, he wanted her, as much now as ever. He stared at her compressed lips and wanted to lick them. "You look sexy in my shirt," he told her, and added in a husky whisper, "but you'd look sexier out of it."

Face flushing, she put her hands flat to his chest. His gaze drifted up to hers, and he saw her narrowed eyes. "You're one fickle son of a bitch, Murphy, did you know that?"

Uh-oh. She sounded really angry. Hopeful of redirecting her thoughts to more carnal ground, Quinton wedged one leg between hers. "No." He leaned in closer, hoping to steal a kiss.

She shoved him back a foot. If she hadn't taken him by surprise, he might not have staggered away so easily, giving her room to duck away and rush off down the hall.

"Ashley." Hot on her heels, Quinton followed her into the kitchen, then watched as she opened and closed cabinets in a furious search.

Crossing his arms, he demanded, "What are you doing?"

"Casing the joint, what else?"

This was not how he'd planned to spend the morning. "If you tell me what you're looking for, perhaps I can help you find it."

"I need a cup, damn it." She stretched up, causing the shirt to rise and putting two very fine half moons on display.

Quinton was so entranced by the image she presented that he almost missed her angry outburst when she added, "You're being a jerk, and I want some coffee to clear my head before I tell you to go to hell."

"*I'm* being a jerk? You're the one who went secretly rummaging through my home—"

"Yeah, stealing everything in sight, right?" She sneered at him, her expression mean and provoking. "You want to check my pockets? Oh wait, I don't *have* any pockets!"

She yanked open another cabinet, saw it held only boxes of cereal, and closed it again.

Quinton dropped his arms in dawning awareness. Ashley was truly insulted, but it was her hurt that made him feel like an ass.

Silently cursing himself, he went to her. Standing very near, he said softly, "No one mentioned stealing."

She whipped around to face him. "But that's what you think, right? Why else would you care if I walked around?"

He reached over her; she ducked, but he only retrieved two mugs from the highest shelf. Handing one to her, he explained, "You invaded my privacy."

She snatched the mug away from him and retreated to the other end of the counter. "Whoopee. I saw your couches and chairs and gazillion bathrooms."

"Six bathrooms."

"For one man?" She snorted. "You're so spoiled."

"They came with the house, Ashley. I didn't add in any extras."

She wasn't listening. "It's not like I went through your drawers or anything." Then she froze, and her mouth flattened. "Well, only the drawers in the kitchen. But that was just to find the coffee. I didn't expect to uncover company secrets or skeletons from your closet or super-private stuff. I mean, it's a *kitchen*."

She gave him her back while she dumped three spoonfuls of sugar into the cup, then poured in the coffee.

Quinton saw that her hands were shaking. "Ash—"

In a quieter voice filled with distress, she said, "I've never had the proverbial morning after, so I didn't know coffee was a grave mistake."

So she wasn't going to mention the toys or

games, the additional twin beds? Did she chalk those up as the vagaries of the rich? Possibly.

Seeing her hunched shoulders, the way she hugged herself with one arm while sipping her coffee, Quinton felt like a bastard. He'd taken her first sexual experience and ruined it with ugly accusations.

"I'm sorry."

She curled a little tighter and muttered, "Fuck off."

Shocked, Quinton stared at her, but within seconds, he started to grin. Leave it to Ashley to take him by surprise at the best and worst of times. "Wow, when you get angry, you go all out, don't you?"

Giving him the meanest look he'd ever seen on a female's face, she downed the rest of her coffee, put her cup in the sink, and thrust up her chin. "I'm leaving now."

"Why don't we talk for a little bit first?"

She struggled to keep her gaze on his face but lost. Staring at his body, her voice filled with disgust, she said, "Why don't you put on some damned clothes?"

"No."

She glared at him. "So you're an exhibitionist? Who knew? I still have to go."

He smiled. "I like the way you look at me. I like it that you like my body."

"Yeah, well, I liked it fine last night, but last night you were nice."

"I'm nice now. You just . . . I've never had a woman roam my home uninvited."

"You already knew that I'm a freak of social behavior," she stated. "So what did you expect?" She started out of the room, but Quinton put himself in her path.

"Please. Let's talk."

She accepted with a scowl. "Okay, later, *maybe*. But for right now, I have to go."

She was dead serious. They'd made love all night, slept curled together, and because of one misunderstanding, she intended to bolt.

Quinton braced his feet apart and crossed his arms. "Where can you possibly need to be the morning after your best friend's wedding, on a Sunday, at barely six A.M.?"

"I have some work to do, and I need to study." She waited defiantly for him to question her on that.

He decided that, in her present mood, it'd be best not to push her. "All right." He wrapped his hands around her upper arms, caressed her, and tried for a compromise. "How about we shower first, then I'll drive you home."

"You shower." Her chin went a little higher, and her nose wrinkled. "I'm going to put my bra and dress back on, then call a cab."

Stubborn. Quinton closed his eyes and counted to ten. "I really am sorry, honey. I reacted badly. The truth is, I've never had another woman in this house."

Her look was one of blatant disbelief. "Right."

"I'm not a liar, love, so please don't infer otherwise."

She opened her mouth, but nothing came out, so she closed it again. After several seconds, she conceded with ill grace. "All right, fine." Before he could relax, she added, "But don't call me love,

Zebra Contemporary

Whatever your taste in contemporary romance — Romantic Suspense... Character-Driven... Light & Whimsical... Heartwarming... Humorous — we have it at Zebra!

And now Zebra has created a Book Club for readers like yourself who enjoy fine Contemporary Romance written by today's best-selling authors.

Authors like Fern Michaels... Lori Foster... Janet Dailey... Lisa Jackson...Janelle Taylor...Kasey Michaels... Shannon Drake... Kat Martin... to name but a few!

These are the finest
contemporary romances available
anywhere today!

But don't take our word for it! Accept our gift of FREE Zebra Contemporary Romances — and see for yourself. You only pay $1.99 for shipping and handling.

Once you've read them, we're sure you'll want to continue receiving the newest Zebra Contemporaries as soon as they're published each month! And you can by becoming a member of the Zebra Contemporary Romance Book Club!

As a member of Zebra Contemporary Romance Book Club,

- You'll receive four books every month. Each book will be by one of Zebra's best-selling authors.
- You'll have variety — you'll never receive two of the same kind of story in one month.
- You'll get your books hot off the press, usually before they appear in bookstores.
- You'll ALWAYS save up to 30% off the cover price.

SEND FOR YOUR FREE BOOKS TODAY!

don't yell at me or accuse me, and for crying out loud, cover yourself up."

Confident that the storm had passed, Quinton relaxed. Leave it to Ashley to lose her anger as quickly as she had gained it. "I'm not uncomfortable naked."

She wiggled out of his hold and went back to the coffeepot. "Yeah, I can tell. But you're enough to make a freshly initiated ex-virgin blush."

"Maybe you just need to take off the shirt, so we're on equal ground."

"Sorry, no can do." She leaned back on the counter and looked him over from toes to head and back again. "I really do have to study, and not even you in all your naked glory will sway me from my course. So get a move on, Murphy. If you want to be gallant and drive me home, I'll give you ten minutes to get yourself decent. After that, I'm calling a cab."

At six o'clock that night Quinton and his assistant, Adrianna Perkins, ushered fifteen boys between the ages of five and twelve into the upscale restaurant. They were spiffed up in the new clothes he'd bought them, wide-eyed with awe, and giddy at the chance to be out and about. They didn't get to eat in restaurants often, and most of their transportation occurred on a bus.

Quinton had rented a limo for them because, as he'd explained, they wouldn't all fit in his Bentley. A few days ago, they'd very much enjoyed taking turns tooling around town with him in his newest car. They were every bit as car crazy as he was, but without his privileges.

They'd loved riding in the limo.

He loved doing things for them and with them.

These boys, part of society's outcasts, some of the forgotten, were his passion. He took more pleasure in handing out gifts to them than he did in sealing a multimillion-dollar long-term deal. They were each and every one of them unique, fun, and so imperfect that they kept him on his toes.

Uncle Warren didn't understand it, but Quinton loved them.

The youngest, Rupert, clung to Quinton's pants leg and walked in tiny, shuffling, uncertain steps. The din from their excited and anxious chatter turned the heads of the rest of the patrons in the restaurant. Not that Quinton minded. He'd called ahead for reservations and had procured the back half of the dining room.

"Let's go." He swung Rupert up into his arms and the hostess, like the Pied Piper, led the way. Adrianna brought up the rear, making certain no stragglers got left behind.

Two long tables were pushed together to accommodate them all, and as they clamored for seats, dinnerware rattled and a tablecloth was almost removed.

The smiling hostess set a stack of menus on the table and said, "Your waitress will be right with you to tell you the specials of the day. Enjoy your meal."

Quinton thanked her and heard an echo from the boys as, one by one, they mumbled or squealed or yelled their thanks as well. He shook his head, as always amused by them and their varying personalities.

"Now," he said, standing at the head of the combined tables, "everyone sit still and listen. Adrianna, get Neil's attention for me, please. Thank you. Now we're going to quietly read the menus—Rupert, I'll read it to you—and we'll each decide what we'd like for dinner."

"What can we haf?" one boy asked around two missing front teeth.

"Anything you want. This is your day out. You have my blessing to go hog wild—" A roaring cheer arose, prompting him to laughingly add, "But please, do so *quietly* so they don't toss us to the curb."

The noise dropped an octave, but it was still pretty up there in the decibel level. They were all so wound up, they couldn't sit still, and as Quinton looked from one animated face to another, he wished he had the time to take them out each night. Somehow he'd find a way to incorporate it into their routines. Each month they had theater day, and museum day, and sports day. Why not dinner day?

He was grinning at Oliver, a boy with a clunky hearing aid in his left ear, when he heard, "Quinton Murphy, what are you doing?"

Shock rippled down his spine. He knew that sassy female voice. But what in the world would Ashley be doing in such a restaurant? She claimed to live a frugal life, and the whole point of the restaurant was extravagance.

Slowly, a staged smile firmly in place, he pivoted to face her—and got another jolt of shock.

She wore a uniform.

Or rather, she wore the homogeneous black slacks and white dress shirt required by the restaurant. *A waitress?* But she already had a job. And school. He shook his head. "What are you doing here?"

"Huh-uh." Arms crossed, one hip cocked out, Ashley tapped her foot. "I asked first."

Quinton felt the blood run out of his face, then rush back into it again. Caught red-handed. Not a single excuse came to mind.

One of the boys yelled, "Hey, Dad, make Marcus quit tugging on the tablecloth."

He froze, and Ashley's eyebrow went up a good two inches. "Dad?"

Desperate, Quinton turned to Adrianna, and she was already at his side, her hand held out to Ashley.

"Hello. I'm Adrianna Perkins, Quinton's personal assistant. I work for him in the office and assist him in his . . . extra-curricular activities."

"Extra-curricular, huh?" Ashley leaned to the side to look around them, and he saw her gaze go up and down the length of the two tables, pausing on each boy.

He waited for her questions.

He waited for her derision.

What he got was a smile so bright, it nearly blinded him. Her brown eyes lit up with it. Dimples appeared in her cheeks. She looked . . . delighted.

Raising a hand, she said, "Hey, guys."

The boys yelled back a cacophony of greetings, guaranteed to break mortal eardrums.

Wincing, Quinton explained, "They're enthused about the restaurant."

"I can see that." Leaving him to dangle in his own deceptions, she pushed around him and went to the table. "All right, fellas. Who's hungry?"

She laughed at their roar.

"Okay then, listen up. The specials of the day are boring, boring, *boring*." She leaned in as if sharing a confidence. "Lobster with tentacles and fish with eyeballs. Yech. But you know what I recommend? Beef. We've got some of the biggest, juiciest hamburgers you'll ever sink your teeth into. And if you're not a burger kind of guy, we also have steaks, and chicken fingers, and the best fries in the whole world. Oh, and milk shakes! My personal favorite is strawberry, but we have chocolate and vanilla, too."

They cheered her.

And she took a bow, accepting their tribute.

Mouth open, brain blank, Quinton stood back in disbelief. Once, a few years back, he'd introduced a woman to this brood, and she'd run away as if her fanny had caught fire. But not Ashley. The brood had changed in the past years, with a few young men maturing and moving on to promising jobs, while others were given into his care. The numbers had grown, yet Ashley leaped into the fray feet first, and seemed right at home amidst the mob.

Struggling with his confusion, Quinton looked at Adrianna. She smiled and shrugged.

"I'm going to start at this end of the table," Ashley announced, "and work my way around. Think about what you want and then tell me when I get to you." She caught a tumbled glass without comment. Ruffled a boy's hair. Put her hand on another's shoulder, earning a toothy grin in response. "After you finish up your meal, I'll come back with a dessert tray, and let me tell you boys, your eyes are going to hit the floor, our desserts are so good."

Another cheer, and above it, he could hear Ashley laughing. She even bent to hug Rupert.

Quinton shook. He wasn't numb any longer. Now he felt . . . things. Stronger than any lust. More profound than any declarations.

It was so powerful, it almost made him ill. In that moment he knew she had his heart in both fists, and she wasn't going to let go.

Putting a hand to his head, he murmured, "I think I'm falling in love."

Adrianna didn't hear him. She went to help Ashley, leaving Quinton standing there, spellbound, stupefied, and lost in his own drowning emotions. A man could only take so many shocks from one slip of a woman, and he groped for a chair, fell into it, and watched Ashley work her magic on all the boys he sponsored, the boys he'd taken into his care, the boys he loved.

Ashley bit her lip as she leaned around the corner and watched Quinton with the hoard of unruly children. God love the man, he was a hero. More than a hero. How could one man possess such good looks, such profound sex appeal, *and* have such a beautiful heart?

It wasn't fair.

Halfway through the meal, he'd tried to talk to her, but a lump the size of a coconut had lodged in her throat and she couldn't choke it down no matter how she tried. The boys made her laugh with their robust enthusiasm, while at the same time, the reality of a changed future made her want to sit down and sob.

Thanks to Quinton, she'd never be the same. She'd taken one look at the boys, all of them watching Quinton with adoring, trusting eyes, and her priorities had all shifted, when she'd spent a lifetime making those priorities.

So whenever he'd tried to approach her, she'd only smiled at him and hurried away with the excuse of filling more glasses.

They called him Dad and Daddy Q and Pops and a whole variety of other fatherly names that ranged from respectful to teasing to wishful. Obviously, they were affectionate terms only. Some of the boys were Caucasian, a few African American, while others were mixed nationalities that she couldn't peg exactly. Not a one of them looked like Quinton.

The little runt currently trying to force smashed fries past Quinton's smiling mouth had red hair and a million freckles. Rupert, she'd heard him called. More than the others, he clung to Quinton, and Quinton didn't seem to mind in the least. The boy appeared to be around four or five and was the youngest in the group.

Quinton dodged the food, leaned down, and pretended to chew on Rupert's neck instead.

His . . . *wonderfulness* struck her yet again, putting a stranglehold on her emotions and bringing tears to her eyes. She drew away, wrapping her arms around her middle and fighting for composure.

"Are you okay?"

Ashley jerked upright and opened her eyes to see Quinton's assistant standing beside her. The woman was drop-dead gorgeous, voluptuous, kind, and probably in her midforties.

Denny would be hot on her heels if he ever saw her.

Ashley summoned up a shaky smile. "I'm great. Super. Enjoying the chaos. How about you?"

Expression gentle and understanding, she touched Ashley's arm. "I was worrying about you, actually. It's apparent you and Quinton have an association, and it's just as apparent that you didn't expect to see him with a group of children."

"Yeah." Ashley looked out at the dining floor again. Quinton, napkin in hand, efficiently cleaned ketchup off a boy's face, ears, chin . . . pretty much everywhere. She sighed. "Threw me for a loop, all right."

"I've worked as Quinton's assistant for many years now. He doesn't advertise his benevolence. In fact, he hides it whenever possible. Warren, his uncle, is opposed to the time Quinton donates to the boys, but since Quinton does whatever he wants—always has—Warren tried to use it as a deduction, a business expense, and promotion for the goodwill of the company."

"I bet that went over real big."

Adrianna's kind blue eyes showed her amusement. "I thought Quinton would leave the company, he was so incensed. Since then, Warren has left him alone about it."

"I met Uncle Warren."

Slim brown eyebrows lifted. "Do tell."

"Yeah, he didn't seem real taken with me."

Adrianna laughed. "He's a stickler for propriety and a bit of a snob. But deep down, he's a good man. And as I said, Quinton neither wants nor needs Warren's approval."

Right before her eyes, a small food fight broke out, and Quinton barely dodged a glass of cola that tipped over. He snatched up cloth napkins and began mopping at the spill.

"He could be mother of the year."

Adrianna grinned. "And father of the year, and big brother, and so on. I don't know if Quinton has explained yet, but he sponsors the boys. They don't have homes or family that cares, so Quinton fills in. He bought this enormous house and hired people to clean, cook, and supervise when he wasn't available. But he spends a lot of time with the boys. Every spare minute, in fact."

A lightbulb went off. "He has a gaming room in his home, and a lot of bedrooms and bathrooms."

"That's for the boys. They often spend the weekend with him, using his pool, hanging out, just being with—"

"Someone who cares."

Sighing, Adrianna looked back at Quinton. "That's about it."

Another glass toppled, and as Quinton rushed to stem the stream, a fork nearly gouged him in the nose.

"Ho, boy." Ashley cringed as the fork barely missed him again. "I better go wrangle some manners."

Adrianna accompanied her and together, they made short work of restoring order. To keep everyone occupied, Ashley announced it was time for dessert, but she couldn't serve it if things didn't settle down a little.

Silence reigned.

Grinning, she went off to retrieve the dessert cart, then had a difficult time making the boys understand that they couldn't just help themselves. She had to wheel the cart with finesse to keep sticky fingers from snatching off the samples.

"This stuff isn't as fresh as you want," she assured them. "Right now one of the cooks is milking the cows for the cream while another is out in the fields picking the berries for the fruit pies."

Only half the boys believed that, but they gave their orders and again, Ashley escaped Quinton's scrutiny. Once she'd served dessert, the boys settled in for a sugar feast, leaving Quinton with enough time to corner her.

"You're a waitress."

Ashley halted on her way through the double doors leading to the kitchen. Well, she reasoned, he was bound to find out sooner or later. She pivoted around with mock surprise. "Wow, Quinton, nothing gets by you. It's nice to know that young minds are safe in the shadow of your astute influence."

He scowled at her. "Don't turn this around. So I brought some boys here for dinner. So what? It's not a big deal."

"But me being a waitress is?" He couldn't be serious.

"You already have a full-time job. And school."

"And goals," she reminded him, "which I have on a time frame."

"And that means you have to work yourself to death?"

Theatrical in the extreme, Ashley examined each of her arms, and then her legs. She touched her throat, her head. "Gee, I don't think I'm near death. I seem pretty hale and hearty, in fact." Dropping the humor, she crossed her arms and tapped her foot. "Let it go, Murphy. A little hard work never killed anyone."

"How many hours a week do you put in?"

She shot back, "How many do you?" Three steps brought her chest to chest with him. They were out of sight of most patrons, not all, but at least the boys couldn't see them. "How many hours do you spend with those kids?"

"That's not work, damn it."

"Oh, ho. Now *you're* offended?" She curled her lip, deliberately antagonistic. But geez, he played dad to a bunch of children and had never told her. "Is this why you were up so early the other day, dressed in casual duds? You were going to see the boys?"

He stubbornly sealed his lips together. Ashley wasn't deterred.

"This is why you freaked out about me seeing your house, isn't it? You thought I'd find out how good you are?"

"I'm not *good.*"

He sounded so insulted, she barked a laugh. "I'd hardly call what you do evil."

"It's . . . nothing." He leaned in, antagonistic, defensive. "It's for *my* pleasure. Because I enjoy it. It has nothing to do with goodness."

Another absurd argument. Nothing new for them. But one point she couldn't ignore: he hadn't trusted her. "Buzz off, Murphy. You're not *my* daddy, so I don't need you monitoring my schedule."

He thrust his hands into his pockets—probably to keep from grabbing her. Teeth locked, he snarled, "What I do with the boys isn't a hardship."

"Working toward my goals isn't a hardship, either." She shrugged. "To each his own."

His eyes suddenly widened. "This is the restaurant that allowed Elton to get your number, isn't it? Back at the wedding, when Tim mentioned how he'd gotten your number. Everyone knew what was going on except me."

"There's nothing going on, so don't make it sound like some big conspiracy to deceive you."

"But you did deceive me, damn it." And with that insistence, he growled, "How the hell can I protect you if I don't even know where you're working?"

Ashley waved away his concerns. "I already talked to the management about all that and the numbers have been moved."

"It's a little too late, isn't it?"

Quinton was red-faced and rigid. She shook her head at him. "Just why are you so mad?"

He drew himself up, opened his mouth, and then closed it with a suspicious look at her. "Why are you?"

Ashley threw up her hands. "I'm annoyed because you didn't trust me. Just like you thought I was casing your place this morning—"

"I did *not* think—"

"—You figured I wouldn't like the idea of you sponsoring needy children. What am I? A fiend? A fiendish thief? I like kids, too, ya know." And with that great parting shot, she turned to stalk away.

Except Quinton caught her elbow and momentum carried her full circle and around into his arms, flat up against his chest. He looked at her mouth. "Damn, you are so hot when you're pissed."

Her eyes flared and she stiffened her arms against him. A quick look around assured her that no one had heard him. "Are you trying to get me fired?"

"No." His hold softened, became caressing, tender. "But honey, I could offer you a better job, making better pay, with benefits."

Ice shot through her veins. *Charity.* The man wanted to give her charity. Almost strangling on her hurt, she whispered, "Don't. Even. Think it."

"Whoa." He lifted his hands away from her. "Calm down, Ash. I didn't mean—"

"Yes, you did." Under her breath, so only he could hear, she whispered, "But I don't need a handout, Murphy. I'm not a young helpless kid." Not anymore.

His gaze softened. His hand, so big and warm, cupped her cheek. He stroked her skin with his thumb and half smiled. "Trust me, I know the difference."

"Yeah. Well." He'd taken all her steam with that gentle caress and coaxing voice. "I like this job just fine. They work around my schedule and I make great tips. And speaking of tips, don't you dare think to leave me something outrageous—"

"I'm always a generous tipper, honey. Don't make me become a cheapskate now."

"I don't need your money."

"You've just waited on, placated, entertained, and supervised fifteen boys. I think you're up for sainthood. But if you hadn't been waiting on us, you'd have waited other tables, and been tipped. At the very least, you should allow me to be fair."

She could see no way to argue around that one. "As long as it's not too much, then okay." And grudgingly, she added, "Thank you."

"What time do you finish your shift?"

"Not till nine. And before you even ask, I need to study afterward, and do some laundry, and . . . a bunch of other stuff."

He looked disappointed but manfully tried to hide it. "When can I see you again?"

"I'm just about due for a break. I can join you for fifteen minutes or so."

"I'll take it." He brought his other hand to her face, too. "But when can I be alone with you?"

"You mean, when can we"—Ashley gave an exaggerated, furtive look around the restaurant—"*have sex* again?"

"Tease." His laugh was quiet and intimate and stirring. "That's exactly what I mean."

"Sorry, Murphy." Her own disappointment was vast, but she wouldn't be swayed. "I told you from jump, my free time is limited. We'll just have to play it by ear."

He stroked her cheeks again and then dropped his hands. "All right. I'll try to be patient. Finish up whatever you have to do, and then join us. The boys will be thrilled."

"Thrilled, huh?"

"You have no idea." He glanced over his shoulder at them, and some deep sadness clouded his eyes. "They crave attention and affection. You naturally doled out both to them. Thank you."

It wasn't the most lavish compliment she'd ever gotten, but coming from Quinton, with so much sincerity, made it cherished. "Hey, my pleasure."

Another hour passed before all the boys had finished their desserts and drinks and were ready to go. Ashley walked them outside, and to her surprise and pleasure, nine-year-old Oliver held her hand. Bursting with energy, he practically skipped beside her, talking nonstop about the hearing aid Quinton had gotten him, the ride in his Bentley, the cool games he had at his house, his pool, and on and on.

They so obviously loved him that Ashley wondered how she would keep from loving him, too. It wouldn't be easy. But he'd made it clear that his attention came with certain limitations. He wasn't ready for "happily ever after," and she'd do well to keep that in mind.

The limo pulled up and as the boys started to pile inside, disagreements arose as to who got what seat. It seemed everyone wanted to sit next to "Dad." Quinton sorted it out with finesse, diplomacy, and firm control.

After instructing all the boys to buckle up, he walked back in Ashley's direction, abashed by the situation, unsure of her reaction, and exhilarated from the outing, all at the same time.

"So." Ashley grinned. "They call you Dad."

The statement took him by surprise, and he ran a hand over his head. The limo door stood open, but she and Quinton were far enough away from the car that small ears couldn't hear them over the music already playing and the raucous conversations.

"I'd rather you not make a big deal of it. It's just . . . they're lacking father figures in their lives."

"I see."

He scowled. "I'm around, so they naturally substitute."

"Okay." Ashley didn't think there was anything natural about it. Not every male who involved himself in their welfare would be loved enough to earn such a title. "Why didn't you tell me about them?"

For several moments, he stared off at nothing in particular then, resigned, he brought his attention back to her. "I wasn't sure you'd understand."

"Understand what? That you're a terrific guy?"

His scowl reappeared. "Damn it. I am not—"

Ashley smashed her fingers against his mouth, hushing his objections. "Relax, Quinton. I'm not going to erect a shrine in your name."

He hesitated, then his frown lifted and he bit her fingertips. Yelping, Ashley jerked her hand away.

"Let me get you alone," he whispered, "and I'll show you what you can erect."

Ashley laughed, but her laughter got cut short when Quinton bent and put his mouth to hers. The kiss was brief and sweet, and still it made her melt. "I'll see if I can find some free time."

"You do that." He trailed his fingers along her cheek, then dropped his hand and turned around to head for the limo. Ashley followed.

But they both froze at the sight of fifteen faces pressed together to the limo windows. The kids were agog with the idea of Quinton smooching, which told Ashley he hadn't done it often in their presence.

In the next instant, the kids roared with laughter while making loud kissing noises, grabbing each other in mock embraces, and all in all being hysterically funny.

"Rodents," Quinton said to them with affection. He shook his head, waved to Ashley, and joined the boys in the limo.

Chapter 11

It looked like a family reunion when Ashley opened Quinton's office door—well after business hours—and found not only Quinton, but Warren and Adrianna still inside.

Quinton was behind his desk, seated in his big leather chair. Warren paced the floor in front of the desk, and Adrianna had one shapely hip propped on the edge of the desk. The men wore dress shirts and ties, but they'd rolled up their sleeves and removed their suit coats. Adrianna wore a black pencil-slim skirt and white cashmere sweater with black high heels.

Ashley wanted to groan. They all resembled fashion plates, while she wore superlow pale beige corduroy pants with flared legs, a black long-sleeved T-shirt covered in small red flowers, and red flip-flops.

Well, shoot. She hadn't seen Quinton since the night at the restaurant, over a week ago. But she really didn't want to see him now, in a crowd.

She tried to back out, but it was too late. She'd taken only a single silent step in retreat when she was spotted.

"Ashley." Adrianna welcomed her with a smile. "Hello. It's good to see you again."

Oops. Busted. "Hey, there. Yeah, uh, I'm sorry to interrupt."

Warren glared at her, rigid with indignation. "I didn't hear you knock."

God, he was a sourpuss. "Maybe that's because I didn't. Knock, I mean. I figured the place would be empty."

"You figured wrong," Warren informed her.

"Yeah, well . . . it should have been empty." She felt guilty and intrusive, and she hated it. "But hey, no sweat, I can come back later—"

"Ignore Warren." Quinton already approached her with a smile. "His shorts are probably too tight."

"But—"

"You're only a little early, Ashley. It's not a problem."

Because she'd hoped to find him alone.

Stupid, stupid plan.

She tried to think of a good excuse, but nothing came to mind. "I guess my watch must be off. But I don't want to interrupt. I can come back to this room later—"

Quinton's mouth on hers ended her refusal. It wasn't a lingering kiss, but neither would she call it a delicate peck.

For her ears only, he whispered, "I missed you."

Warren hissed a sound of disgust, making Quinton roll his eyes.

Holding Ashley's hand so she couldn't escape, he turned to his uncle. "I think we're done here."

Warren went florid. "Of course we aren't. We haven't even begun to—"

Adrianna interrupted with a laugh. "It is getting late, Warren." She fluffed her hair and turned coy. "You know I need my beauty sleep."

Warren's color increased while he harrumphed and stammered an incoherent reply.

Interesting, Ashley thought. The two of them didn't relate as easily as did Adrianna and Quinton. But then, who could relate easily to Warren Murphy? The man was a real stick-in-the-mud.

"Fine." Back straight and shoulders tensed, Warren strode to the desk to gather up papers. As he stuffed them into a leather briefcase, he continued to grouse. "But this deal won't seal itself. If we want to purchase the property, we need to make a decision."

"I want more figures on it first." Unruffled, Quinton tugged Ashley into the room and toward his desk. One-handed—because he wouldn't release her—he moved aside a folder and uncovered a sheet of paper filled with data. "Give this to McCreedy and tell him to check it out. I want every financial projection he can get."

Adrianna took the paper. "First thing in the morning, Quinton."

"Thank you." He turned, draped an arm around Ashley, and waited for the others to exit. Warren rudely took his time putting on his suit coat while glancing at Ashley, and then Adrianna.

Only the ringing of a cell phone broke the awkward silence.

Adrianna reached for her purse, Warren reopened his briefcase, and Quinton lifted the phone from his desk. They all realized their phones weren't ringing, and looked at Ashley.

"Oh. It's me." Sheepish at being the center of attention, she slid her purse strap off her arm and dug out her phone. She answered it on the third ring. "Hello."

"So you haven't changed numbers yet. Good."

Not again. Her mouth went dry, and she had trouble swallowing. If she hung up, Elton would just call back. Determined to keep her private business just that, she covered the receiver and said to Quinton, "I'll just take this out in the hall."

She tried to sidle away, but he took one look at her and caught her shoulders.

"Who is it?"

She could hear Elton's muffled voice demanding her attention. She felt Adrianna and Warren watching her, waiting. And Quinton, so sharp-eyed and observant, made it clear by his expression alone that he did not intend to let her out of his sight.

Praying he wouldn't cause a scene in front of the others, Ashley shook her head at Quinton, at the same time saying into the phone, "What do you want now?"

"You," Elton purred. "And I'll have you. Eventually."

Adrianna and Warren must have felt the tension because they both kept their gazes glued to her.

"Put it on speakerphone," Quinton whispered, but she didn't want to do that. Warren distrusted her enough without her advertising this mess.

Determined to keep Elton talking in the hope

that he might give himself away, she turned her back on the room and lowered her voice. "You think you're that good, huh? Then how come you're running around penniless, driving an old Buick and looking like death?"

She heard his gasp and knew that it had been him outside the Squirrel the morning she'd had breakfast with Quinton.

"You want to know why, you little bitch?"

His rage and madness vibrated through the phone, sending an icy chill into Ashley's soul. But she wouldn't let Elton know that he terrified her. She wouldn't give him the satisfaction. "I asked, didn't I?"

"It's because of *you.*"

He sounded so vile, she forgot everyone else. "Nah. It's because you're a lunatic."

"You fucking—"

"Your little fascination with explosives backfired on you, didn't it, Elton? Instead of killing Jude, you killed an innocent man and a young woman who you claimed to care for. I'd say that makes you one sick puppy."

Voice cold and flat, he stated, "You will die."

Oh God, oh God, oh God. Ashley squeezed the phone tighter and refused to look at Quinton. She moved a few feet away from him, needing space to breathe.

"You know what they do with nutcases like you, Elton?" The words trembled, but she continued. "They wrap them in straitjackets and lock them away in a padded cell. Forever. You'll never live the high life again. No more fancy cars or nightclubs. No more admiration from society. No more young starlets."

"Shut up."

"Everyone will see you for the insane murderer that you are. But hey, at least you'll be off the streets and eating regularly. For a fat cat like you, living lean has to be rough."

For two heartbeats, Elton sucked air, breathing deep and hard and fast. Then he laughed. *Laughed.*

"Your rich boyfriend won't be able to help you, bitch. I'm going to enjoy every second of your punishment."

The phone went dead—and Ashley's knees almost gave out.

Quinton was there, quickly leading her to a chair. The second her butt hit the seat, he took the phone from her and checked the call. Ashley already knew it'd be anonymous. Elton was insane and vicious—but not stupid.

Furious, Quinton threw it across the room. It hit the wall and shattered. Ashley cringed. Adrianna pressed a hand to her heart.

"Jesus." Warren's voice shook. "What in blazes is going on here? What is she talking about, murder and insane asylums? What—"

Shaking off her stupor, Adrianna said, "Hush, Warren. There'll be time for explanations later."

To Ashley's amazement, Warren obeyed Adrianna and clamped his mouth shut.

All business and efficiency, Adrianna asked Quinton, "What can I do?"

"Get her a drink, please."

"That's all right. I don't need—" Ashley gave up when Adrianna strode from the office. But she didn't want Quinton's assistant waiting on her. She'd never before been pampered, and she didn't want to start now. "Quinton," she practically hissed, "I can take care of myself."

As if he hadn't heard her, he crouched in front of her and carefully took both her hands in his. His thumbs rubbed over her knuckles, and his expression was one of deep concern. "Are you all right?"

Other than feeling like a cowardly fool, she was fine. "Of course." She tried to laugh, but it came out sounding eerie and weak, and she made a face at herself. "Sorry. I just . . . Elton gives me the creeps, that's all."

"What did he say?"

"Same old same old. I ruined his plans, so I have to be punished." She flattened her mouth, knowing she had to share the rest. "And he said . . . a rich boyfriend won't do me any good."

Quinton's face darkened and suddenly red-hot anger buried concern. "I thought you were going to get rid of that goddamned phone!"

She blinked at his outburst. "I was. I am."

"When?"

At his tone, her spine straightened. She had planned to replace the phone after she got her next paycheck, but she said only, "On my next day off."

His hands tightened on hers. "I don't fucking believe this."

"Quinton!" Scandalized, Warren stood over them like a disapproving papa. "What's gotten into you?"

Adrianna came rushing back into the room. Ashley noticed that even in her high heels, she jogged gracefully.

She presented an icy can of Coke, and Quinton

pressed it into Ashley's hands, then pushed back to his feet. He took two long strides to his desk.

Shrugging, trying her best to look cavalier instead of really, really pissed, Ashley popped the tab on the cola and sipped.

Using his desk phone, Quinton punched in a number, then barked into the receiver, "He just called and threatened her again."

Ashley realized he must have called the guards, but she doubted they could be of much help with a phone call.

"She got here only a few minutes ago. Did you see anything?" Quinton listened, asked a few more questions, and then dropped the phone back to the desk in disgust. "Nothing." This time he kept his distance from Ashley, pacing the room like a big caged cat. "They say you weren't followed—"

"Except by them," she pointed out, because otherwise how would they know that Elton hadn't been behind her?

"Did you see them?" Quinton demanded.

And she admitted, "No," then cleared her throat. Time to take control of the situation. Time to speak for herself. "Adrianna, thank you so much for the Coke. I really appreciate it. Warren, I'm sorry about the confusion. Really. I didn't mean to cause theatrics in the office."

Warren held his face so still, he looked like stone, and when he spoke, his voice reeked of loathing. "Did you mean to drag my nephew into your problems?"

"Of course not. I just—"

As cold as Elton, he said, "And yet you did."

She couldn't really deny that. "Yeah. Maybe."

"Knock it off, Uncle Warren." Quinton gave her

a long look while addressing the others. "Ashley and I need to talk. Alone."

Warren dropped his briefcase and puffed up his chest. "You're my nephew and I'm not leaving here until I know what she's gotten you into."

Still with uncharacteristic temper, Quinton turned on him. "I said to leave."

Ashley jumped out of her seat. She put herself between the two men but faced Quinton. "You could be in danger, too, Quinton. Warren's your family and he has a right to his concern."

For a long, heart-stopping minute, Quinton just worked his jaw. He was always so controlled that seeing him now left her off-kilter.

Finally, he let out a long breath and nodded. "Ashley should call the police first. Because this is an ongoing situation, there's a detective keeping track of everything." Quinton indicated a chair for his uncle. "Make yourself comfortable. It's a little complicated."

She'd need to call Denny, too, or that old coot would never forgive her. But she'd wait until after Warren and Adrianna's departure.

The detective handling the case wasn't in, so another officer took a report for him, and he promised to have men scour the area for the old white Buick. Naturally he didn't hold out much hope of actually apprehending Elton, and Ashley knew Elton would now ditch the car. If they didn't find him tonight, tomorrow he'd be in a different vehicle.

While she'd talked with the police, Quinton began explaining the history behind Elton's behavior. Ashley settled back into her chair and drank her Coke until he finished.

Every couple of seconds, Adrianna looked at her with sympathy, while Warren made no bones about his growing animosity. He rightfully blamed her for putting Quinton at risk, and guilt nearly smothered her.

"From now on," Quinton told them, "Ashley will be using my cell phone. I'll pick up a new one tomorrow."

"Now wait a minute—"

As if she weren't even in the room, Quinton disregarded her objections. "I'll let you know my new number as soon as I have it."

While Ashley stood there flabbergasted at his audacity, Adrianna said, "She might need to reach you. Keep your phone and I'll give her mine." And she dug out her phone from her purse.

Ashley backed away from them all. "I can get my own damn phone, thank you very much."

"But you haven't yet."

"I *will*." She blinked hard and fast. With virtual strangers staring at her, offering help, she felt cornered. She felt . . . *helpless*—much as she had as a child. She hated it. "First thing tomorrow."

Quinton would have argued further, but whatever he saw in her eyes made him pause. She knew he wasn't backing down, but he had the good sense to realize that he'd infuriated her.

After a long look, he turned back to his uncle in an effort to clear the room. "Thank you, Adrianna, but we'll figure it out. Whatever we decide, I'll call and let you know." He took his uncle's arm and tried to urge him toward the door.

Warren jerked out of his grasp. "Be smart, Quinton. End this idiocy right now."

Quinton stiffened. "This doesn't concern you."

"You're my nephew, my business partner. Of course it concerns me when I see you behaving so stupidly."

"Warren . . ." Adrianna warned, but he wasn't listening.

"You've had your fun with her. Now get rid of her before it's too late."

"Get out."

Ashley stepped forward and put a hand on Quinton's biceps. "That's enough."

Her quiet voice dropped into the shocked silence.

Quinton turned to face her. "Stay out of this, honey." And then to Warren. "You're leaving. Now."

"Damn you, Quinton, the day hasn't come when I need a man to speak for me." Eyes narrowed, she closed the distance to Warren. He stiffened—and backed up. But in the confines of the office, he couldn't get away from her. "It's clear you don't like me, Warren. And with all your uppity breeding, you can't bring yourself to be polite. Hey, that's no skin off my nose. I don't really give a damn what you think."

He stopped retreating and looked down his nose at her.

"But you're Quinton's uncle, so I *will* be polite. I might not have your breeding, but I have something better. Decency."

His chin tucked in. "You're insulting me!"

"Yeah." She smiled. "I am." Never in her adult life had Ashley felt so volatile. And it wasn't because of Elton's call, or the insults Warren had dished out.

It was Quinton's involvement, and his over-the-top display in front of others that now had her behaving badly.

Warren looked past her to Quinton, probably hoping for assistance. But Quinton wasn't in the mood to offer help.

He looked ready to say things that would cause irrevocable damage to the family dynamics.

"God, do I have to do everything?" With a huff, Ashley turned to Quinton. "Your uncle is worried about you, Quinton."

Warren snatched up her defense. "I am. This entire ghastly situation sounds dangerous. I don't want you hurt. If you won't protect yourself for me, then think of your Aunt Ivana."

Adrianna made a rude noise. "Both you and Ivana should know that Quinton is more than capable of taking care of himself. He's never been one to blindly turn away from injustice."

"If you mean those brats he coddles—"

"That's more than enough, Uncle Warren."

Ashley was pleased to hear the calm in his tone. When he slipped his hand into hers, she didn't draw away.

"You've made your feelings clear. Now you need to go home before we say things we'll later regret."

"Fine. I'll go. But for God's sake, be careful." Incensed, he shot Ashley one last venomous look before opening the office door.

"Wait for me." Adrianna gathered up her belongings in a rush. "If there's danger, I'd just as soon not walk out alone."

Sighing, Warren nodded in agreement, but he stepped outside the office.

Adrianna touched Ashley's arm. "Thank you for

being so understanding. I know Warren sometimes isn't the easiest man to tolerate."

No, he wasn't. But she figured she wouldn't see
him that much anyway. "No sweat."

Next, Adrianna addressed Quinton. "I hope you
know that he means well. It's just that he's old and
stuck in his ways—"

Warren poked his head back inside. "I can hear
your every word, Adrianna."

She grinned, winked at Quinton, and hurried
out.

The second everyone left the room, Ashley
turned away from Quinton. Arms wrapped around
herself, she whispered, "How could you do that?"

Quinton wasn't sure if it was hurt or rage that directed her now. He just knew that he never again
wanted to see that particular look in her eyes.
"Should I apologize yet again?"

"No." She kept walking around the perimeter of
the room until she encountered her ruined phone,
lying in pieces on the floor. "I could have traded it
in, or just gotten another number assigned to it."

Every muscle in Quinton's body clenched.
Regardless of the time limits of their relationship,
he knew Ashley. She wasn't a timid woman who
held herself in check. She was a woman who went
full steam ahead on everything and everyone. She
left her emotions exposed and when they got
trampled, she pretended she didn't care and kept
on trucking.

As she had in confronting his uncle.

He didn't like seeing her so contained. He didn't
like worrying that her feelings were hurt, or that

she might consider him and his stuffy uncle too much trouble.

Knowing the exact reaction he'd get, Quinton moved closer to her and said, "I'll buy you another one."

When she turned on him, brimming with fury, he was ready for her. Her mouth was open, but whatever invective she had planned turned into a gasp when he snatched her into his chest.

He locked his arms around her waist. He was bigger, stronger, heavier, and he had no problem backing her into the wall and pinning her in place.

She struggled, but he just tightened his hold. Putting his mouth near her ear, he whispered, "I'm sorry, Ashley."

"Let me go."

"That's not going to happen, sweetheart. It doesn't matter what my uncle says or what you think." He kissed her cheek and smiled when she jerked her head away. "God Almighty, I've missed you."

Her fist clunked against his shoulder, but he held her so close that she wasn't able to get any force behind the blow.

"Do you realize how long it's been? And I no sooner get to see you, than all hell breaks loose. I'm tortured."

"You're nuts, that's what you are!"

"Agreed. But when I think of Elton hassling you, threatening you, I want to rip him apart with my bare hands. I can't stand it that he's out of my reach, that I can't get to him."

She went still, her chest heaving, her stance stiff and hostile.

"And I don't want anyone, not even a damned relative, to insult you. It infuriates me. I'm only a man, honey. Grant me the right to temporarily misguided behavior."

He could tell she was listening, really hearing him, and he kissed her again, this time close to the corner of her mouth.

"I know you're independent, and I'm sorry that I embarrassed you. I should have waited until we were alone. I should have kept myself in check and controlled my temper until then."

"You should have let me handle Elton myself."

"No. I can't." And he precluded more fury by saying, "Especially when I planned to ask for your help."

Suspicion ripe, she levered her head back to see him. "Help you how?"

"With the boys. If you can spare the time. You see, I want to do a Thanksgiving dinner for them. I realize we have some time, but the holiday will be upon us before long, and I know the boys enjoyed your company and—"

Ashley grabbed his face and kissed him. "That sounds wonderful."

"Really?" He'd sort of made that up, and her kiss had boggled him, but . . . it wasn't a bad idea. And if she agreed now, it'd be like cementing their relationship for weeks to come. That idea pleased him. "Do you think you'll be able to get some time off work?"

She shrugged. "Let me know your schedule and I'll see what I can do."

Damn it, now he had something else to fret about. If she missed work for the boys, would she still be able to make ends meet? Feeling his way, he said, "I realize you're on . . . limited funds, so perhaps—"

"Don't." She tried again to shove him away, but he only snuggled in closer to her. She quit pushing and instead knotted her hands in his shirt, then pulled his face down to hers. "If you're smart, you'll let that one go, Murphy. I mean it."

"All right." Quinton covered her hands with his, easing her grip, and because he couldn't wait, not even long enough to finish his apologies, he kissed her.

She didn't exactly kiss him back, but she didn't turn away, either.

"Tell me you'll forgive me." Being so close to her, holding her and breathing in her scent, had his heart thundering in a now-familiar way. "Right now."

"Why?"

"Because you don't start work for another half an hour and I'm dying to get my hands under this little flirty shirt of yours."

"Oh." She glanced at the office door, licked her lips, and looked back at him. "Does it lock?"

Her quick acquiescence had Quinton groaning. In a heartbeat he reached the door and clicked the lock into place. He flipped off the overhead lights, leaving only his desk lamp on, and faced her again.

She had her bottom lip caught in her teeth, but he could see the excitement in her dark eyes and in the thickened way she breathed.

For a second, Quinton just looked at her. She peered around the room, then slid her purse strap off her shoulder and put it on a chair. Lacing her fingers together, she sized up the desk and frowned.

"Quinton?"

He eased toward her. "Hmmm?"

"I've got the whole bed thing figured out now. But I don't know about your desk chair. It swivels, right? I mean, it looks like we could get dumped to the floor pretty easy."

"Trust me." He stepped up behind her and gently brushed her hair forward over her shoulders so he could kiss her nape. Her crewneck T-shirt covered her chest, but she was once again braless, and the hem just met the top of her hip-hugger pants.

"Have you done this before?" She tipped her head, making it easier for him to kiss her neck and the side of her throat. "In your office?"

"No." He slid his left hand around her, under the thin cotton T-shirt, and palmed her bare stomach. Her skin was warm and silky, and he loved the way she always wore loose-fitting pants, which would be much more accommodating than skintight jeans. Teasing her and himself, he pressed his fingertips under the waistband.

She inhaled sharply. "Then how do you know—"

He gently bit her ear. "Men have an instinct for these things."

Her elbow connected with his ribs.

Laughing, Quinton pinned her arms to her sides so she couldn't inflict more damage on him. "I gather you want to know exactly what we'll do?"

"Yes."

"All right." He started her forward toward his desk and then guided her behind it. Still standing at her back, he cupped her left breast in one hand, slid his other inside the front of her pants, and whispered, "I'm going to bend you over the desk."

Chapter 12

The pulse in Ashley's throat quickened, drawing his lips. "What do you think of that?"

"I don't know."

Her voice was high and thin with excitement, and he felt her bottom press back into his groin.

His mouth very close to her ear, he continued. "I'll drop your pants to your ankles so you can open your legs enough. From my position, I'll be able to see all of you . . . even me going into you."

She groaned, and her nipple puckered tightly beneath his fingers.

"You'll brace your hands on the desktop so you can take my thrusts. It's deep this way, Ashley. Very deep. If I hurt you, I want you to tell me—"

"Do it now."

He smiled at her urgency. His fingers were inside her pants, but over her panties, and he gently caressed her. "Mmm. I can feel you, already warm and damp. And this . . ." He pressed his fingers to her distended clitoris. "You're nearly ready."

She moved against him, seeking his fingers, wanting more.

"Let me just rearrange you a bit." He pulled his hands from her pants and she moaned at the loss, but caught her breath when he opened the snap at her waistband and then eased down the zipper. "Don't move."

She stood frozen as he pushed the pants down over her slim hips, then lower, beneath her knees.

"Let me see how far you can open your legs." When she just stood there, all but panting, he said, "Ashley. Open your legs."

And she did, easing them apart.

"More."

Her hands curled into fists, but she widened her stance more, as far as she could with the restriction of the thick material around her ankles.

Quinton coasted a hand over her quivering belly, then down between her legs and over her crotch. He boldly stroked once, twice, then drew his hand away. "Yes, that'll do. Especially once you're bent over with your sexy tush in the air."

"Oh, God."

"Only twenty minutes left before you have to start work. Let's take off your shirt. I want to be able to touch your naked breasts."

"This is so kinky," she moaned.

"It's only feels kinky the first time, I promise."

She made a sound that was part moan, part laugh. But as Quinton bunched her shirt up under her arms, leaving her breasts exposed, she started breathing hard.

"What do you think?" he asked her, while rasping his open palms over her stiffened nipples.

"I'm ready."

She was close, but he wanted her climax to be a sure thing. He wasn't about to enter her until he got her almost there. "Not yet." He caught her nipples between fingers and thumbs and tugged her forward. "Brace your hands on the desk."

She did so quickly, flattening her hands on the hard surface and stiffening her arms.

"Now arch your back for me."

"You're pushing it."

"I'm pushing you, but I promise you'll enjoy it." He continued to toy with her nipples, rolling them, pinching lightly, all the while keeping his erection—still inside his pants—snug against her bottom. "Now come on, honey, get that sweet ass up there."

Her head dropped forward, but she did arch her back—and she looked so ripe, so sexy, Quinton had a difficult time reminding himself to put her first.

He hooked his hands into her panties and eased them down her legs, then kissed her knee, her thigh, and her bottom on his way back up.

Finally, he stood back to just look at her. The lighting was dim, but he could see her pale, smooth flesh, her long, lean thighs.

And her vulva.

He had to close his eyes a moment to collect himself or he knew it'd be all over for him. He'd drop his pants and be on her, and in less than two minutes, he'd be grinding out an orgasm.

"Quinton?"

They had a limited amount of time, so he had to man-up to control himself until she reached her own release. "You are so beautiful." With one hand at the small of her back to keep her in place, he trailed the fingertips of his other hand up the back of her thigh. "Do you know how you look to me, Ashley? Pink and wet and so tempting, I want to come right now."

"Okay," she said in a breathless rush, her voice shaking. "Then how about—"

"Shhh. Not yet. Now just let me touch you." He watched as he searched his fingers through her pubic curls to her damp, swollen lips. Forcing himself to go slow, he explored her, stroked her, worked one finger barely into her, then glided it over her clitoris until she trembled all over and couldn't stay still.

He, too, braced one hand on the desk, and with the other, he found a rhythm that suited her. He wished they were naked. He wished they had hours to spend. But they had only here and now, so he'd make the most of it.

When her breathing became choppy and he could feel the small contractions building, he stepped back and quickly opened his pants. In less than twenty seconds, he'd opened a condom from his wallet and rolled it on.

"Ashley." He held her hips in his hands, his thumbs keeping her open, and watched as her body accepted his cock. By small degrees, her slick, delicate flesh opened around him, allowing him in, letting him sink deeper and deeper with each careful thrust.

Ashley moaned, saying, "I can't . . ." and then she just folded her arms on the desk, lowering her upper body but keeping her legs straight and stiff, and he knew he was lost.

Clasping her hips tightly, he thrust in, hard and fast. He heard her groan but he couldn't seem to slow himself. *"Ashley . . ."*

He didn't want to hurt her, but she was moving with him, groaning with each forward thrust, her body grasping him on each retreat. He felt her contractions begin, squeezing him, milking him, and he locked his teeth on a mind-numbing orgasm. Something fell from his desk and hit the floor with a thud. A paper fluttered away.

Still inside her, both of them now wet, he collapsed over her.

Her legs were trembling. He realized that about the same time that Ashley snickered, and then laughed. "Hey, Quinton?"

She sounded sweet and teasing and replete. "Hmm?"

"In maybe two seconds we're both going to go the way of the stapler, which hit the floor along with a folder or two."

"Right." It wasn't easy, but he dredged up the energy and raised himself, dropped back in his chair—which, thankfully, was behind him—and pulled her into his lap.

Rubbing her nose into his throat, she asked, "I don't suppose you have anything in this office that we can use to clean up?"

His arms were tingling. His legs were blown. His heart was still trying to come out of his chest. "I'm wealthy."

"I know."

"I have a bathroom in the inner office."

"Oh. Cool."

"Please tell me I don't need to carry you there." She snickered again. "No, but I hope you know how hard it's going to be for me to work a solid eight hours tonight."

His eyes opened. He hadn't even considered that. He wanted to go home and go to bed, and she had work to do. "Want me to stay and help?"

Her snort nearly parted his hair. "Now wouldn't that go over big with Uncle Warren! Can you imagine how he'd react to you playing janitor?"

Offended, Quinton sat up and cradled her in his arms. She smiled at him, a sweetheart without a care. "It doesn't matter what he thinks, not about this, not about you."

"Quinton, I'm not going to let you help me do my job."

He frowned. It had been a wayward, spur-of-the-moment offer anyway. But . . . "Could I help you study?"

She sat up a little straighter. "Get real. You're a big-shot company guy."

"I'm your lover."

Her eyes went big, then softened. "Well . . . yeah." Her hand settled on his chest, and he wished like hell that he'd taken the time to remove his shirt. He loved the way she touched him. "But that doesn't mean—"

"I would enjoy it," he promised her. And he realized that he would. He'd happily help her fold clothes, cook dinner, or anything else she needed to do. He simply wanted to be with her. "I promise I'm not offering just to get in your pants again."

Her mouth quirked and she gave him a look. "Like you need anything more than a smile to get there." Shaking her head, she said in playful dismay, "I'm so easy, it's embarrassing."

"You're not easy, just honest in your feelings."

He smoothed her hair behind her ear and then couldn't stop stroking her hair. It was thick and long and very feminine. "I'm glad you're seeing things as they should be seen."

"You mean sex?"

"Yes."

"That's because I picked a super stud to show me the ropes."

He wanted to laugh, but he thought of how different things would be if she'd chosen her first time to be with some other man, and all he could do was hug her tight.

They sat in his office, in his leather chair, in the dark, and they both had their pants down around their ankles. Yet with Ashley, he didn't feel the least bit silly.

They had only a few minutes left before she'd want to clock in, so he got on track with some things they had yet to cover. "Will you do me a favor, honey?"

"I don't know. What is it?"

"For me," he stressed, "so that I don't worry more than necessary, and because I'm the one who broke your phone, will you take mine until I can buy you a new one?"

"No on both counts."

"You've told me repeatedly how smart and independent you are. Don't let stubborn pride prove you wrong now." He tilted her back to see her face. "Elton is out there, obviously bent on plaguing you in one way or another. I want you to have a phone on you, with the numbers for the guards keyed in. I want to know that you can reach me if necessary."

She ran her fingers along his loosened tie, thinking over what he'd said, and finally she nodded.

"Yeah, you're right. I can be too stubborn some-times. I'll take your phone, and since you did break mine, you can buy me another. Want to meet me at the mall tomorrow morning, before my first class?"

When the hell did she sleep? He wasn't used to worrying about women. Family, yes. The kids he sponsored, sure. But not a woman. With Ashley he was either lusting for her, trying to talk his way around her, or worrying about her. She'd age him before his time.

"I'll be there. And since we're sitting here bare-assed, chatting in the dark, how about we work out a timetable?"

"What kind of timetable?"

"I know your work at the restaurant varies, but our classes and your hours here are set, right?"

"For the most part."

"My hours are flexible."

Using his tie as a leash, she pulled him down for a smooch. "Because you're the boss."

"And being the boss has its perks. If you share your schedule when you get it, I can adjust mine. We enjoy our time together, right?"

"I'm bare-assed, aren't I?"

He smiled with her. "If I help you study, and you occasionally help me with the boys, we'll be able to get together more."

Given her wide smile, the idea pleased her. "Other than making me a little messy, this pre-work visit wasn't bad, either."

"Next time we can try the chair. And there's a leather sofa in the inner office that Adrianna uses—"

Ashley swatted him. "You big shot CEO types really like taking chances, huh?"

"I'm starving for you. Again. Already." He covered her small breast and caressed her. "Work with me here."

"Okay, okay." Before he could further his seduction, Ashley caught his wrist and removed his hand. After awkwardly scrambling off his lap and pulling up her pants, she said, "Long as we're really careful, I'm game for some office hanky-panky every now and then. But for tonight, I need to go get clocked in and start cleaning."

Quinton stood too, and pulled up his trousers. "Have I told you that your exceptional work ethic turns me on?"

Ashley laughed. "I'm beginning to wonder what doesn't turn you on."

Without responding, he took her hand to lead her to the restroom. He already knew that everything about her struck him bone deep.

The thought of Elton getting anywhere near her sent him into a rage. First thing tomorrow, he'd double the guards protecting her. And now, with her agreement to allow him further into her life, he'd be able to keep a closer watch on her, too.

Until Elton was behind bars, he didn't want her alone for a single second.

The moon rested low in the black sky when Elton opened the rusty metal door of the abandoned trailer he now called home. Screeching hinges disturbed the otherwise silent night. The rank odors from within followed him down the wobbly steps, then dissipated in the fresh air. Behind him, disturbed cockroaches scuttled over the floors and counters.

He barely heard them anymore.

Not long ago he'd lived in a mansion furnished by one of the most respected interior designers known. He'd had a cook and a housekeeper and money to burn. He'd gotten weekly haircuts, manicures, and he'd eaten the finest food.

But not anymore.

Now he was fifty pounds lighter, which actually worked to his advantage, changing his appearance drastically. To help in that regard he'd dyed his blond hair a dark brown. It was longer, unkempt. He wore a beard that itched, glasses that did nothing for his eyesight, and he shared space with rats and insects.

At least he'd been able to procure clean blankets for sleeping, a bucket for personal use, a jug of water, and a cooler to store supplies. It wasn't the environment he'd become accustomed to, but he was warm and dry.

And within minutes of where Ashley Miles lived.

When the time proved right, she'd be within easy reach.

Overgrown weeds and roots tried to trip him as he stepped into what had once served as a yard. The thorny branch of a wild shrub left a bloody scratch on his neck and caught in his tangled mane. He cursed low, but he didn't dare use any lights that might draw attention to his presence. He didn't want anyone poking around the trailer and possibly finding his stash. Already he'd acquired all the ingredients necessary for a variety of different explosive devices. They were so easy to get that no one even blinked an eye as he stocked up on the things he'd need.

Most chemicals were found in the grocery store, and others could be made from mixing cleaning supplies. Construction sites afforded plenty of pipe pieces and scraps of metal. He collected everything from rusted nails and burned-out lightbulbs to glass shards and rat poison.

The empty CO_2 canisters had been the most difficult to obtain, but then he'd found the used cartridges from air guns that kids had tossed out behind a sports center.

Yes, he had bombs, and he intended to use them to hurt Ashley Miles.

But in the end, she wouldn't enjoy the quick, painless death of an explosion. This time he intended to take his time, to make it last.

To make her pay.

But first, he not only had to ditch the car, but he needed a new plan. Her loaded boyfriend had her well protected. Guards watched her 24/7, never leaving her alone, making it impossible for him to trail her. For now, she was safe.

But the boyfriend was not.

All he needed was one small chink in the defenses and he'd have them both. With different transportation, uncovering Murphy's schedule would be easy. He already knew where he lived and where he worked. The rest would come.

Elton considered going to Tim for a car. God knew it had been easy enough to manipulate that spineless worm once already. But Denny had taken Tim under his wing, and Denny was one scary individual. He detested Elton, and if given a chance,

Elton knew Denny would cut his heart out without remorse and worry about the consequences later.

Best to steer clear of Tim.

And who needed Tim anyway, now that he had Ashley?

Parked within the thick brush surrounding the old trailer, he located the Buick and unlocked the door. Mind churning with plans, he drove cautiously along the empty back roads of Stillbrooke until he found just the right spot.

In the deep churning water of a muddy creek that ran under the railroad tracks, he dumped the car. Standing on the shore, Elton watched as the rusty Buick slowly sank farther and farther under the water, until not a single part of it showed. By the time anyone found it, Ashley would be dead, and he'd be long gone.

Whistling wind cut through his clothes on his walk back, and with each step he took, his hatred and determination expanded. He was still a good distance from the trailer when luck shone on him.

There, on the side of the road beside her car, stood a woman alone. Beneath the opalescent light of the moon, she looked to be in her late thirties, cheap in the way of a barfly, with big hair, exaggerated eye makeup, and clothes that squeezed her too-full figure. Even with the chill in the air, she wore a low-cut shirt that showed more than it covered. She kept trying to use her cell phone and muttered a rank curse when it wouldn't work.

Clouds blew in to cover the moonlight, filling the area with black shadows.

Elton pulled off the glasses and slid them into a pocket. Affecting an air of charm, wearing a friendly smile, he approached her. "Car break down?"

She jumped at his sudden appearance, so skittish that he thought she might turn and run away in her high wedge shoes. She squinted her eyes, trying to see him. "Who's there?"

He maintained a respectable distance. "I live up the road a ways. My dog got loose. He's a big German shepherd. Old and friendly. You seen him?"

"Oh." He heard the relief in her tone. "No, I sure haven't. My tire went flat and I've been trying to reach someone to lend a hand."

"Can't get any reception, can you?"

"I suppose the woods are too thick." She took a step toward him. "I've never changed a tire in my life. I'm sure I'd end up breaking a nail."

Excess drink slurred her words and kept her stance unsteady. Perfect.

He eased closer. "Now, we can't have that. I'll take care of it for you. Or if you'd rather, you can come up to the house and use my phone to call a boyfriend."

"I don't really have a boyfriend." She turned her head to look down the dark, vast expanse of empty road. "I was going to try to reach a friend, but she's probably out partying still herself."

"Leaving you helpless." He tsk-tsked.

"You really wouldn't mind lending me a hand?"

"Not at all. It's the least I can do for a damsel in distress." Gravel crunched beneath his feet as he strode to the back of the car. "Pop the trunk."

Giddy with relief, she gave a gushing, "Thank you," and opened the driver's side door. Light spread out over the road. He could see her smile, the flash of her bright hair.

Her gratitude was pathetic, making Elton almost chuckle. She got behind the wheel, pulled a lever, and the trunk unlatched. Elton dug around inside until he found what he wanted: a tire iron.

Yeah, it was his lucky night.

The stupid whore never saw what hit her.

When her doorbell rang early that morning, Ashley had to remind herself not to run. Quinton already knew how eager she always was to see him. No reason to throw herself at his feet.

But this would be the first time for him to be in her apartment, and she was anxious. It was a new step, when it felt to her like they constantly took new steps. She wouldn't admit to falling in love with him. Not yet. But with each day that passed, the idea of love had grown on her.

Today Quinton had offered to go over test questions with her, to help her study for an exam, but she had more than schoolwork on her mind. Though they'd made a pact to spend more time together, Murphy's Law had constantly worked against her, and it had taken another ten days to make it happen. In the meantime, she'd seen him at work, talked with him on the phone, and even managed another breakfast out. But other than a few stolen kisses, they'd had no intimacy.

She needed him. Somehow she'd become addicted to his touch, his scent, and she craved him all the time.

Crazy—but also exhilarating.

Quinton had said nothing about love or commitment or happily ever after, but she knew he cared. She felt it. It scared her a little, but she couldn't pull back now.

Smiling broadly, she swung the door open—and instantly deflated. "Denny. Tim. What are you two doing here?"

Jovial, Tim stepped inside without an invitation. "We've been doing morning workouts. Lifting, sparring, and then jogging. Denny said we could take a break and so we decided to see how you're holding up." He looked around with blatant nosiness. "This is . . . nice."

His "nice" sounded very lackluster, but then, Ashley knew her rehabbed furnishings and ancient carpet wouldn't appeal to most. She turned to Denny with accusation in her eyes. The last thing she needed was Tim dropping in on her.

Denny deflected any comment she might have by grabbing her into a bear hug. "Good to see ya, kiddo."

Good grief. Had her one hug at the reception turned Denny into an affectionmonger? Had she driven them past the polite stage to the overly familiar?

She opened her mouth to say something sassy, and Tim whirled her around into his long arms for another bruising embrace. "It's been forever, Ash. But you look good. Healthy, I mean, not . . . well, I don't mean sexy or anything. Just good, like you're happy and stuff." Tim snapped his mouth shut, looked guilty for a moment, then grinned at her.

To her surprise, Denny didn't castigate Tim for his blather. He just puffed up like a proud papa and asked, "Got any coffee? I could use a jolt."

"Me, too." As if he'd been in her place numerous times, Tim went to her sofa and plopped down, stretching out his long legs and dropping his head back. "Denny can run for hours. He wears me out."

"Don't be such a girl. You need more wind if you're ever going to compete."

Ashley finally noticed that Tim and Denny both wore running gear and were on the sweaty side.

"Coffee." Ashley gave a tight smile while wondering if she could just pour the drinks down them and shove them back out the door. "Coming right up."

She'd already made a pot for Quinton, so within minutes she returned with two mugs on a tray with creamer and sugar. It was a novel thing to have company and at any other time, she might have enjoyed it.

Tim sat forward to load his mug with cream, but Denny took his black, sipping as he paced the crowded space in Ashley's apartment. "Do you realize that Jude and May will be home in a week? And Elton's still on the loose. Where the hell is he hiding?"

"Who knows?" Trying to be discreet, Ashley glanced at the clock on her wall. "Maybe he's not around here at all. Maybe he called from somewhere else, and he just wants to scare me."

Quinton should arrive any second now. She had only an hour before she had to get to class. She'd cut back on her sleep to see him, and now she had company, when no one *ever* visited her. What were the odds?

Where Murphy's Law was concerned, she didn't stand a chance.

"Have you heard from him again?" Denny demanded, drawing her out of her ruminations.

"No." She paced over to look out the window by her desk.

"Are you sure? You're acting jumpy."

She wasn't jumpy, she was impatient. For Quinton. "I told you the last time he called."

"Not right away," Denny reminded her. "You should have called me the second it happened."

Ashley turned to stare at him. It amazed her how devoted Denny was to her welfare, for no reason that she could fathom. She didn't know if she'd ever get used to it.

"We've been through this, Denny. Quinton was there, and we called the cops, and I told you first thing the next morning—"

He closed the space between them. "If it ever happens again, call me immediately."

He looked so insistent, she shrugged. "Yeah, sure, Dad. Whatever you say."

Her flippant words gave him pause, and he set down the coffee to confront her. "You know, I wish I was your dad."

Tim watched them with wide eyes, his gaze bouncing from one to the other and back again.

"I was being a smart-ass, Denny. Having you for a friend is good enough for me."

He raked back his thinning hair, frowned, looked ready to confide the secrets of the world—and Quinton knocked.

Ashley's heart did a somersault in excitement, but Denny shot around to face the door.

"You expecting company?" he whispered with intimidating disquiet.

"Yeah, I am. So cool your jets, okay?" She started for the door, and Denny held her back.

"Let me answer it."

"Oh, for the love of . . . Knock it off, will ya?" She pulled away from him, saying over her shoulder, "If I'm not allowed to answer my own door, I wouldn't have been able to let you in, right?"

Unfortunately, her apartment was old and therefore well insulated. Quinton hadn't heard a single thing, and the second she got the door open he was on her, kissing her while backing her into the apartment.

With his mouth devouring hers, she couldn't protest or alert him to spectators. She did manage a mumbled, "Mmmhmmm . . ."

Quinton kicked the door shut, slid his hands down to her butt—and finally heard Denny's loud snort.

He went still.

His mouth still on hers, Quinton opened his eyes, looked behind her, and groaned. "Denny. Tim. I didn't realize Ashley had other company."

Still smashed close to Quinton's body, Ashley couldn't see anyone else. But she heard the amusement in Tim's voice when he replied, "That's obvious enough."

"We won't stay long," Denny told Quinton, but anything more than a few minutes would probably guarantee a lost opportunity for intimacy. She absolutely would not run the risk of being late to class.

Ashley tipped her head back, saw the banked anticipation in Quinton's eyes, and said, "Maybe you should let go of my behind?"

"Right." His fingers flexed—then opened and he lifted them away, holding them in the air as if at gunpoint. "Sorry about that."

She patted his chest. "Want some coffee?"

Under his breath, he muttered, "Of course. Coffee. That's exactly what I wanted."

Snickering at his woebegone air, Ashley slid out of his arms and escaped to her tiny kitchen to fetch another mug. When she returned, Denny had sprawled onto the couch too, while Quinton roamed the room, touching her furniture, peeking out her one window, and looking at her photos, books, and the scattered notes on her desk.

Her tiny apartment had to be as shocking to him as his mansion was to her. She could fit her entire living space into one of his rooms. Other than the living room, she had a standing-room-only kitchen, closet-sized bath, and a bedroom just big enough for her full-sized mattress and tall dresser.

To her, the apartment represented a stepping-stone to her end goals.

To Quinton, it probably represented poverty.

Mouth quirked, Ashley poured his coffee and carried it to him. "So what do you think?"

To her surprise, he said, "This is nice."

"Nice?" She did another quick look around the place and saw crowded spaces, used furniture, and an overabundance of study materials.

Quinton touched her cheek. "Very nice. I see you everywhere."

She would never understand him. "Meaning?"

He lifted one butter yellow curtain panel. "It's tidy but colorful." His fingers trailed along the surface of her wooden desk. "Utilitarian and efficient, but feminine. You have your computer set up to be the focal point because you're serious about your studies." He smiled at her. "Everything is organized, but still very comfortable."

"Like me?" She wrinkled her nose at him. "I don't know that I like being compared to well-worn, rehabbed furniture."

"Your furniture is cozy and inviting. And like you, an eclectic mix of colors."

She glanced at the sofa where Denny and Tim sat. She'd covered it in striped material and tossed around some plump pillows in a mix of florals, checks, and prints.

"I do most of my required reading on the couch," she explained. "If I read in bed, I'd fall asleep."

Quinton picked up a silver framed photo that she kept beside her computer. "This is you, isn't it?"

"And May." As always, the picture gave her the warm fuzzies. "I was sixteen when that was taken. May was eighteen. She had a copy framed for me when I moved away from my folks."

Quinton ran his thumb along the engraved script at the bottom of the frame. "Sister of my heart."

Ashley's smile came easily. "Yeah." Her next breath trembled, but damn it, some secrets were getting harder and harder to keep. "The only photos I have are the ones May took or copied for me. I'm not sure we even had a camera when I was a kid."

"No school portraits?"

"Nope. But May always shared her yearbooks with me, so it didn't matter." Shaking off the poignant memories and niggling guilt, she set the photo down on a file folder and tried to coax Quinton away from her workspace.

But he'd already given his attention to the magazine pages tacked to the corkboard behind her desk. He lifted the first ad for curtains, then the garden shot of spring flowers around a bird bath. He flipped through several more with interest. "What are these for?"

"Nothing." Damn, why hadn't she remembered to remove them? "Just ideas."

Denny and Tim twisted on the couch to see. "Ideas for what?" Tim asked.

Heat tinged her cheeks, but she refused to admit to any embarrassment. "For my house." She rolled her eyes. "When I get a house, I mean."

"Really?" Curiosity brought Denny off the couch and around to the desk. He studied a kitchen makeover that had appealed to her.

Tim, too, sauntered over. "I wanna see."

Another glance at the clock showed her time with Quinton slipping away. "All right, I'll show you. But there better not be any jokes." She pulled the tack out of the stack of ads and articles and carried them to the couch.

The men all settled back on the couch, so she seated herself on the coffee table beside the tray, facing them. She passed Quinton the first photo of a small cottage.

"This is what my dream house would look like. It's not exact, but it is the right size. Small and neat and homey." With a glance at first Denny and then Quinton, she said, "No offense, but those hotels you guys live in would make me feel lost."

"It's a fine-looking house," Denny announced. "You have good taste."

Tim took the page from him. "I like it. The porch is nice."

Ashley stared at them in amazement. They didn't tease her. They didn't tell her how unattainable her dreams were. In fact, all three looked really interested, especially Quinton.

Something unfurled inside her. "I want a porch swing," she explained to Tim. "I can just imagine sitting out there at night and looking at the stars."

Quinton lifted the photo of a midsized bedroom. The colorful quilt on the bed had drawn her eye first, but she also loved the light oak color of the furniture and the rag rugs on the floor.

"I'd put a vase of flowers here," she said, pointing to the top of the dresser. "And maybe a hanging plant in that corner."

For several minutes they looked over her photos and discussed options, the pros and cons of her preferences, and price brackets, and Ashley enjoyed every second of it.

Other than May, she'd never shared her ideas of the perfect little dream house. Since she'd lived in the apartment, no one but May had ever visited her. Definitely, no men had ever been inside.

Now she had three big males scrunched together on her couch, oozing testosterone into her air and sharing her dreams of the future.

She couldn't stifle a laugh.

Quinton tilted his head at her. "What's funny?"

"You three. This situation. I think my entire world has gone topsy-turvy."

He reached for her hand. "I have no doubt that you'll one day have your house."

His confidence warmed her. "You think?"

"I know."

"And when you do," Tim told her, "we can have a housewarming party and we'll bring you gifts." He looked at the other two. "That's what family does, right?"

Denny's elbow shot into Tim's ribs, and Tim stuttered, "I mean, you know, I want to be the one to buy you the porch swing. That's all." He blinded her with a winning smile.

"*Okaaaay.*" Ashley had to wonder what had gotten into him lately. He'd gone from flirting with her shamelessly to treating her like a best friend. Or maybe a kid sister. Weird. Had Denny's influence brought about the drastic change? "Thanks, Tim. That'd be really nice."

Hopeful of salvaging a little time with Quinton, she rose from the table and returned her pictures to the corkboard behind her desk. No way did she want to offend either of them, so she tried for a little diplomacy.

"You know, it was nice of you guys to drop in, but—"

Her phone rang.

Everyone froze.

Quinton and Denny shot off the couch at the same time, almost tripping over each other in their efforts to get to her desk where the phone sat.

Ashley beat them to it. With her hand pressed to the top of the receiver, she halted them with a glare. "Knock. It. Off."

"It could be Elton," Denny insisted.

"I haven't heard from him in over a week," she said.

"That doesn't mean—"

"He's *never* called me on my landline. It's unlisted. And besides, no one has even spotted his car lately. I think he might have finally wised up and hightailed it away from here."

"I'll make no assumptions," Quinton told her.

Ashley rolled her eyes. "I realize you guys consider me a social outcast, but I do get the occasional phone call, so stop overreacting."

"Pick it up," Quinton told her, "and if it is that bastard, hand it to me."

And he'd do *what?* Ashley wondered.

"No," Denny said, rubbing his hands together. "Let *me* talk to him."

Seeing another debate about to start, Ashley turned her back on both men and snatched up the phone on the sixth ring, right before her answering machine would have picked up. "Hello?"

"I was just about to hang up. Did I wake you?"

"May." Ashley sent a smug look at all three men, who turned mute at having a potential crisis aborted. Then her gaze went to the photo they'd been admiring, and she sighed. Eventually, she and May would have to talk about some things. But not now. Not yet. Maybe not ever.

May had enough family to drive her crazy. Ashley refused to add to her burden.

Chapter 13

"Of course I'm up," Ashley told her. "But even if I hadn't been, I'd be happy to get your call. How are you? How's that hunky husband of yours? And how's Japan?"

"Jude and I are wonderful, and as to Japan . . . who knows? Other than a few business meetings and one art expedition, we've barely left the suite."

May sounded dreamy and very much in love. Ashley grinned. "So it's nonstop sex, huh?"

The words had no sooner left her mouth than she glanced at the men. Denny and Quinton had rejoined Tim on the couch. They all shifted in appalled discomfort. Apparently, they weren't used to hearing women discuss sex. They blinked at each other, then focused on Ashley with undivided attentiveness.

Unaware that Ashley had an engaged audience, May laughed. "Jude is tireless. And speaking of sex . . ."

"Were we?"

"How are things going with Quinton?"

"Well . . ."

"No hedging, Ash! I want to hear all the juicy details. Come on, spill it."

Because they looked like the three stooges poised to break into an act, Ashley peered at each man in turn and said, "The sex is great, but sporadic. See, I finally had a little free time this morning to be with Quinton, and as luck would have it, Denny and Tim decided to grace me with a visit."

Quinton choked, Tim went red, and Denny roared with laughter.

Shocked, May whispered, "Ashley!" And she laughed as hard as Denny. "They really are in your apartment, because I can hear them in the background! You are so bad to tease Denny like that."

Staring at Denny with wry humor, Ashley asked, "Who's teasing?"

Denny rose from the couch, then hauled Tim up, too. "I think that's our cue to leave."

Ashley waved them back to their seats. "I have to head out in just a few minutes, myself, so forget it. You may as well stay."

Denny shrugged toward Quinton. "You should have said something."

Gaze centered on Ashley, Quinton said, "Next time I will."

May laughed again. "Their timing might not be the best, but I'm glad you have company."

"Yeah, me, too. It's not what I'm used to, but it's nice. Especially with you out of town."

Going solemn, May whispered, "I miss you a lot."

"Same here." And she really meant it. So many things had changed lately, and it didn't seem right not to have May there, sharing it with her.

"I know you can't really talk with the guys all listening in, but I'll be home soon, and when I get there, I want to hear everything."

Ashley smiled. "I'll start taking notes so I don't forget anything."

Grinning ear to ear, Denny and Tim leaned around to look at Quinton. He tossed up his hands and flopped back on the couch, but he was laughing, too.

"Yes, you do that. And while you have a pencil in your hand . . ." May drew a deep breath. "Jot us down for Thanksgiving."

"May . . ."

"Come on, Ashley. Please. It's different this year. It won't just be my folks, it'll be Jude and Denny, too, and I want you there."

Ashley had expected the invitation. At every holiday, May wanted her to join her family, but Ashley always made an excuse to miss it. For more reasons than May knew, Ashley found it painful to be around them all. Crazy as her family could be, they treated her as an extended family member, when she knew she'd never be any such thing.

Without thinking it through, going on gut reaction, she gave May her most legitimate excuse. "I would love to, hon. But this year I'll be with Quinton and the boys."

Quinton shot to the edge of the couch cushion, his expression daunting.

"Boys?" May asked, "What boys?"

Uh-oh. Ashley nearly groaned over her big mouth. She shouldn't have said that, definitely not with

Denny and Tim listening in. May could keep a secret with the best of them, but now everyone knew.

Quinton didn't appear happy with the disclosure, but as usual, she couldn't read his expression well enough to know if she'd truly angered him.

"Ashley?" May persisted. "What boys?"

She mouthed a silent apology to Quinton and, keeping the tale as simplified as possible, said, "He sponsors some underprivileged kids. They don't have much in the way of family, so Quinton promised them a big fancy Thanksgiving dinner with all the trimmings. He invited me to join them, and I said yes."

"How wonderful! I love the idea. In fact . . . Hang on, okay?" A muffled noise came through the phone while May spoke with Jude. Good grief. In no time at all, the whole world would know about his generosity.

Covering the phone with one hand, Ashley said, "Quinton, I—" But what could she say?

He lifted a brow at her, but when Denny turned to him to get the details, he sighed his surrender and spilled his guts.

May came back on the line with barely banked excitement. "Jude wants to help, too. He said to tell Quinton he'll get with him when he gets home."

Oh, boy. Quinton was not going to like the added involvement of others. "I'll tell him."

"I better go now. Love ya, Ashley. I'll call you as soon as we get in."

"Love you, too. Have a safe trip home."

She hung up in time to hear Denny say, "Maybe Tim and I could put on an exhibition for the boys. You know, nothing too bloody—"

Tim muttered, "Thank God."

"But just to show them some moves. It's a good way to expend energy, and you know, I've trained plenty of guys who had a rough childhood. They love the discipline of the sport, the camaraderie."

After giving it some thought, Quinton nodded. "A few of the older boys are carrying around a lot of resentment. It worries me."

"Exactly." Excited by the prospect of getting involved, Denny further ingratiated himself. "There's no better way to shed the rage than on a heavyweight bag. I'll even donate the bag and some other gear. What do you think?"

Quinton eyed him, then, to Ashley's surprise, shook Denny's hand. "That'd be great. Thank you."

Tim all but burst with excitement. "An exhibition? I'll be in an exhibition?"

"Your first," Denny told him, "so we better get back out there and work on your stamina. I don't want you to shame yourself."

Grinning ear to ear, Tim grabbed Ashley up, swung her in a circle, plopped her back on her feet and then headed for the door.

"Good grief!" Watching Tim in amazement, Ashley dusted herself off.

"He's coming around," Denny told her, and he gave her a more sedate peck on the cheek. "Sorry we threw off your plans."

"I enjoyed it," she promised him. "But next time, maybe you could—"

"I'll call first." He winked, clapped Quinton on the shoulder, and took off after Tim.

Quinton shut the door behind them and turned the lock. "Alone at last," he said as he drew her back into his arms. "Do you really have to leave right now?"

"Unfortunately, yeah." She bit the side of her mouth. "I sort of thought you'd follow them out the door. I wouldn't really blame you if you were mad at me."

He clasped his hands at the small of her back. "You mean because you told the whole world something I'd managed to keep secret so long?"

Guilt made her grimace. "I'm sorry. I didn't mean to let the cat out the bag. It just sort of came out without my permission. You know I love May, and even Tim is starting to grow on me. But I get hives when I have to be around Olympia and Stuart, and it's for certain that for any holiday function, May's parents will be there—"

To hush her ramblings, Quinton pressed a firm kiss to her mouth. "It's all right, honey. The boys will be thrilled to know Denny, and I can't even imagine their reactions to meeting the famous Jude Jamison. This'll be fun for them. I should have thought of it myself."

"Really?" His attitude floored her. How could he possibly be so generous and wonderful? "You're not upset with me?"

"I'm not upset." The corners of his mouth lifted in a wry smile. "Hell, I'm not sure why I was still keeping it secret anyway."

She glanced at the photo on her desk. "It was private to you. I understand that. Some things are just better kept secret."

That threw him. For the longest time he stared down at her, his expression so probing, Ashley looked away. He used the edge of a fist to nudge her face back up again.

"Ashley?"

She frowned at him.

"What secrets do you have?"

She tried to joke that off. "If I told you, they wouldn't be secret any longer, would they?"

His annoyance was palpable. "I thought we were beyond this."

Ashley put her arms around him and tucked her head under his chin. "Don't get all surly. It's not just my secret, but someone else's, too."

"Someone you care about?"

"Yes."

"Someone you love?"

She nodded.

"One day you'll tell me."

Because she also loved him, Ashley smiled at the arrogant statement. "Yeah, probably." To change the subject, she kissed his throat and whispered, "I was so looking forward to being with you again."

Quinton crushed her close for a moment. "Me, too, honey."

"You know . . ." She looked up at Quinton, saw the restrained lust in his expression, along with a good dose of tenderness and regret, and her plans got tossed out the window. "I can spare a few hours tonight if you and the boys don't mind company."

He held her back the length of his arms. "What time?"

"I don't need to work at the restaurant tonight." She had thought to use that time to finish a paper and study for the next exam, especially since she hadn't studied this morning. But at that moment nothing seemed more important than being with Quinton. "My last class ends at three."

He treated her to a kiss that set her insides all

aflutter and had her almost ready to skip class after all.

Against her lips, he whispered, "I'll pick you up."

"*Ooooh*," she teased. "In the Bentley?"

His smile was lazy and warm. "Of course. And this time you'll be the driver."

Ashley smiled as she steered the luxury car down the street toward Quinton's driveway. The day had been more wonderful than she'd ever imagined. The kids were, without a doubt, a handful. Loud and boisterous, but also loving and hilarious. They'd ordered in pizza, watched a video, and shot baskets in the yard of the special housing where they currently resided.

Quinton had top-notch people supervising the boys throughout the day and tending to their needs. They were well schooled, cared for, comfortable, and safe.

But they went bananas when Quinton showed up.

Quinton's home was on the way to hers, so he'd asked her to stop there. She had an hour before she had to be at work, and she couldn't resist the chance to be alone with him, even for a short time.

"Stop here at the end of the driveway. I need to check the mail before we go in."

"Okay." She pulled the Bentley up close to the tall brick and stone masonry structure that housed his mailbox. A duplicate structure sat on the other side of the drive, only without the mailbox inside. In a tall dome shape and surrounded by flourishing greenery and fall flowers, they added a showy touch to the entrance of the drive. It struck Ashley funny that even Quinton's mailbox seemed fancier than her home.

Quinton unhooked his seat belt, rolled down the window, and reached out far enough to loop a finger into the decorative fixture on the front of the box. He started to pull it open—and Ashley noticed the trampled plants around the base. She frowned, certain the mailman would have no need to walk on the landscaping.

Why then . . .

Everything clicked into place in a single heartbeat.

"No!" Ashley yanked Quinton back, but she wasn't fast enough.

The mailbox exploded with an ear-shattering boom, sending out a spray of hardened projectiles. The windshield cracked in several places, and debris shot in through the open passenger-door window. Ashley felt a stinging burn on the side of her neck and face. Fire flickered from inside the box, filling the air with swirling black smoke.

Because of the blast and the way she'd jerked him back, Quinton lost his balance. He landed half on Ashley, crushing her into the driver's door.

Cursing, blood running down his face, he struggled to sit up. Ashley frantically threw the car into park.

Quinton shoved himself upright, and she moaned as a throbbing pain raced through her left arm.

"Ashley!" Twisting toward her, Quinton looked her over, smoothing her hair back. "Oh, Jesus. Ashley, honey, are you all right?"

Ashley blinked, trying to comprehend the situation.

"Ashley, answer me!"

She looked at him and nodded, doing her best to catch her breath. She was just so . . . shocked. Her ears still rang from the blast and the acrid scent of smoke burned her nostrils and lungs. Then she saw the blood from Quinton's forehead and new panic set in. "Oh my God!"

He sounded harsh and angry as he touched her chin and tipped her face. "Don't move, okay?"

"You're bleeding!"

"I'm fine." He caught her fluttering hand and gently controlled her. "I'm *fine*, honey, I swear. Now sit still. I have to call for an ambulance."

An ambulance? Dear God. How badly was he hurt?

Numb, aching all over, Ashley sat there, and she knew Elton Pascal had done this. He wanted her, but because Denny and Quinton had her so well protected, he'd turned his attention to Quinton. Unfortunately, when she was with Quinton, the guards were off duty.

If she hadn't noticed the signs of trespass, if she hadn't pulled Quinton back in time, the explosion might have maimed him. Or killed him.

Bile rose in her throat, and she covered her mouth with a hand, swallowing hard. "I'm sorry." Her whisper emerged so low, she didn't think Quinton had heard her.

While lifting the hem of his T-shirt to his forehead to staunch the trickle of blood, he glanced her way with worry. He had the cell phone to his ear, explaining what had happened, but Ashley barely heard the words. She watched him and realized that she was being useless, that he was hurt, too, and still he took control.

She dragged a deep breath into her lungs, then

another and another until the panic began to recede. Head wounds bled a lot. She knew that.

But she'd never seen Quinton bleed.

He could be hurt badly, but given how easily he moved and the clear way he spoke, his wounds were likely superficial. Realizing that did a lot to calm her.

Experimentally, she flexed her left arm. *Ouch.* Okay, so maybe she had fractured something when Quinton landed against her outstretched arms. A distal radius fracture would be the most likely. Not life threatening, but painful. It'd mean a cast, which would be a nuisance, but she could deal with it.

Her cheek and neck stung. Broken glass and pieces of metal were all around them. She couldn't move without getting pinched or poked, but a quick exam of her hands and lower arms showed no serious injuries

She looked again at Quinton. Several small cuts oozed blood on his face, but other than the cut to his forehead, none of them were very deep.

"You're going to need stitches," she told him. "And if we keep sitting here, we'll probably get more cuts from all the debris."

But if they got out of the car, would Elton be waiting?

Quinton finished the call and turned to her again. His steely gaze went to her cheek. "Hang on, honey. An ambulance is on the way." He unhooked her seat belt, settling the strap away from her with care.

"I'm okay," she promised him, while scanning the area for any suspicious shadow in the form of a murderous worm. This was way beyond obnoxious phone calls. This showed Elton's sick desperation.

But what if he hadn't left any evidence? He was accused of killing two people with an impact bomb, but . . . would that be proof that he did this? Would the police blame Elton? Would they understand now just how far he'd go?

"Ashley, honey, listen to me. Something is jamming my door." Quinton touched her hair, moving it back. He winced. "Will yours open?"

"I think I broke my wrist." The pain had settled into a blunt, cold throb. "Can you reach around me and get the handle?"

He briefly closed his eyes, his face hard with rage and helplessness. But when he spoke, his tone was gentle and soft. "Yeah. Hold on, baby. I don't want to hurt you."

"You won't." She pressed back into the seat to give him room. He reached one long arm across her waist and shoved the door wide.

The beams from the Bentley's headlights still shone across the yard, and as far as she could see, nothing moved except the drifting smoke. Keeping her arm tucked close to her stomach, Quinton's hand on her right elbow to assist her, Ashley stepped out. She used care so that she didn't accidentally grind against anything sharp in the seat.

Quinton was right behind her, his arm around her waist as if to support her. "Come on, honey. I want you to sit down." He tried to guide her to the curb, and Ashley noticed that his hands shook.

She frowned at him. "If you're shaking because of me, I really am fine. But if it's because you're hurt, then *you* need to sit down."

His jaw worked, flexing as he locked his teeth. "I'm shaking because I want to kill him."

The quiet, convicted rasp startled her. With the

blood marring his face, and that particular tone, Quinton looked more than capable of taking Elton apart. "Oh, well, then. Me, too."

Sirens split the night, and seconds later, the ambulance was there with two cruisers and a lot of confusion. Paramedics took one look at them and immediately went to work. Ashley found herself separated from Quinton and led to sit on the open back of the ambulance.

Quinton shrugged off the hands of the poor EMT who wanted to check his head. At least his anger reiterated his strength, comforting her on so many levels. If anything had happened to him . . .

"I'm fine," Quinton insisted to the man. "It's just a damn cut. Take care of her." He nodded to Ashley, and the paramedic immediately switched gears, joining the female EMT who now wanted to usher Ashley into the ambulance.

"No, wait," she said, but no one was really listening to her. "I'm okay," she tried to tell them. "It's just a simple break, that's all."

Quinton stopped the medics long enough to tip up her chin. He looked so severe, so enraged. "Your face is cut, honey."

That startled her. She blinked. "It is?"

"Let them take care of you."

Confused, she started to reach up, but Quinton caught her hand. "Shhh. It's all right, Ashley."

"I felt something hit my upper cheek and my neck, too." She frowned and realized her face felt stiff. The way Quinton acted, she had no idea if her head was about to fall off. "Is it bad?"

Grim with resolve, his eyes blazing, Quinton shook his head. "No. You'll be fine. I swear it."

Never had she seen a man more pained. Her smile went crooked. "Well, I never doubted that I'd live. But you look a little unconvinced."

A police officer approached, a dozen questions tripping off his tongue at once, trying to pull Quinton's attention away from her.

"Go on," Ashley told him. She wanted the cops to get started on collecting evidence as soon as possible before any more of it was destroyed by well-meaning people. "Don't worry about me. I'll get in the ambulance like a good girl."

Quinton hesitated, so Ashley reasoned with him. "Elton might still be around. There could be tracks or fingerprints or . . . I don't know. Elton could still be around here somewhere. Tell them everything now so they can start hunting for him."

Quinton again touched her chin. "I'll be right back."

The EMT said, "We won't leave without you."

He nodded his thanks. While he answered the officer the best he could, the paramedics helped Ashley into the ambulance. They left the door open, though, and she could hear the officer speaking.

"We'll have some experts take a look, but I think this was the work of a homemade bomb. Several in fact, to get that much of an explosion. You two are lucky you weren't hurt worse. Even killed."

No, Ashley thought, feeling ill again. Elton Pascal didn't want her dead. He'd said she would be punished, and a quick death wasn't on his agenda. This was a scare tactic.

And it worked.

Knowing he'd do this to Quinton, to the people she cared about, was the scariest thing imaginable.

To distract herself, she smiled at the female EMT carefully cleaning the blood off her face. "How bad is it?"

"You'll be fine."

Oh, for the love of . . . How many times did they think to tell her that?

"Right. Fine." She leaned away from the woman's busy hands. "But come on. Stitches? A scar? What?"

The EMT tried to go back to swabbing her face, but Ashley avoided her.

"I'm a nurse," she lied. She wouldn't graduate for a while yet. "Whatever it is, I can take it."

The woman met her gaze, wavered, but finally gave in. "You'll need stitches. I can't say for sure, but as long as there's no nerve or muscle damage, and you don't get any infections, I think the scar should be minimal."

"I remember something hitting me, but I don't remember what. It's a laceration?"

The EMT nodded. "Pretty deep, too. Something jagged must've caught you from the force of the blast. I'm not sure if it's still embedded in there or not. There's a lot of swelling . . ."

Just dandy. "I guess they can do some X-rays at the hospital." Ashley leaned her head back and closed her eyes. "What about my neck? The same?"

"A deep scratch, that's all. On your shoulder too. I don't think they'll need stitches. They've already stopped bleeding."

Bounding up into the ambulance, Quinton took a seat beside Ashley on the gurney. "Let's go." He'd retrieved her purse from the Bentley and she took it from him, clutching it in her lap with her good hand.

The doors closed and a moment later, the am

bulance pulled away with sirens screeching and lights flashing.

Quinton now had a bandage on his head, most of the blood swabbed away. He sat rigid beside her, all but vibrating with fury.

"Your car?" she asked, wondering how much damage the Bentley had suffered.

At her query, he looked ready to combust. "I don't give a fuck about the car."

He was so distraught that Ashley couldn't stand it. She turned her head toward him and said, "See, that's the difference between us, Murphy. You can blow off the destruction to a car that costs more than most houses, but I'm already worrying about the work I might miss because of this mess."

"Ashley?"

"What?"

"Don't provoke me."

She couldn't help it; she laughed.

"Not now," he added, ignoring her humor. "Not while I'm considering kidnapping you so I can keep you under lock and key."

"Lock and key, huh?"

"Safe."

"I hate to break it to you, Murphy, but it was your mailbox that exploded, not mine."

"The bomb squad's headed to your place right now to check out your mailbox, too." He picked up her hand and carried it to his mouth, pressing a firm kiss to her knuckles. His eyes closed, his jaw went taut. "If you moved in with me—"

"Whoa!" *Moved in?* Where had that come from? Are you in shock or something? You can't be serious."

The EMT pretended to do some reorganizing of her supplies, but Ashley caught her slight smile.

"Of course I'm serious." Quinton was furious again. "If you lived with me, if you cooperated just a little bit, I could keep shit like this from happening!"

"Gee." Ashley eyed him up and down. "That's about the most romantic invitation to cohabitate that I think I've ever heard. I'm all aflutter. I don't know what to say."

For a second, Quinton's expression remained frozen in harsh lines. He breathed hard, and his hold on her hand was bruising. Finally, he relaxed on a short laugh, closing his eyes again and muttering, "I am so goddamned sorry."

She knew he wasn't talking about his misguided invitation. "That's my line, Murphy. Elton's after me, not you. You're nothing more than an innocent bystander." Her arm really hurt now, and her head pounded, and she felt sick to her stomach. "But he failed this time because we're both okay. So don't make emotional declarations that you might later regret. All right?"

Ashley waited for his reaction to all she'd said, and she waited, and waited. She raised her brows. "Cat got your tongue?"

He shook his head. "No. I've just never heard you spout so much nonsense at one time before."

"Nonsense?"

He patted her hand and gave her an insincere smile that reeked of resolve. "We'll both get patched up, then go back to my place and get some sleep. In the morning we'll talk about . . . everything."

"So I'm sleeping over?"

"Yes."

It went against her independent nature to admit it, but Ashley said, "I'm glad." Then she leaned her head on Quinton's strong, solid shoulder and drew from his strength—while wondering how she could possibly protect him when he was so determined to protect her instead.

Chapter 14

Clipboard and pen in hand, the emergency room doctor continued with her never-ending list of questions. "Is there a possibility you could be pregnant?"

Ashley stopped fidgeting with the long ties to the hospital gown. Because her wrist hurt so badly, a technician had helped her change and she now wore the hideous cotton contraption that didn't want to stay closed.

Utterly mute, she stared at the female doctor. "What?"

Glancing up from her clipboard, the doctor smiled. "Please understand. When a patient is female, I'm required to ask if there's a possibility of pregnancy. I'm not making assumptions about your sexual activity or orientation."

"No."

The doctor paused, then moved to sit on the edge of the narrow metal bed by Ashley's hip. "X-rays can pose a risk to a developing fetus, so we try to take every precaution. We ask this question of *all* women."

Ashley shook her head.

Folding her hands over the clipboard, the doctor asked gently, "When was your last period?"

It was . . . New panic burned in Ashley's stomach. She pressed her right hand to her forehead, but she just didn't know, when usually she was regular as clockwork. "I . . . I can't remember. I'm late, I guess. But I'm *not* pregnant. I'm sure of it. We've been careful."

"If you've missed a period—"

Desperate, she said, "I'm new to this sex stuff. That ought to be enough to throw off anyone's cycle."

The doctor lifted her brows. "You've only recently become sexually active?"

"That's right."

"I don't think that would have any bearing on your regular cycle. And you should know, the only foolproof birth control is abstinence. So even if you've been using protection, it could still be possible."

"Oh, God." Ashley bit her lip. "It hasn't been that long. Are you sure you'll even be able to tell if I'm pregnant?"

"A test can detect pregnancy as early as six days after conception, or one day after your last missed period." She squeezed Ashley's hand. "It's better to be safe, yes? The test won't take long, I promise. Then we'll know, and we can take the necessary precautions before X-raying your wrist."

"I came here with a man . . ." Ashley snapped her mouth shut, but the doctor had already picked up on her train of thought.

"We finished stitching him up some time ago. He's pacing the hallway waiting to see you." She squeezed Ashley's hand again. "Your records are entirely confidential. He'll know only what you choose to tell him. Now just relax. I'll be right back."

The next few minutes left Ashley numb. Even after the test, she sat there in silence, unsure of her feelings, wishing she could see Quinton now, but unwilling to involve him.

When the doctor returned, Ashley knew something wasn't right. She pulled up a chair beside the bed, tipped her head in a thoughtful way, and finally met Ashley's gaze with clear concern.

Ashley held her breath, at least until the doctor said, "You're pregnant."

Then she let it out in a whoosh.

Pinpoints of light danced in front of her eyes and a rush of heat made her dizzy. For a moment, she thought she might faint.

The doctor eased her back to rest against a pillow on the cot. "Take some deep breaths."

Ashley gulped instead. No way. This couldn't be happening. "You're sure?"

"Yes. I take it this is unexpected news?"

She gulped again.

"Ms. Miles, listen to me. An unplanned pregnancy presents a lot of complicated decisions and often ambivalent feelings. Pregnancy counseling is available to talk over your alternatives or to get referrals for additional support and information. They can help you explore your options and feelings regarding an unexpected pregnancy."

Ashley stared at her. Counseling? Good grief.

The doctor continued. "You don't have to decide anything right now. You've just been through a very traumatic experience. You're injured and in need of medical care. For tonight, let's just take care of that."

"But . . ."

The doctor patted her hand. "Tomorrow, or the day after, you can think more about the pregnancy. If you choose to keep the baby and you don't already have an obstetrics and gynecology physician, I suggest you contact your primary care doctor. He or she can refer you to someone right away."

That sounded too ominous by half, and Ashley bolted upright again. "Why the rush? Is there something wrong with the baby?"

"No, I didn't mean that. The objective of prenatal care is to monitor the health of the pregnant mother and fetus. The doctor will monitor your weight and blood pressure, and he'll be able to tell you exactly when you're due."

"Okay." Ashley drew another, slower breath this time. "Thank you."

"You're all right?"

She honestly didn't know how she felt about the idea of a baby. *A baby*. Dear God, just thinking about it scared her to death. She could barely take care of herself, and she had all her plans for the future, but now . . .

Ashley shook off the renewed panic. As the doctor said, she didn't have to have all the solutions tonight. She knew only one thing for sure. "I'll keep the baby."

The doctor smiled. "So you're not unhappy about the pregnancy?"

"Shocked stupid. Taken off guard. Scared spitless." She felt herself smiling and didn't know why. "But no, I'm not unhappy."

"I'm glad." After patting her hand, the doctor moved away from the bed. "We'll use a lead apron to protect the fetus during the X-rays."

"What about my face?" Ashley could still feel the burn from where they'd cleaned the wound and closed it with over twenty-five tiny sutures. The shot to numb the area had stung, as did the solution they'd used to clean it. Now bandaging pulled at her skin every time she spoke or moved her mouth.

But luckily, the doctor hadn't detected any serious damage.

"I can give you the name of a plastic surgeon if you're worried about a scar. After twenty-four hours you can get the stitches wet, but be sure to dry them well and apply antibiotic ointment twice a day. In five days you'll come back to have the sutures removed. It'll be red for a while, but with time to heal, I think it'll barely be noticeable."

Ashley waved a hand. "That sounds fine. No need for a plastic surgeon. I'm not real worried about it. I was just curious."

"Then we're ready for our X-rays."

It was another hour and a half before the doctor confirmed a break and put her left wrist in a cast. Ashley chose hot pink for the cast, which fit in around her fingers and came up to, but not over her elbow.

By the time she finally rejoined Quinton, Denny and Tim had arrived to keep him company.

She came to a halt in the hallway and stared at them all. Exhaustion weighed her down, her arm and face thumped with pain, and her emotions were on a wild roller-coaster ride.

But she noticed the bandaging on Quinton's forehead, the bruises on his cheekbone, and the harried way he paced. His hair stood on end, and he'd exchanged his bloodied shirt for a clean one, probably supplied by Denny.

She'd already decided against telling Quinton about the baby tonight. After everything else that had happened, she didn't have the courage, and he didn't look up to hearing the news anyway. They'd both been through the wringer; no reason to heighten the tension further.

Still, the second Quinton met her gaze, she wanted to run to him and share all her worries for a future that had drastically changed in a matter of minutes.

With all three men watching her, their concern and worry plain to see, it took all Ashley's resolve to stiffen her spine and crack off a smart reply.

"Jesus," she teased, propping her hot pink cast against her hip. "Did I die and someone forgot to tell me? I've seen happier mugs on the convicted."

With feigned calm, Quinton started toward her. An awful strain, almost like fear, showed in her expression, and it kept him from rushing to her and hauling her into his arms. He knew Ashley, and she had to be thinking about the difficulties of getting along with a cast, maintaining her hectic non-stop schedule, and dealing with more possible attacks from Elton. The situation would be daunting to anyone, but especially to someone without resources, without family backup.

He wished Jude and May were home because Ashley could use May now more than ever. Denny and Tim were there for her, and God knew he'd do everything in his power—everything Ashley would allow him to do—to make everything easier and safer for her. But he'd witnessed himself the special closeness of the two women.

Ashley held herself in careful restraint, as if she might shatter if he said or did the wrong thing. She was by far the proudest woman he knew, and if she broke down now, in front of Denny and Tim, she'd be doubly upset with herself, and possibly with him.

Casual as he could contrive, Quinton walked to her, tipped up her chin, and said, "You look beautiful, Ashley. Are you sure you needed to be back there so long? Did you take a nap and leave me out here to worry needlessly?"

Her mouth quivered into an uncertain smile.

Unfortunately, Denny and Tim had followed on his heels, and at almost the same time, Denny said, "Damn, girl. You look like shit."

Blue and black bruising from her cut had spread out to her eye, along with some substantial swelling. She partially squinted while saying, "Gee, thanks, Denny. That's so good to know."

"He's right." Tim grimaced and looked ready to throw up. "Your face is all puffy and colorful, and scraped in places. There's still some blood in your hair, and it's all over your shirt—"

Quinton rolled his eyes, but because Tim had worried right along with him, he didn't strangle him. "Good going, guys. That'll make her feel better."

"Oh." Tim grimaced again, visibly racked his

brain, and shrugged. "I'm sure you'll look like your old self once you heal, right? I mean, you won't be scarred up or anything, will you?"

Ashley's grin went lopsided, likely because of the stitches in her upper cheek. Thank God, the projectile that had cut her had missed her eye. When Quinton thought of how badly she could have been hurt, rage infused him to the point that he couldn't talk, could barely breathe.

One way or another, he'd get to Elton and remove the lunatic from her life.

"I dunno, Tim," she teased. "Will you quit being my friend if I look like Frankenstein?"

"No!" He replied without hesitation. "I swear, Ash, it won't matter to me."

This time she laughed, and though it sounded weak and scratchy, Quinton felt better for hearing it.

"Relax, Tim." She curled her uninjured arm through Quinton's and edged up close to his side. "I was just funning you. Before long you won't be able to tell that I was ever hurt."

"That's great." Tim nodded to her colorful cast. "You gotta wear that for six weeks?"

"Nope. Four, which is a whole lot better, but bad enough." She looked up at Quinton and gently touched his forehead. "Ouch. That looks painful."

"I didn't need stitches. The cut was shallow, thanks to the way you pulled me back." He rubbed her left shoulder, down to the start of the cast. "That's when you broke your wrist, isn't it? From the way I landed against you?"

"From the way I stupidly braced myself." She went on tiptoe to kiss his chin, surprising him. "The X-rays are what took so long. Then they had to put on the cast. I'm just relieved it's my left hand and not my right. I can't imagine trying to finish up my semester without being able to write."

Denny, as enraged as Quinton, drew a deep breath. "If there's anything I can do to help, you let me know."

"You're already doing it. Thanks."

Quinton noticed the way she favored her injured wrist. "It's hurting?" He tried to keep his tone light, but from the inside out, he felt scraped raw.

"Nah. It's fine."

He could tell she lied, but he didn't call her on it. "Come on then, let's go home."

She held back, and he realized his choice of words might have taken her off guard. With Denny and Tim crowded close, he bent down to her and said firmly, "My home, honey. And don't argue. Everything's already arranged."

"He's right," Denny chimed in. "The police can't do a damn thing. They don't have proof that Elton was involved with the mailbox bomb, not yet anyway. They're still looking for him, but who knows how much he might have changed, or where he could be hiding?"

Quinton glared at Denny. "It doesn't matter. I'm not going to let anything happen to her."

"That's my point," Denny shot right back. "We've got people watching the house, and they'll trail both of you wherever you go. As long as you stay with Quinton, Elton Pascal won't get within shouting distance of you again. I swear it."

Quinton shored up Denny's claims. "He's right, honey. I can guard you better than the police, if you'll let me."

She started to tuck back her hair, remembered it was stiff with blood and iodine, and struck a cocky pose instead. "Amazing. You're all three waiting for me to argue, aren't you?"

"Because you usually do," Tim pointed out. "I think you like to be contrary."

She laughed. "Well, not this time. Not when my safety is an issue. I don't particularly want to be blown up, you know. Until the police catch up with Elton, I'm all for playing it safe."

"Glad to hear it." Quinton put his arm around her and coaxed her toward the door. He wanted her in his house, in his bed, and in his arms. Until he got her there, he wouldn't start feeling right again.

Ashley was unusually subdued on the ride home. Denny drove, with Tim in the front seat beside him. Quinton couldn't keep his hands off Ashley, and though she stayed glued to his side, she seemed withdrawn, as if she'd suddenly erected new barriers against him.

He tried to write it off as the circumstances. She had to be in discomfort. Hell, his head still pounded from the explosion, and he couldn't seem to loosen his muscles. He was rigid enough to fracture, but he tried to hide that from her.

They needed to be alone, to talk, but he wouldn't take chances with her safety.

When Denny pulled the car into the driveway, another car pulled up to the curb. Headlights stayed on as a man stepped out and approached.

"It's okay," Quinton told her.

Regardless of his reassurance, Ashley stiffened,

but when Denny opened the door to greet him, she sighed.

"I suppose he's part of the new security you mentioned?"

Quinton lifted her right hand to his mouth and kissed her knuckles. "He and his men will be outside the house all night. In the morning, new video cameras will be installed that'll include the entire yard. I'll cancel my postal delivery and use a post office box instead, until Elton is behind bars. I want you to do the same thing."

She nodded. "Good idea."

Denny returned to the wheel and put the car back in drive. "He says the cops are circling the block, too, watching the yard. He introduced himself to them."

Ashley closed her eyes and rested her head on his shoulder. She looked minutes away from falling asleep.

He asked Denny, "Would you mind coming inside and going through the house, just to be sure? I want to get Ashley cleaned up and then into bed."

Tim snickered, and it was all Quinton could do to keep from smacking him in the head. Denny did it for him, which started Tim apologizing to Ashley.

With her head still resting on Quinton's shoulder, her eyes closed, she flapped her good hand toward Tim. "No apology necessary. Truthfully, was thinking the same thing."

Quinton did a double take. "Don't be ridiculous. You're hurt and you've been through hell—"

"Right. Sorry about that." She snuggled closer

"I didn't mean to pressure you. If you need to rest tonight, I'll understand."

Tim started laughing. "You see. I wasn't the only one who—"

Quinton and Denny said together, "Shut up, Tim."

He nodded, but then asked, "Is anyone hungry?"

Quinton was too busy staring at Ashley, wondering if she'd meant that, if she truly wanted to make love with him. God knew, he wanted nothing more than to be close to her, as close as two people could get, to touch her all over and assure himself of her well-being.

"I could get some food together," Tim continued. "We were at the hospital for hours, and my stomach is starting to rumble, so I just thought the rest of you might want something to eat, too."

Ashley smiled. "Actually, now that you mention it, I'm starving."

Knowing he had to pull himself together, Quinton kept his gaze on Ashley, but told Tim, "Feel free to root around in the kitchen and see what you can find. I'm not sure what's there, but help yourself."

They parked in the garage. Quinton keyed in the password to his alarm system, then stood back and allowed Denny to go in first. While he and Tim checked through the house, Quinton waited in the garage with Ashley. She curled her pink cast in close to her body and valiantly tried to hide her exhaustion.

Wishing he could read her thoughts, Quinton tipped up her chin with his fingertips. "Starving, huh?"

She smiled at him. "Ravenous."

Much more of her teasing, and he'd lose it. "I don't want to hurt you, honey."

"Then plan on putting me out of my sexual misery. You're the one who got me addicted. And Murphy's Law aside, it's been way too damn long to suit me."

"But your arm . . ." As gently as he could, he touched her cheek. "Your *cheek*. You have to be hurting."

"Damn right." She stared at his mouth. "But it's nothing you can't fix."

Quinton didn't know what to make of her mood. She was so determined to be intimate that she obliterated his resolve to pamper her. Most women would've been in constant tears, or even in shock, after what she'd been through.

"I know what you're thinking, Murphy, so knock it off. I wasn't the only one there tonight. You were right beside me, and you were injured, too. But you're not whining or huddling into the fetal position. You don't see me coddling you like you're a fragile piece of glass."

"I'm a man."

The black eye and bandaging gave her an especially feral look. "If you weren't already so battered, I'd smack you for saying that." She caught the front of his shirt in her right hand and hauled him down to within inches of her. "Speak up, Murphy. Do you want me or not?"

How could she ask something so ridiculous. "Always." He touched his mouth to hers. "I want you so much I can't think of anything else. I asked Denny to check the house because he'll be sharper tonight than I can be."

"Great." She bobbed her head once in satisfaction. "Then let's go get cleaned up, eat, and kick our beloved guests out on their cans." Her wide grin taunted him—but it was the emotion in her dark eyes that grabbed him around the heart.

Holding out a hand for Ashley to precede him, Quinton followed her into the house. They reached the kitchen just as Denny returned from his check, with Tim in tow.

"The upstairs and this floor are clear. I'm going to poke around downstairs, too, but nothing looks disturbed to me."

"Thanks, Denny. I appreciate it."

"No problem. Better safe than sorry. Soon as I'm done, I'll help Tim in the kitchen." He winked. "You two take your time. We'll wait for you."

Once Denny had sauntered off, Quinton escorted Ashley to his bedroom. More docile than she'd ever been with him, she sat on the end of his bed while he ran a warm bath and dug out clean clothes for her.

She seemed lost in thought when he reentered the bedroom, but the second she saw him, she stood. "Will you help me get out of my clothes?"

"Yes."

That alluring smile teased over her mouth again. "I have a black eye, stitches, and yucky hair, and you're half hard already."

Quinton glanced down at himself and cursed. "It can't be helped, not when I know you'll soon be naked."

"It wasn't a complaint. I'm just surprised. I figured guys wanted a woman who looked nice. Not one who looks like she's been through the wringer."

Quinton carefully peeled her shirt upward, revealing first her pale belly, then her small breasts.

"I suppose it has to do with being male, and no, that's not cause for smacking me. When a man feels protective toward a woman, and she's looking small and vulnerable, well then, dominant male tendencies come out." He clasped her rib cage just beneath her breasts and smoothed her skin with his thumbs.

"Mmmm." Ashley stepped out of her shoes. "I like the sound of that." She gestured toward the fly of her jeans. "Wanna lend me a hand here?"

"My pleasure." Deliberately brushing her with his knuckles, Quinton unbuttoned her fly and eased down her zipper. The loose-fitting jeans gaped open. Going to his knees in front her, he tugged the jeans down to her ankles. Ashley lifted each foot in turn, and he shoved the jeans aside, leaving her in nothing more than a minuscule pair of pale pink panties.

He wanted to play the game with her, he really did. His sexual encounters with Ashley had shown him the meaning of true satisfaction. He loved making love to her, hearing her soft sighs and harsh moans, the way she clutched at him, her willingness to explore.

But when her small hand sank into his hair, possessiveness crashed through him and he crushed her close, his cheek to her belly.

"Quinton?"

Damn it, he couldn't get a single word past the lump in his throat. Tonight he could have lost her, and he'd been battling a riot of emotions ever since. He shook his head, hating the way he felt so overwhelmed and uncertain and too exposed.

"We're both okay, you know." Her gentle voice

washed over him. "And now that I'm here with you, I'm better than okay."

She reassured him, unmanning him with her understanding, and Quinton couldn't bear it. It made him weak, which was something he couldn't abide. He naturally countered by sliding his hand inside the leg of her panties to palm one plump cheek. At the same time, he pressed a kiss to her navel. "You are so soft."

She laughed. "I'm also impatient."

"Right." Pulling himself together, Quinton tugged her panties down her legs, stood, and scooped her into his arms to carry her into the bath.

"I feel pampered."

He nuzzled a breast and said, "No, you feel hot."

Making sure she kept her cast propped on the ledge surrounding the tub, Quinton lowered her into the warm water. He knelt next to the tub and stroked the side of her neck where an ugly bruise marred her delicate skin. "Want me to wash your hair for you?"

"Thanks. I'm not sure I could do it without getting my cast wet."

Reaching over his shoulder to grab a fistful of his shirt, he yanked it off over his head and tossed it to the bench. "Just relax, and I'll do everything."

He took his time, and to his surprise, Ashley didn't once protest. Near her injured skin, he took special care, using a cloth to dab around her stitches, removing the iodine stains. After her hair was clean, he soaped up the cloth to give her shoulders and lower back a sudsy massage. He washed her slender legs and played with her small toes, enjoying her giggles.

And when he brought the cloth to her breasts, and then between her legs, he tried to be detached—but couldn't.

Ashley leaned forward and said, "Kiss me, Quinton."

He did, but he kept the kiss light and easy, then retreated. "If Denny and Tim weren't downstairs, I'd delay this forever. I enjoy taking care of you. Given these tight nipples"—he stroked the cloth over her breasts again and heard her deep inhalation—"you enjoy it, too."

"I suppose if we kept them waiting, they'd know exactly why."

"They're guys, so of course they'd know." He opened the drain in the tub, stood, and shook open a big fluffy towel. "Come on, honey. Let's go eat."

As Ashley stepped out of the tub and he wrapped her in the towel, Quinton thought it was just as well that company curtailed his inclinations. Seeing her like this, so weary but still stoic, her good humor intact, made him that much more anxious to be with her, skin to skin, heartbeat to heartbeat. He worried enough for her that he wasn't sure about sex, but he cared enough that he craved the special closeness of lovemaking.

Quinton shook his head at himself and concentrated on drying her without further arousing himself. Even with stress and exhaustion leaving circles under her eyes, he loved seeing her so casually at ease with him.

By the time they reached the kitchen, Tim had put together a stack of cheese sandwiches, pickles, nachos, and colas over ice. Bundled in flannel pants that drooped low on her narrow hips, and one of his oversized sweatshirts with the left cuff cut away to accommodate her cast, Ashley looked adorable. She tucked her wet hair behind her ears, padded barefoot to the table, and immediately dug into a sandwich, devouring it in no time.

Studying her with near fascination, Tim put another on her plate, along with some pickles and chips. He smiled as he watched her eat.

Quinton knew that Tim was seeing Ashley with new eyes, and it pleased him that Tim had accepted things so easily, that he seemed intent on building a special bond. He only hoped that Ashley would be happy about it when she caught on to the changed circumstances.

After gobbling down two of the sandwiches, Denny crossed his arms on the top of the table. "I don't suppose you plan to sleep in tomorrow?"

Ashley shook her head. "I have class. The semester ends soon. If I miss anything now, I might blow the finals."

Quinton had to wonder if she'd ever allowed herself to have a lazy day spent in bed, maybe with someone waiting on her. He'd like to do that, and if he could talk her into it, the sooner the better. But he knew it'd have to wait until her classes were over.

"What time's your first class?" Denny asked.

"Ten-thirty." She paused in the process of munching her third crisp pickle spear. "Wait a minute. You're going to follow me to school, aren't you?"

"No." Denny thrust out his chin. "I'm going to drive you. Your car isn't here, and Quinton has his own work, not to mention some things to do to finalize the security additions."

Quinton shook his head. "I can take a day off."
He had a meeting scheduled, but between Warren
and Adrianna, they could handle it without him.

"I don't mind driving her at all," Denny explained.

And Tim added, "Let him drive you, Ash. It'll
give me a break from the workout."

Ashley slanted a look at Quinton, then waved
the pickle spear at all of them. "Let's get something straight here, okay? However I get to class tomorrow, when I finish up, I'm going to get my car
and I'm going to drive myself back here. I won't be
sitting helpless in Quinton's home."

"Helpless?" Quinton snapped to attention. It relieved him that she planned to come back to his
home, but she made it sound like he'd have her
chained to the wall. "What the hell does that
mean?"

"It means I like having options."

"Well, hell, if you decide you have somewhere to
go, I can take you. Or I have plenty of cars you can
use."

"I want *my* car. But," she said, interrupting any
objections, "I don't plan to go anywhere unless
one of you knows about it. Until that crazy SOB is
behind bars, I'm going to be very, very careful."

Quinton wasn't sure if he'd won that one or not,
but Denny seemed satisfied, so he let it go.

"Good enough." Denny stood and stretched.
"We're getting out of here, or you won't get any
sleep at all." He set the empty dishes in the sink
and patted Ashley's shoulder as he passed her.

Tim pushed back his chair, circled the table
and bent to kiss Ashley's cheek. In an uncharacter

istic display of concern, he said, "For God's sake, Ash, take it easy, will you?"

Bemused, Ashley nodded. "Uh, sure thing, Tim."

Quinton smiled. "I'll see you guys out." The men discussed last-minute details, but as soon as they'd pulled out of the garage, he set the alarms again, locked the door, and came back to Ashley.

She stretched, too. "I need a toothbrush."

"Use mine."

"Wow." Pretending great surprise at his offer, she put a hand to her heart. "In some countries, sharing a toothbrush is part of an elaborate bonding ritual."

Quinton pulled back her chair and picked her up again, holding her close to his chest. "In this country as well."

"No kidding? I didn't know that."

He kissed her to stop her teasing—and then he couldn't stop kissing her. It had been too long, and he'd been patient enough. Relishing her gentle weight in his arms, he strode down the hall, kicked his bedroom door shut behind him, and carried her into the bathroom. "Do whatever you need to do. I'll turn down the bed."

She shooed him out, shutting the door behind him, and Quinton busied himself with the covers, his mind racing ahead to the point he felt nearly explosive. Rather than stand there waiting for her, he got into bed and propped his arms behind his head.

Staring at the ceiling, he listened to the sounds of his blow dryer, water splashing, and finally, Ashley opened the bathroom door. As she stood there in the lighted door frame, he saw that her hair billowed out, as if she'd had a hell of a time using his blow dryer one-handed. She'd also removed the flannel pants. Beneath the hem of his sweatshirt, her long legs looked pale, and too damn sexy.

For a while she simply stood there, staring toward him in silence. "I not only used your toothbrush, but your lotion, too. Now I smell like you."

Why that would make him hard, Quinton didn't know. But he was so aroused he hurt. He pulled back the covers and patted the mattress. "Come here."

He sounded savage, a man on the edge. A man overcome with lust.

Ashley smiled and turned out the bathroom light, leaving the room in darkness.

Guarding her cast, she lowered herself to the bed beside him. He braced himself over her, smoothed back her now-dry, very fluffy hair, and waited for her to call the shots.

She stared up at him, then whispered, "Alone at last."

Chapter 15

Rich in shadows, cool and quiet, Quinton's bedroom felt like the safest haven around. Using care not to clunk him with her cast, she put her arms around him. "I've missed you so much."

His fingertips played over her face. "How do you feel?"

"Like I'll die if you don't make love to me."

There was a moment of perfect stillness, and then Quinton snugged the sweatshirt up over her breasts. She could feel his hot breath when he said, "Tell me if I hurt you."

She started to say okay, but his mouth latched onto her breast and she could do no more than arch beneath him. She was more sensitive than she'd ever been, the sensation of his mouth on her so acute, so delicious, that her aches and pains faded away, her worries lifted. He drew softly on her, tugging at her nipple, curling his tongue around her.

"Quinton?" She tangled her right hand in his

hair. "Let's take off our clothes. I want to be naked with you."

He lifted his head, and though she couldn't see his eyes, she knew his thoughts.

"I need to feel all of you. Please."

"All right." He sat up beside her. "Careful now."

He helped to get her back out of the sweatshirt before standing beside the bed. She heard the rustling as he removed his own flannel pants and boxers, the opening and closing of a drawer, and when he came back to her, she felt the heat of his body and the tautness of his muscles.

"Much better."

"Let's get you comfortable." Using a soft, plump pillow, he cushioned her head, then went one further and placed another pillow under her hips. "Put your arms beside you. I don't want to bump your broken wrist."

"You aren't going to hurt me."

"I know." Sensual command had entered his tone, seducing her as thoroughly as the fingers that trailed over her belly, just above the curls between her legs. "That's because you're going to be very still while I make you feel good."

She closed her eyes and relaxed. "Okay."

With a hand on each thigh, he eased her legs open. "I wish I could see you, but just knowing that you're lying here, open and waiting, is good enough for now."

"What am I waiting for?"

He said, "This," and licked her nipple before gently nipping with teeth. He added, "Here," and his fingers pressed between her legs, but only briefly, long enough to touch her clitoris, to roll over it, tease and send a shock of feelings through her.

He withdrew his hand to plump up a breast and suck.

Ashley bit her lip. Knowing what he intended, what he'd eventually do, heightened all her senses. She was so anxious, she couldn't keep still. He stroked her skin, cuddling her breasts and kneading her belly, but he didn't touch between her thighs again. Whenever the waiting became too excruciating and she couldn't bear it, she clamped her legs together. But he seemed to know it and each time, he urged her to part them again.

She was left open and waiting—just as he wanted.

Finally, he left her breasts and kissed each rib, tickling her, making her squirm. His fingertips drifted over her straining thighs as if in approval, as if urging her to widen them even more.

He dipped his tongue into her navel, trailed damp, hot kisses over to her hip bones, and then downward. Ashley moaned, pressing her head back and digging her heels into the mattress.

"Don't hurt your arm," he reminded her.

"No. No, it's fine." She couldn't even feel her arm. All she felt was a great throbbing need right—*where he kissed her.*

"You're wet," he murmured with deep satisfaction, and he parted her with his fingers, then lapped slowly at her, licking his tongue along her vulva, up and over her clitoris. With each leisurely pass, her tension heightened until she couldn't bear it.

But as usual, Quinton seemed to know exactly what she needed and when. With care, he worked two fingers into her, stretching her, rasping along sensitive nerve endings. He slid his fingers out, pressed them in again, and she felt his rough tongue stroking her, seeking, then his mouth closed over her so he could suck at her, and the tension snapped.

With a deep groan, her body trembling and shaking uncontrollably, she climaxed.

Quinton stayed with her, keeping the pleasure keen, until she moaned and pleaded with him.

In the next instant he was over her, gliding easily into her. He kissed her mouth and her throat while rolling his hips, gently riding her. The pillow kept her hips tilted to his advantage, letting him go deep, building the pleasure yet again. Another climax hit her, when she thought for sure she'd be dead to the world.

She clamped a hand to his backside and urged him in closer, harder, but he refused to let her set the pace.

"I won't hurt you, honey. I won't. I won't . . ." His words trailed off, he put his head back, and ground out his release.

His excitement swept her along until her every muscle went limp. Almost immediately afterward, he carefully moved off her. Cool air touched her heated damp skin, making her shiver. She reached for him. "Quinton?"

"I'll be right back."

"Where are you going?"

"To get rid of the condom. Just lie still."

Condom? He must have put it on when he removed his clothes because he sure hadn't paused before entering her. She smiled, liking that idea, imagining him hard while kissing her there . . .

The mattress dipped when he sat beside her. With his fingers he combed her hair away from her face. "You're okay?"

"You tell me."

She heard his smile when he said, "All right. You're wonderful."

"Yes, I am. Thank you. That was mind altering."

"You don't say." A cool, damp cloth touched between her legs and she lurched. "No, be still. I'm just making you more comfortable before we go to sleep."

"I can do that myself, you know. I'm not handicapped."

"I want to do it."

It didn't seem worth the effort of argument. "Yeah, all right. Knock yourself out."

He chuckled. "So, has your mind altered enough that you'll agree to move in with me?"

Though he said it casually enough, Ashley heard his reservation, his uncertainty with her and her acceptance of him. The lethargy left her, and a great thumping entered her heart.

Now would be a good time to tell him about the baby. She had no right to keep the news from him. He needed to know. The sooner the better.

But she couldn't get the words out.

She knew his thoughts on unplanned pregnancy, on unwanted babies. *She* wanted her baby—but how would he feel about it?

No way could she commit to living with him. Not until he knew. It wouldn't be fair. But neither did she want to cause a void between them tonight. She needed him. She needed to feel secure and loved—for just a little while.

"Give me some time, Quinton."

He left the bed and went back into the bathroom, but returned in only moments. The bed dipped again, and he stretched out beside her, propped on an elbow. "Time for what?"

To get used to the idea of being responsible for two, instead of one. But again, she held that back.

"Everything has changed so much." It seemed easier to converse with the lights out, the darkness concealing. "For the longest time, it was just me. I mean, I had May for a friend, but I didn't have anyone else. No family, not even any close associations. And that was okay. It worked for me."

His large, warm hand, so strong and capable, settled on her belly, and her heart lurched. His touch was so protective, so caring, when he had no idea a baby rested beneath his palm.

Tears filled her eyes, and she swallowed with difficulty—then put her hand over his. "I had no thoughts of dating, of involving anyone else in my life." Her voice broke, and she wanted to curse herself. "Now there's not only you, but Denny and Tim keep turning up."

"Like bad pennies?"

"Like caring friends." Feeling like a fraud, feeling dishonorable, she turned toward him and nudged nearer. Tucking her face into his throat, she whispered, "It's so different from what I'm used to, I need to adjust to it all."

His hand drifted to her bottom, pressing her closer. One of his legs went over hers. "If you're here, I can help you adjust."

"Quinton." She finally turned her face up to his. "Don't you see? This could be more of your macho protectiveness toward the poor little woman."

"No." He stroked her skin, lazy and confident of his purpose, familiar in a way she'd never imagined. "It's because I want to be with you, Ashley Miles, and your crazy schedule makes it almost impossible."

Yet her schedule was about to get crazier still. "I'll think about it, okay? And while I do, I want you to consider all the ramifications."

"You in my bed every night, with me in the morning for coffee, safer with me. I know what I'm asking, honey."

Desperation brought a tremor to her voice. "It's not that easy." His tenderness wore her down. She had to find a way to make him back off before she blurted out her news and destroyed their quiet time together. "Do you know that I got a C- on a test the other day? I've never scored that low, but instead of studying, I was . . ." Guilt choked her, but she forced herself to continue. "I was daydreaming about you, trying to cut corners so I could be with you. And my grades suffered."

The silence following her accusation felt like a scream, resounding in her head. Quinton moved to his back beside her, still there, but not quite touching. "I'm sorry."

Oh God, it wasn't his fault. In frustration Ashley started to curl her hands into fists, and her broken wrist protested with a sharp pain.

"*I'm* to blame, Quinton. It's my damned stupid plan that suffers when I get off track. I should—"

He rolled over her, touching her all over without hurting her at all, silencing her with his size and looming position, and his caring. "We'll work it out, okay? Let's give it a week to sink in, then we'll sit down together and discuss things."

He had no idea they'd be discussing baby things, but she was a horrible coward, so she gratefully took the postponement. "Okay."

He gave her a loud smooch. "Get comfortable and I'll settle around you."

That made her laugh, but tears infused the sound. She only hoped Quinton hadn't heard them—or if he did, he said nothing.

Because the stitches on her face made sleeping on her right side nearly impossible, Ashley turned to her left side and positioned her cast in front of her. Quinton spooned her, settled his arm around her waist and, with a kiss to her shoulder, said, "Sleep. If you need anything during the night, let me know." Within minutes his breathing had evened into sleep.

Because she couldn't take any pain meds, Ashley had no intention of waking him. With her mind churning on consequences, deceptions, and guilt, it took her much longer to fall asleep. But finally the warmth of Quinton's touch and the even rhythm of his breath lulled her.

Something woke Ashley bright and early the next morning. She hadn't heard Quinton leave the bed, but she instinctively knew she was alone. She was still tucked in, and the remnants of sleep made her sluggish, but Quinton's overwhelming presence and the peace she felt when with him were gone.

Then she realized a conversation in the hallway had roused her. Dull pain throbbed throughout her body, centering in her head, her arm. Her heart.

Struggling into an upright position, she listened hard and detected Quinton's voice, as well as others. Had the workers arrived to install new security measures? From the little bit of the conversation she could detect, that seemed the case.

Groaning with each movement, she crawled from the bed, dragging the blankets with her.

The door opened and Quinton peeked in. "Sorry we woke you."

She felt like hell warmed over, but managed a smile. "What time is it?"

"Only eight o'clock. You want some coffee?"

She groaned for an entirely different reason. "I'd *kill* for coffee."

His grin did much to revive her. "Everyone will be back out of the house in a few minutes. I'll bring the coffee to you here so you can get started."

Keeping the blankets in place with one hand wasn't easy. "My hero."

"I hope so."

While Quinton saw to the coffee, Ashley ducked into the bathroom. A look in the mirror didn't reassure her. Denny had nailed it—she did look like shit, and a night of restlessness hadn't improved anything.

Sometime during the night the bruising had turned a vivid blue and crimson, and in places, purple. The skin around her eye had puffed up, giving her a squinty, uneven look, and her hair resembled a witch's.

She shrugged, knowing there wasn't anything she could do about it. No amount of makeup would cover the discolorations, and with her cast, her hair was about as good as she could get it. With no help for it, it wasn't worth worrying over.

Then she glanced at the rest of her body. Almost in slow motion, she lowered the blankets and searched for signs of pregnancy. She was as slender as ever, her boobs still nonexistent, her belly concave. She felt different inside, but outside, nothing showed.

How long did she have before noticeable changes occurred?

She put her hand over her abdomen. Would the baby look like Quinton? He was so beautiful to her that she hoped so. She didn't care if she had a boy or a girl. It was odd, but she already loved the baby more than she knew was possible.

When the tears dribbled down her cheeks, she realized she was crying. Stupid, stupid. The doc had said she'd have emotional highs and lows, but she hadn't said anything about her becoming a damned crybaby.

Ashley dashed a hand over her face, washed, brushed her teeth, and stepped back into the flannel pants. When Quinton returned, she was sitting on the end of the bed, unable to get the sweatshirt on.

Two steps into the room, he paused. His gaze went over her belly, exposed by the low-hanging pants, and then to her breasts. One brow lifted. "Damn, that's a good look for you."

Ashley gave him a sour frown. "Quit leering and help. I'm freezing here."

Smiling, he said, "All right." He set the coffee aside and eased the left sleeve over her cast. It hurt to move her fingers at all, not that she could much, anyway. But it seemed aches and pains had settled in overnight, and it made her cranky.

As he assisted her, Quinton said, "It occurred to me that you wouldn't have anything to wear to school this morning."

Ashley groaned. "I hadn't even thought of that. She snatched up the coffee and gulped it so fast she burned her tongue. But damn it, she had to get it together. She had too many responsibilities to just fall apart. "I better get on the ball so I can run by my place first."

"Actually, I put your clothes from last night into the wash. If the stains come out, they'll be good to go in half an hour. At the very least, the jeans should be okay, and you do look fetching in my sweatshirt. In fact, feel free to look through all my shirts and make use of anything that appeals to you."

"You really are my hero." She went on tiptoe to kiss him—and nausea hit her with the force of a tsunami. "Oh, hell."

She caught only a glimpse of Quinton's startled concern before she plopped the coffee cup back onto the dresser, lurched into the bathroom, and fell to the floor in front of the commode. Her knees stung from the impact of connecting with the tile floor, and she clunked her cast on the seat, sending pain screeching through her. She'd barely gotten the seat up before the awful heaving racked her body.

She felt Quinton behind her, standing there in appalled silence, and she violently gagged again.

Her hair in her face, her stomach churning, Ashley snarled, *"Get out,"* in a tone of horror-movie magnitude.

She didn't think he would leave her, but then he stepped out of the room and pulled the door shut, giving her the privacy she needed. The morning sickness seemed to go on and on. Each time she started to stand, her stomach roiled.

"Oh God," she whispered, and she wondered how she'd ever survive this. She had homework to do. She had two jobs. Never mind her grand plans for her future; she had a baby to think of. "Oh God, oh God."

"Are you praying," Quinton asked gently, from just outside the door, "or merely expressing yourself?"

Ashley struggled to her feet. Thank the heavens, her belly didn't protest. She flushed the toilet, took a couple of deep breaths, and tried to stop shaking. Bracing her hands on the sink, she said, "I'm okay."

"No. You're not."

She turned on the water and rinsed out her mouth. "I am if I say I am." But she sounded raspy and Quinton came in uninvited.

"You're ill."

"It's nothing," she lied, hating herself even as she fabricated the fib. "Just leftover upset from last night. Those cheese sandwiches . . ." She almost gagged again and had to swallow convulsively. "They're coming back to haunt me."

Quinton got a fresh washcloth out of a drawer and rinsed it in cool water. She took it from him and wiped her face. Her hands shook and her mouth felt gritty. "I guess you'll be buying a new toothbrush, huh?"

Ignoring her jest, he put a hand to her forehead. "You don't feel feverish."

"Because I'm not."

"Let me take you to the doctor."

Oh, no. Hell, no. She shook her head. "I'm okay now." And she really did feel better. With any luck, the morning sickness would stay away for the rest of the day. She pushed past Quinton and left the bathroom. The coffee cup remained where she'd left it, but rather than gulp this time, she sipped—and her stomach agreed to that method.

"See." She summoned a smile, knowing she looked ghastly but unable to do anything about it. "I'm okay."

Quinton eyed her. "I don't like it, Ash. You're pale under all the bruising. And you didn't sleep well last night."

He'd noticed that? She thought he'd slept through her bouts of discomfort and fear.

"You should take it easy today."

"I will," she promised. "I have some time between my classes, and I'm not working at the restaurant."

He rubbed his head. "You need a day off, some time to recoup."

"Are you taking the day off?"

"I will if it'll keep you home."

"Oh." She hadn't expected that. She couldn't afford to start slacking off now, but neither did she want him to worry. "Tell you what. If I feel sick again, I'll call in. But honest, I think it was just the way I gobbled the food last night, on top of breathing all that smoke and getting stitches and everything. Right now I want to stay busy to keep my mind off Elton and his sick attacks."

Quinton didn't appear convinced, but one of the workers called his name, forcing him to concede. "You're sure you're okay now?"

"Yes. Right as rain."

He held her face and brushed his thumb over her bruised cheek. "All right. If you feel up to eating anything, maybe some toast, I'll be in the kitchen."

The thought of food didn't thrill her, but she knew she had to try. "That sounds good. Thanks."

"You've got it." He kissed her forehead and
walked out of the room, leaving Ashley alone with
her thoughts and her guilt.

She put a hand to her flat belly, protective, scared,
and more uncertain than she'd ever been in her
life.

After class, she'd set an appointment with a doctor. Once she had the pregnancy confirmed and a
delivery date for the baby, she'd tell Quinton.

No more cowardice.

No more evasion.

She would do the right thing—and deal with the
consequences, whatever they might be.

Three days later, mind made up, new plans in
the works, Ashley went to Quinton's office before
her shift. Her heart pounded with dread, nervousness, and hope—all at the same time. She simply
couldn't keep the secrets to herself any longer.

Since the mailbox bombing, she'd remained in
Quinton's home. Not on an official basis, because
she hadn't yet agreed to move in with him. Keeping
to his agreement, he hadn't pressured her for an
answer. But her hours were such that the only way
to see him was to catch him at work, or climb into
his bed after her late shift ended. She couldn't do
that if they weren't in the same place.

Making love in the mornings seemed to be their
best bet. Rather than going right to bed after her
shift, as was her usual habit, Ashley stayed up to
enjoy some time with Quinton.

He got up earlier than need be for his schedule,
doing what he could to adjust to her off hours.

That worked out for her because it ruled out the possibility of waking with morning sickness, and it reduced her chances of rousing Quinton's suspicions. Unfortunately, the morning sickness didn't content itself with mornings only and had interrupted not only her class time, but both jobs.

With the current arrangement, neither of them got enough sleep. Ashley was used to that; she'd sustained a hectic schedule since moving away from home. Only now, she never felt fully rested. She longed to linger in bed after waking and had the awful urge to nap throughout the day. More often than not, she felt like a walking zombie, unable to do anything with competence due to growing weariness.

She had to make some adjustments, the sooner the better. So regardless of her continued reserve, she knew she couldn't continue the sham.

Just hours ago, she'd seen the ob-gyn recommended to her by her family physician. The doctor was kind, not judgmental, and Ashley liked him a lot. After an examination and a few tests, he'd presented her with a delivery date of July twenty-second.

Knowing when the baby would arrive made it all so real.

She'd left the doctor's office with a prescription for vitamins, pamphlets on what to expect, including the cursed morning sickness, and an appointment for another office visit in a few weeks—along with a good dose of new resolve.

Priorities ruled her life, and sometimes that meant adjusting. Right now her priorities were Quinton and the baby. The reality was that she couldn't keep up both jobs, her schoolwork, a romance, and the physical toll of pregnancy. So her job at the office building would have to go.

If she worked a few more hours at the restaurant, she'd make just enough in additional tips to keep up with her expenses, plus she'd have more time for Quinton and school.

Once the baby was born, she'd have to cut back on school, too. Unlike some new mothers, she had no relatives to assist her, and she couldn't afford sitters. She was realistic enough to know she couldn't do it all. So it'd take her a little longer to become a nurse. That wasn't the end of the world.

And if it turned out that Quinton was happy about the baby, that he wanted them to be a real family . . . but she wouldn't let herself start on that particular fantasy just yet.

On the one hand, she wanted to call May in Japan and share the news right now. Without a single doubt, she knew how May would react. Her friend would scream with excitement and joy. She'd take charge, assuring Ashley that everything would work out. May would start going over names, colors for a nursery, the whole nine yards.

Ashley needed May's enthusiasm and optimism.

But on the other hand, it would be grossly unfair to tell May before she told Quinton. The baby's father deserved to hear the news first. She needed things settled with him before she started celebrating.

And if the baby caused a rift between them, she'd need May more than ever before.

Hell, given the circumstances, she might even need Jude—to keep her safe until the police found and arrested Elton, removing him as a threat.

No, she couldn't see Quinton washing his hands
of her, leaving her to fend for herself. He was the
most honorable guy she knew, and the most responsible. But she had to consider every angle, and
she had to accept that his interest in her had never
extended toward children of their own.

Now that she had details from the ob-gyn, she
needed to share them with Quinton before she
lost her nerve. It'd only be a matter of time before
he found out, anyway. With guards trailing her
everywhere she went, they were bound to mention
to him that she'd seen a doctor. Better that she tell
him herself than to let him hear the news from
outsiders.

However, a quick look around the office proved
Quinton wasn't in.

Unfortunately, his uncle was.

With only Warren staring at her, Ashley's courage
shriveled, and she tried to make a hasty retreat.

Warren stopped her with a gasp of exclamation.
"Good God, girl. What happened to you?" He eyed
her up and down while moving closer to the doorway where she hovered.

The weather had cooled considerably in the past
week, so Ashley wore ankle boots with her jeans,
and two layers of T-shirts since a long-sleeved shirt
wouldn't fit over her cast. Unlike Quinton, she
had no desire to take scissors to her wardrobe, especially when the cast would be removed in a few
weeks.

Hoping to conceal her unease, she shoved her
right hand into her pocket and lounged against
the door frame to address Warren. "Didn't Quinton
tell you?"

"About the bomb? Yes, yes he did. But I didn't

realize . . ." New concern pinched his expression. "You look wretched."

"Now, Warren, so much flattery will turn my head."

Her sarcasm flustered him. "It's hardly a matter of jest."

"Yeah, well, I wasn't laughing." She raised the cast in front of her. "It's just a broken wrist, nothing too serious. And most of the bruises are superficial."

"Meaning?"

"They'll fade soon." She looked around again, specifically toward the inner office. "So. Quinton's not here?"

"He'll be back shortly." Warren fought with himself, but good manners, and perhaps concern, won out. He ushered Ashley to a chair. "Sit down, sit down."

That surprised her. "Thanks, but I'm fine."

Carrying a large box that blocked her view, Adrianna bumped into Ashley from behind, forcing her into the office after all.

Peering around the side of the box, Adrianna said, "Oops. I'm sorry." She spotted Ashley, and her frown lifted with a smile. "Ashley, how nice to see you again."

"You, too." How that woman could look so chic all the time, Ashley didn't know. She always wore heels, which set off her shapely legs, and her slim skirts proved that although she might be in her midforties, her figure remained trim and youthful.

Warren rushed to Adrianna to relieve her of her load. "Let me help you with that."

Going icy cold, Adrianna held on and said, "I

can handle it." She set the cumbersome box on the edge of Quinton's desk. After frowning at Warren, she turned to Ashley, and another smile brightened her face before she glanced at her watch. "Was Quinton expecting you?"

Ashley shook her head. The lies were adding up, but she saw no hope for it. "One of my classes was canceled."

"I see. Quinton will be so disappointed he wasn't here. We're working late tonight to free up time later in the week. He ran out to get us some dinner."

Was Quinton making time in his schedule for her? He had so many responsibilities, so many things that he took on himself. Ashley hated that she'd added one more responsibility.

Trying to draw Adrianna's attention, Warren clasped his hands behind his back and rocked on his heels. She did look at him, but only to say, "You should head on home, Warren. We don't need you."

Oh ho, Ashley thought. Trouble between Warren and Adrianna? Not that she should be surprised. He was such a pompous ass that a saint would have trouble getting along with him. But still . . . She almost felt sorry for Quinton's uncle as he floundered at Adrianna's cut.

Blustering through his unease, he said in grave tones, "I have a vested interest in this business."

Adrianna's smug smile set him back a foot. "Not tonight, Warren." She patted his chest in dismissal. "We're dealing with some things for the boys, and everyone knows how you feel about that." Her smile tightened. "Besides, I'm sure Ivana is waiting for you."

Wide-eyed, Ashley watched as Warren flushed pink from his throat to his hairline.

Adrianna made no pretense about enjoying his discomfort.

"I need something to drink," Warren barked, and he left the office without his suit coat, storming down the hall to the elevators.

Ashley whistled low. "Wow. Is there a bar in this building that I don't know about? Will he come back snookered?"

"No. He's just after a cola from the vending machines downstairs." Adrianna glared in the direction where Warren had disappeared. "Pay no attention to him. He'll cool down before he returns."

Somehow, Ashley doubted that.

Adrianna perched on the edge of the desk. "So how are you feeling? Quinton told me what happened, but I see you're not letting a little thing like a bomb slow you down."

Ashley grinned with her. "It didn't slow Quinton down, either."

"I know. If anything, he's gone nonstop. But then, this time of year is crazy for him because of the boys. He puts in extra hours with them around the holidays, plus he organizes special dinners and gifts and gatherings. I admire his loyalty and dedication a lot. So different from *other* men I know."

Somehow that sounded very odd to Ashley. She started to question Adrianna further when her stomach began another revolt. The worst part of the nausea, in Ashley's opinion, was how quickly it came upon her. She had no time to explain to Adrianna before she slapped a hand to her mouth and dashed into the inner office to the private restroom. She slammed the door behind her while praying Quinton wouldn't return just yet.

Adrianna rapped anxiously at the door. "Ashley! Are you all right?"

"Flu," Ashley lied, in between bouts of gagging. "Please, I'm fine."

To her relief, Adrianna said nothing more.

As soon as her stomach quieted enough, Ashley emerged, only to find the main office vacant. Where had everyone gone? They hadn't left for the night because Warren's suit coat rested over the back of a chair, and the box Adrianna had carried in to the desk hadn't been moved.

Maybe Adrianna had gone to look for Warren, so they could resolve whatever differences they had tonight. Whatever their reasons for not being there, Ashley was grateful. It spared her from telling more clankers in explanation of her sickness. At the moment, she wasn't up to believable deceit.

Her skin remained clammy, her stomach iffy, and a quick check of her watch showed she still had plenty of time before she started her shift.

Her new ob-gyn had recommended nibbling crackers and drinking a caffeine-free cola to settle her nausea. She had both in her locker downstairs. Adrianna had said they'd be in the office late, so she'd have a chance to speak with Quinton yet. Better to do it when she wasn't barfing, she decided, and she left, taking the back stairs, before anyone had returned.

Chapter 16

Quinton entered his office, arms laden with food, only to slam into his uncle's blast of anger.

"She stole it!" Warren shook a fist. "To think I was stupid enough, gullible enough to sympathize with her, and then she robbed me blind."

Quinton came to a standstill. "What the hell are you talking about? Who stole what?"

"Your little inamorata," Warren sneered. "She was here—"

"Ashley?" Damn it, he'd stepped out for only an hour, long enough to get dinner for Adrianna and himself. But surely she hadn't left the building. She'd be starting her shift soon, so he'd find her.

"Yes, yes, that's who I mean. She waltzed in and hung around long enough to get what she wanted. I've searched the building over for her, but now she's nowhere to be found."

A hot rush of anger flooded through Quinton. Since that damned hospital trip, he hadn't seen Ashley long enough to get a true sense of her feel-

gs. In many ways it felt as though she held back
om him, as if she deliberately cultivated their
me constraints, while he did everything in his
ower to spend more time with her.

When she wasn't around, he missed her. When
e was near, he couldn't keep his hands off her.
espite her injuries, she made love with him each
orning, and each time was better than the time
efore it.

But damn it, physical satisfaction wasn't enough.
e needed to sit with her at the breakfast table
d chat over coffee. He wanted to curl onto the
fa with her in the evening and share the events
their days. He wanted to talk to her about the
ys, and learn more about her childhood, and . . .
e wanted her to love him.

Damn it.

Holding himself in close check, Quinton walked
the desk and carefully set down the bags of
hinese. It required two breaths before he felt
mposed enough to face his uncle's absurd alle-
tions.

He turned, leaned back on the desk, and folded
s arms over his chest. "So, Warren, are you telling
e that Ashley held you at gunpoint?"

"Don't be idiotic. She was here, I went to get a
la, and when I came back, she was gone. I de-
ded to leave too, but when I put on my suit coat,
ealized the pocket was empty."

"The pocket?"

"Where I had a fifteen-thousand-dollar bracelet
r Ivana!"

Quinton raised a brow over that. "Why were you
rrying a bracelet of that value around with you?"

"Good God, what does that matter? I had t
thing and now it's gone."

When Quinton just waited, Warren huffed in
ritation.

"If you must know, I bought it during my lun
break today." He flushed. "Saw it in a window d
play and knew Ivana would love it."

Aunt Ivana had always bartered forgiveness f
diamonds and gold. Because she and Warren we
often at odds, Ivana always dripped with sparkle
For Warren to choose such a costly apology,
must have really dug himself into a hole.

Instinctively, Quinton knew Ashley would nev
let him off that easy. If he angered her, no gift
the world would take the place of a sincere exp
nation, and when necessary, an apology.

He rather liked that about her.

With a half smile, Quinton said, "Ivana has y
in the doghouse, does she?"

Warren gritted his teeth. "It's a Christmas p
sent, damn it." Righteous anger raised his voi
another octave. "Or at least it was until your pa
mour stole it from me."

The smile disappeared. "Don't call her name:

"All right, all right." Warren moderated his to
"I'm sorry. But she took it. I know she did."

Quinton shook off the accusation and turned
open the food packages. It wasn't worth discussi
"Forget it. Ashley would never do that."

In an effort to convince him, Warren point
out, "When I saw her, she was jumpy. Nervous."

That disclosure only made Quinton more p
tective. "Of course she's nervous. A madman is t
ing to kill her." For his part, Quinton fou

himself observing every shadow, studying every face he passed, constantly listening for whispers.

"That only emphasizes my point," Warren insisted. "Her life is now at an all-time low—when from what I can tell, it was low enough from birth."

Quinton tensed, fighting the urge to take his uncle apart. "I'm not listening to this, Warren. You're dead wrong. Now drop it."

"It's a fifteen-thousand-dollar bracelet, Quinton. I can't just pretend it didn't happen."

"Ashley didn't take it. You probably misplaced it somewhere."

He took a step nearer to Quinton. "I left it right here in my coat pocket." His hands balled into fists. "It's worth enough to set her life straight, to give her a fresh start. I'm telling you, she took it."

Quinton turned back to Warren. So there'd be no misunderstandings, he narrowed his eyes and infused his tone with grave sobriety. "Listen carefully, Warren. I know you don't like her; you've made that plain enough. But I won't tolerate your idiotic accusations. You'll be polite to Ashley, you'll accept her, or our relationship will suffer."

"That's absurd!"

"I've asked Ashley to live with me. She's an important person in my life. Deal with it."

Warren backed up to a chair and fell into it. "You're joking."

"No."

"But that's . . ."

Quinton cut him off. "You were warned, Uncle Warren."

He snapped his mouth shut, then watched Quinton in stunned silence until, in a huff, he stood and stomped back into the inner office. He slammed the door so hard that it didn't catch and instead bounced open again.

Quinton stared at that door, wishing his uncle could be just a little easier to deal with.

"Am I catching you at a bad time?"

Quinton jerked around and found Ashley standing in the doorway. She looked . . . dreadful. Pale and limp, and pinched with worry.

"Of course not." Had she heard his uncle's ravings? "Ashley, I—"

"I need to talk to you, Quinton."

She sounded so upset, he started toward her. "Are you all right?"

"No!" She held up a hand to keep him at a distance. "Please. Just . . . stay there."

Had Elton threatened her again? Had that bastard gotten near her?

Disregarding her order to keep away, Quinton stormed up to her. "What's happened?" he demanded. "What's wrong?"

But when he reached for her, she ducked his hands and backed up as if in fear.

"Ashley?"

Her delicate throat worked as she swallowed. She held her cast bent close to her waist, and with her right hand, hugged herself. "I have to tell you something."

"Elton?"

"*No.*" She shook her head hard. "I'm sorry. I didn't mean for you to think . . . . It has nothing to do with him."

With her behaving so oddly, Quinton felt not one iota of relief. She wasn't even looking at him.

he realized. She stared at his throat. "All right,
Ashley." He retreated to lean against his desk. "This
sounds serious."

"It is." She turned her back on him but immediately faced him again. "I'm sorry. Please believe
that. I didn't mean for it to happen and I . . ."

Good God. Quinton stared at her, every sick suspicion worming through his mind. "Sorry about
what?"

She rubbed at her forehead, practically in tears
when usually, nothing got her weepy. "If I didn't
feel so wretched, I'm sure I could do this better.
But I was sick again and . . ." She dropped her
hand. "Don't be angry with me. Please."

Unease stiffened Quinton's spine. He'd never
heard Ashley be so apologetic, and hearing it now
actually scared him. "You can tell me anything, you
know that."

She nodded, curled her hand into a fist. "I have
a confession."

Those four words echoed in his head like a bass
drumbeat: loud, hollow, and deep. Seconds ticked
by while he ran through a dozen possible scenar-
ios, but only the worst conclusions came to mind.
"A confession?"

"I hope you'll understand. It's not something I
planned. It just sort of happened." And with desperation, "I'd never want to betray your trust."

His heart began thumping too hard. "I do understand." If she took the bracelet, she had to have a
damn good reason. Never would she steal for personal gain, so it had to have something to do with
Quinton. Was he somehow blackmailing her?

"I know this isn't the best place for a private conversation, but I was afraid that if I waited until we were home, I'd lose my nerve." Her mouth trembled. "This isn't easy."

His patience ran out. "Why don't you just tell me what you're talking about?"

"Okay." She reached into her purse. "But first, I . . . I have to give you something."

Warren erupted from the inner office. "I *knew* it."

Jesus. He'd forgotten all about his uncle. Quinton didn't think he could draw in a deep enough breath, but he managed to growl, "Shut up, Warren."

Ashley backed up, appalled to see that they weren't alone after all. "Warren. You're still here? I thought . . . that is, I just assumed you were gone."

"Not without my belongings."

She turned to Quinton with pleading eyes. "This is a private matter, Quinton. I need to talk to you alone."

Warren advanced on her. "You stole my bracelet. Admit it, and then give it back, and maybe I won't press charges. For my nephew, you understand. Out of consideration for him."

Appearing lost, Ashley glowered at him. "What are you blathering on about?"

Quinton caught her shoulder. "Warren, you will back the hell up, shut the hell up, or I swear to you, you'll be sorry."

Holding up his hands, smug in his vindication, Warren went to a chair and sat. He gestured for Quinton to continue.

Ashley looked from Warren to Quinton. "What's going on here?"

"As if you don't know," Warren piped in again. "You've all but admitted to it."

"Admitted to *what?*"

"You with your grand confession. Your big secret. You hope Quinton will forgive you, and God help him, he probably will. But I insist you return the bracelet immediately."

Quinton took two long strides to reach Warren and he hauled him out of the chair by his arm. *"Get out."*

Ashley said, "No."

They both turned to her.

To Quinton's surprise, all signs of nervousness and fear were gone, replaced by chilling pride. "I want to hear what your uncle has to say."

She was so impassive, so . . . alone, that Quinton couldn't bear it. "You don't have to do this, honey. We'll talk about it alone, in private, as you asked."

"It?"

"My damn bracelet that you stole," Warren supplied, and Quinton wanted to strangle him.

"Ah, so I'm a thief again?" Ashley laughed at Quinton's dark expression. "Oh, come on, Quinton. Don't kill him because you agree with him."

Damn it, why could things never be easy with this particular woman? "I don't."

She laughed again, the sound hollow and hurt. "Yes, you do. I can see it in your eyes. Some bauble's missing, and you think I took it."

"I . . ." Quinton stopped, gave himself a moment to gather his thoughts, then asked calmly, "Did you?"

For a single instant, she looked as though he'd struck her. But it was only an instant, then her eyes sparked with anger, her shoulders went back, and her chin lifted. "How many times do we have to go over this, Murphy? I'm not a thief."

"Then what do you have to give him," Warren demanded, "if not my bracelet? What is this big tearful confession you want to make, if not that you stole from me?"

"It doesn't matter," Quinton barked at him, again ready to toss him out on his ear. "She said she didn't take it, and that's it."

"Let me put his mind at ease." Ashley strolled over while withdrawing a piece of paper. She snapped it open. "I was going to show Quinton my letter of resignation for this job. In two weeks, I won't be working here anymore."

She'd quit one of the jobs? Quinton's first reaction was elation—but Ashley's expression kept all joy at bay.

"I'm glad," he told her. "You work too hard."

Warren, however, wasn't satisfied. "Do you plan to make up lost income with the sale of *my* bracelet?"

"I work for what I want, you ass."

The insult affected Warren mightily, given his outraged gasp. "I don't believe you. Why the hell would you apologize for quitting a job? That doesn't make any sense. Why would that require my nephew's forgiveness?"

At her sarcastic best, Ashley laughed. "It's Murphy's Law, ya know? I had more to say to Quinton besides quitting this job, and like an idiot I chose the same time that your stupid bracelet goes missing. Of course, I had no way of knowing I'd be blamed for something like that—"

"It's not a stupid bracelet," Warren charged. "It's worth over fifteen thousand dollars."

Ashley whistled. "Fifteen grand? And you lost it? Damn, Warren, you should be more careful."

His teeth locked. "You took it."

"That's it." Ashley propped her good arm on her hip. "I'm damn tired of hearing you say that. If you believe it, call the cops. Right now." She strode to the desk, picked up the phone, and tossed it toward Warren. It almost struck him, but at the last second he caught it, juggling it a second or two before getting a firm hold on it.

"Maybe I will," Warren threatened.

Ashley's smile looked more like a snarl. "I insist that you do."

Quinton knew he had to take control of the situation before it entirely exploded. He could feel Ashley's emotional retreat, could feel her slipping away from him, and he refused to let that happen.

With iron will and forced calm, he said, "No one is calling the cops."

"If he doesn't, I will." Ashley tightened her mouth. "I don't have anything to hide. And I'll be damned before I stand here accused."

Adrianna appeared in the doorway. "Accused of what? What's going on here?"

Warren clammed up, but Ashley had plenty to say. She gestured toward Warren. "This idiot thinks I lifted his stupid bracelet. He even has Quinton convinced."

"He does not," Quinton denied.

She rounded on him, vibrating with fury. "Don't you lie to me, Murphy. You think I took it." Her voice broke and she went red in the face. "After everything, you still believe I'd do something like that."

"You were ready to confess!" Warren reminded her.

Once again, Quinton tried to take control. "Adrianna, get Warren out of here before I strangle him. And Ashley, for God's sake, stop jumping to conclusions about my thoughts."

Ashley opened her mouth—and Adrianna said, "I took it."

Everyone turned to her in shock.

"That's right. Me. I took the bracelet." Her stride long and graceful in her spiked heels, she glided through to the inner office.

Mouth hanging open, Warren followed her as far as the door.

Adrianna went to her desk, opened a drawer, and lifted out a beautiful gift box. It came winging through the doorway and smacked Warren in the belly. He said, "*Oof*" and let it fall to the floor.

Warren had his share of projectiles aimed at him today, but he didn't seem to notice. He stepped over the box without retrieving it. "Adrianna, I can explain."

"No need, Warren. We're through."

"But . . . !"

"But what? You *love* me? I've heard it too many times, over too many years. You love your good name and social standing too much to ever divorce Ivana, and you know what, Warren? You shouldn't. You two deserve each other."

Frozen in disbelief, Quinton watched the drama unfold. How could he have been so obtuse? Yet . . . Many things now made sense: looks between his uncle and Adrianna, how Warren often volunteered to stay after work when he and Adrianna worked on a project, the way Adrianna could handle Warren when no one else could.

He frowned over his own stupidity—until he realized Ashley had turned and walked away.

"Goddamn it!" On his way out, Quinton paused,

grabbed Warren by the shoulder, and yanked him around to face him. "You've got some explaining to do."

Shamefaced, Warren said nothing.

Quinton pointed at Adrianna. "Don't you dare think about quitting on me just because of this. I need you. The boys need you."

She shooed him away. "We'll talk later, Quinton. Right now you have more important things to do. She's getting away."

With another curse Quinton bounded out of the room. He barely reached the elevators before the doors started sliding shut, with Ashley inside.

He leaped—and made it in.

Ashley reached for the "door open" button, but Quinton caught her arm. "Oh, no, sweetheart. We need to talk. And the elevator surely provides more privacy than my office did."

"I have nothing more to say to you."

"Bullshit." She glared at him, and he glared right back. "You had some grand confession, remember? You were full of apologies for something. I want to know what's going on."

"It doesn't matter now."

"The hell it doesn't. Ignore my uncle and his vagaries. Tell me what has you upset."

She shoved him back a good foot. "Damn you, you should know me better than to think I'd steal!"

"You won't let me know you." He crowded her into the corner of the elevator, uncaring where the car took them or what might be transpiring in his office. "I'm constantly working my ass off to get closer to you, and you're constantly shutting me out."

She turned away.

But Quinton caught her chin and brought her face back to his. She was bruised and tearful and now red-faced with anger. And she was so beautiful to him, she took his breath away.

"I would never deliberately hurt you, Ashley. You have to know that."

She worked her jaw, and tears clung to her lashes.

A sucker punch to the gut couldn't hurt as much as seeing Ashley cry. "Oh, no, baby, please don't cry. I'm sorry."

The elevator dinged and the doors opened. She sniffled, wiped her eyes with her good hand, and said, "Let me out, Quinton."

"Why?"

"I'm going home. *My* home. I don't . . ." She avoided his gaze. "I don't feel well."

Damn it. He searched her face and saw the truth of her words in her big dark eyes. Flu? Sheer exhaustion? Whatever ailed her, she did need to rest, so he moved aside to let her pass but then followed her from the elevator. "What is your big confession?"

She turned to face him.

He waited, and waited some more, until once again his patience wore thin. "Goddammit, whatever it is, just say it! I swear I won't—"

"I'm pregnant."

The bottom dropped out of his world. He inhaled and then choked. Wheezing, he tried to grasp her words. *"What?"*

Her pitiful, defiant expression changed to one of antagonism. "You heard me, Murphy. I'm preggers. Knocked up." She thrust her chin toward him in challenge. "There's a bun in the oven."

"But . . ." Too much had transpired in the past hour, and he couldn't catch up. "I was careful."

"Apparently not careful enough."

He looked beyond her, saying as much to himself as to her, "I never touched you without a condom. Never."

She flagged her hand in dismissal. "So maybe one of them was faulty or something. What do I know about rubbers?"

Pregnant? It wasn't possible. He thought of her damned plans, how he'd already interrupted them, and how this would throw her completely off course. Shit, shit. "Are you positive?" And then with hope, "Have you seen a doctor?"

"I'm positive, twice over."

"What the hell does that mean?"

She shrugged. "They checked me at the hospital, before the X-rays, and then I went to a doctor today, too."

Quinton's vision crowded in. She'd known for days now, but had kept the news from him? He tasted bitter betrayal. He stung from her deceit. "That's why you were sick?"

"Yes."

"And I suppose that explains why you're quitting this job?"

"Yes."

"It's why you've been so quiet and solemn." Pieces came together, and with it, anger. "You found out at the hospital, but you didn't think I needed to know? I am the father, yes?"

"You bastard."

He slashed a hand through the air. "I'm to be a father, but you figured I didn't need to know?"

She raised her voice to match his until they were shouting at each other. "I didn't know how to tell you!"

"Right." Quinton took in her arrogant stance, that balls-to-the-walls attitude. "You being such a quiet, timid woman and all."

He regretted the words immediately, but especially with the way she smiled at him—the same way she'd smiled at Warren. "Don't sweat it, Quinton. The baby doesn't have to concern you. I can handle it on my own."

That brought his anger right back to the boiling point. She intended to cut him out? Like hell. "You can barely take care of yourself. How the hell do you think to care for an infant alone?"

Chapter 17

Never in her adult life had Ashley felt so de-
raded, so ashamed, or so hurt. Her parents' lack
f love had left her hollow, but it hadn't made her
el like this.

And it wasn't because of Warren's idiotic accu-
tions. She'd expected no better from him, so
ow could he insult her?

No, Warren could say whatever he liked. He
attered not a bit to her. But Quinton's skepticism,
s meanness, made her feel contemptible—be-
use it hurt her feelings. Because she loved him.

Because she had hoped he might love her, too.

Ashley began backing up. If she didn't get away
om him, she'd be bawling her eyes out like a fool,
d she'd rather eat dirt than let him see that.

As detached as possible, she gave him details.
he baby is due in July. It's really early to know,
t a fact all the same. Just think, if it wasn't for
ton and my stupid broken arm, I might not have
own for another month or more."

"Where are you going?"

"Away from you." She continued to retreat. "Pregnancy does funny things to women. It makes them tired. It makes them maudlin. It makes me want to kick your sorry ass. But with only one arm, I doubt I'm up to it."

"You want to slap me? Fine. Do it and get over it so we can talk."

He looked like he'd really let her. "We don't have anything else to talk about. I told you, so now you know." She shrugged. "I'm going home for a nap."

With each step she retreated, he advanced. "My home?"

She laughed. "No, my home. And don't worry, I've already forgotten all about your offer for me to move in. You're off the hook with that one."

Quinton rolled his eyes. "It's not over between us, so quit acting like it is."

"Feels over to me."

"That's because you're upset. And maybe you're feeling a little guilty for not leveling with me right off, as you should have. But if you'll just stop to think—"

"I can think, Murphy, just as I can see, and the look on your face said it all. You believed your uncle."

Taut with irritation, he growled, "No, I did not. Not until you started apologizing and saying you had something to confess. But even then, I assumed that if you had taken the bracelet, you had a good reason. I had no way of knowing you had something bigger than a stolen bracelet to share with me. You"—he pointed at her—"are the one at fault here. You're the one who lied to me by omis-

sion. So don't keep throwing my uncle's idiotic assumptions in my face."

"And what about the baby?" she challenged.
"You sure as hell don't look happy about it."

"You blindsided me. Unlike you, I haven't had
days to process it, to get used to the idea." His
green eyes glittered at her, bright with blame.
"What I have processed is your emotional evasion
the last few days, and it's put me through hell.
With a fucking lunatic trying to blow us up, I'd
rather know you're unexpectedly pregnant than to
be left wondering what's really going on."

She supposed she deserved that. "You're right."
She clenched her jaw but forced the words out.
"I'm sorry. I should have told you right away."

"You're damn right." He stared down at her,
then shook his head. "You're ready to fall off your
feet. Go take that nap, and we'll talk when I get
home."

Quinton took her elbow and walked her to her
car, but he didn't say how he felt about the baby, or
even how he felt about her.

For sure, her timing sucked. To think of Warren
accusing her . . .

And what about Warren and Adrianna? She
hadn't seen that one coming. Adrianna was so
warm and kind, and generous, and Warren was . . .
well, almost unbearably obnoxious. Relationships,
she now knew firsthand, were tricky to navigate.
She didn't even want to know how difficult it must
have been for Adrianna.

When Ashley unlocked her car and got behind
the wheel, Quinton called the guards to make certain they knew of her early departure.

"Drive careful," he told her. He hesitated, still frowning, then bent and put a perfunctory kiss to her forehead, closed her car door, and stepped back to watch until she drove out of sight.

Well, Ashley thought, that was awkward. And she knew she was mostly to blame.

But damn Warren. If he hadn't declared her a thief at just that precise moment, she would have told Quinton everything and maybe, just maybe, the outcome would have been different. Instead of talking out the circumstances of an unplanned pregnancy, they'd argued viciously, and a strained tension now existed between them.

She knew that, despite the rough path her confession had taken, Quinton expected her to go to his house for her rest. It would be too surly of her to do differently. Perhaps by the time he got home they would be able to talk without the animosity.

Ten minutes later, when Ashley was almost to Quinton's place, her phone rang. She had to pull over to the side of the road to answer it. Driving with a cast on her lower arm was awkward, but driving and talking on the phone at the same time would be stupid and dangerous.

Assuming it'd be Quinton, hoping that he'd be following her home after all, she dug the phone out of her purse and said, "Hey."

But it wasn't Quinton who said, "Hello, Ashley."

She raised her brows in surprise. "Stuart?" Why in the world would May's father be calling her? Fear struck her heart, and she said in a rush, "Is May all right? Has something—"

"I assume May's fine. I haven't heard from her in a few days."

"Then . . ." Ashley frowned. He sounded odd, not like his usual obnoxious self. "What did you want, Stuart?"

"Ashley, I'm sorry."

She went cold in renewed dread. "Yeah? Sorry for what?"

She detected the sounds of a scuffle for the phone, and then Elton laughed.

No.

"Yes, Ashley. Stuart is so very, very sorry."

Enough was enough. Ashley gripped the phone tightly. "You miserable swine. What have you done to Stuart?"

"Why not a thing. *Yet.*" He laughed again. "But I'm prepared to do any number of things if you don't follow my instructions. If you hang up— which I know you're anxious to do—I'll kill him. Without a moment's hesitation, without remorse, probably with a good deal of pleasure, I'll snuff the life right out of him."

No, no, *no.*

"And Ashley, won't your dear, dear *friend* despise you for letting her daddy be murdered?"

Ashley had to keep him talking while she figured out what to do. "Why Stuart? Why pick on him?"

"You switched phones and I couldn't reach you. But I assumed, rightly so, that you'd share your new number with those people important to you."

"And you think Stuart fits the bill? You're more deranged than I realized."

"Ah well, Ashley, I know you care for May. And I now she cherishes her family, despite their many faults. So you can see the connection. Besides," he added with a shrug in his voice, "you walked away from your parents, so Stuart seemed a fitting . . . substitute."

God, her head hurt. "Bastard."

"You shouldn't call me names." As he said it, she heard Stuart moan and knew that Elton was the cause.

Pleading with him, showing him any weakness, would do her no good. She instinctively knew her best chance was to remain strong. But Elton was right; May would be crushed if anything happened to her family. "Listen up, you worm." Ashley put a deliberate dose of scorn in her tone. "Hurt him again, and I'll hang up on you and damn the consequences."

"Would you really?"

"Good-bye, Elton."

"Wait!"

Panicking, heart racing, Ashley gave silent thanks that her ploy had worked. "Enough. Tell me what you want and let's get this over with."

Pleasure evident in his tone, Elton told her, "Go to your apartment, park your car, and then slip out the back of the building. Cross through those empty overgrown lots, and then meet me at the abandoned drive-in theater a block or so from you. I'll give you fifteen minutes, and then he's dead."

"That's not enough time."

As if she hadn't spoken, he continued, saying, "If I kill Stuart, that'll mean we'll have to start all over again. And maybe next time, I'll grab one of the children."

"Children?" She held the phone awkwardly with her left hand and with her right, put the car back in gear. She didn't have any time to waste. She eased back into traffic, trying to calm the rioting of her heart, the nausea that burned the back of her throat.

"Don't play stupid, you bitch. It doesn't suit you. Your boyfriend has a whole group of motley unfortunates that he likes to coddle. Plucking one of them away will be easy enough, I promise you. If you don't care about poor Stuart, surely you care about them?"

Her foot slammed onto the gas, speeding the car along. Never would she let Elton hurt the boys. "I'll be there."

"You, and only you. No cops. If they follow you in, and I know I'm caught anyway, I'll take Stuart with me, don't doubt it."

"I understand."

"Good. Don't be late."

He hung up and Ashley dropped the phone so she could better steer. She glanced in the rearview mirror several times, but she didn't see any guards. They were good—but good enough to fool Elton? Good enough that they could be there, and she wouldn't see them at all?

She just didn't know. Why did everything have to happen at once?

She parked carefully so as not to give herself away. Cars passed her, but none that seemed conspicuously watchful of her. Still, Quinton said he'd be followed home to ensure her safety.

Surely, the guards would report to Quinton that he hadn't gone to his place, but to her apartment instead. But would he even care, or would he assume she was in a snit, and stewing?

It wasn't until she'd cut through her apartment building and was about to go out the back door that she wondered if Elton had booby-trapped her building.

Would the door explode when she opened it? Her pulse raced until she felt light-headed. Backing up, she retraced her steps and slid out the front door. Again looking for any signs of guards, she walked around to the back of the building, then jogged into the empty, overgrown lots that led to the main road. She got a stitch in her side, but she paid it little mind.

Through the heavy shrubs and overgrown trees, she could just see the road and the drive-in on the other side of it. Pushing branches and weeds out of her path, she started forward again—and Elton spoke from her left.

"Right on time."

As Ashley whirled around to face him, her sleeve caught on a bramble, her foot on an exposed root. She stumbled but stayed upright.

Good God, Elton looked more miserable than she'd thought humanly possible. His blond hair had been dyed a dull brown, and it hung long, greasy, and unkempt. His unclean skin glowed with oily perspiration, while madness brightened his eyes.

Even from several feet away, Ashley could smell him. "You look like shit."

"Thanks to you and your fucking meddling." Elton held a length of pipe in his right hand and something else, something strange, in his left. Stuart stood beside him, sweating, pale as a ghost.

"I thought you said to meet you at the drive-in."

He licked his lips in expectation. "I changed my mind about that. In case you squealed, I decided we'd do better to stay right here." He prodded Stuart forward with the piece of pipe.

"You aren't good enough at planning to get away with this, Elton. You know that."

"You have no idea what I'm planning, so shut the fuck up and start walking. I want to put more distance between us and your apartment building."

Ashley considered her options, looked at that piece of hard pipe in Elton's hand, and shook her head. "And if I refuse to go with you?"

Elton smiled at her and raised his left arm into the air. Ashley could see that he clutched two cylindrical devices, about six inches long, three-quarters of an inch in diameter with wires attached to a nine-volt battery. His thumb rested on the switch.

A bomb.

Ashley thought of her baby, of Quinton, and knew she would *not* die today. She finally had things she wanted, things she'd never known were important to her because they'd seemed so unattainable. They were within her grasp, and she wasn't about to let Elton rob her of them.

Yes, she wanted her career as a nurse. She wanted money in the bank and her cute little dream house. But she didn't need those things, not the way she needed Quinton and her baby.

Forcing a shrug, she smiled at Elton. "If you detonate that clumsy thing, won't you blow up, too?"

"Not if I throw it at you first."

If he threw it, wouldn't he have to take his thumb off the switch first?

As if he'd read her thoughts, Elton laughed. Then again, if you won't cooperate, maybe I'll just go straight to the children and explode a similar bomb that I have planted there."

An odd calm came over Ashley, obliterating the mind-scrambling panic and making it easier for her to rationalize.

"I don't think so," she said slowly, thinking things through. She had to trust in Quinton and his awesome capacity for caring. "You don't have a bomb planted there, because Quinton would never leave the children unprotected. You're lying through your teeth."

Elton's temper snapped. "You're right, you fucking bitch. He has an army protecting that place."

Ashley closed her eyes in relief. She wasn't safe, not by a long shot, and Stuart looked like he might have wet himself at Elton's outburst. But they were both adults, not innocent children.

She should have known sooner that Quinton wouldn't leave the boys unprotected. He had money and he enjoyed it. But most of all he enjoyed using it to care for and shelter others.

"So what do you want, Elton?" She hoped to distract him enough to keep him from going farther from her apartment. "I don't have all day."

Her bluster, even while delivered with a shaking voice, enraged him further. "You're worth a lot now girlie."

She snorted. "Yeah, right. Whoever told you that misled you big-time."

"Your lover is loaded," he snapped.

"Right. He is. But that's got nothing to do with me."

"You're going to contact him for me." Elton eased closer, rabid in his planning. "You're going to get enough money from him that I can get away from here. You're going to—"

"Dream on," Ashley interrupted. "I've never asked for a handout and I won't start now, especially not for the likes of you."

"You'll do it, all right." Using the pipe, Elton gouged Stuart in the small of the back, and Stuart staggered forward with a grimace. "You'll do it, or 'll cave in his skull right now."

Resolutely keeping her eyes off that bomb, Ashley hesitated.

But this time Elton wasn't fooled. "Act as ballsy as you like, little girl. Pretend you don't care. Pretend that having a daddy doesn't matter to you." He grinned, showing teeth that hadn't experienced the touch of a toothbrush in weeks. "I know better."

Shock rippled through Ashley. Elton spoke as if he knew . . . but that was impossible. No one knew. She stared at Stuart, at the man who should have been her father, but who had always treated her as an outsider. And she laughed. "You're joking, right?"

"For God's sake, Ashley," Stuart cried out. "Just do what he—"

The panicked words dropped like stones from a cliff when Elton swung the pipe and cracked Stuart in the back of the head. With a dull grunt, he collapsed to the ground.

"No." Ignoring Elton's cackling laugh, Ashley ran to Stuart, dropped to one knee at his side, and grasped his shoulder with her uninjured hand. "Stuart?" She jarred him the best she could. "Answer me, Stuart."

His groan proved he was breathing. Thank God. May would be so upset if anything happened to him.

And damn it, Elton was right.

Stuart had never claimed her. She owed him nothing, less than nothing. But . . . she didn't want him injured. She cared about him. Such an idiot.

"Come on, Stuart." She slapped his cleanly shaven jaw, trying to rouse him. "You don't get to take the easy way out. Open your damned eyes."

Heavy lids fluttered open, showing eyes the same color as hers, and identical in shape.

In a voice weak with confusion, he rasped, "I'm sorry, Ash. I should have . . . should have told you . . ." He swallowed hard, his glazed eyes pleading with her. "Please don't let me die."

Keeping Elton in her peripheral vision, Ashley sat back on her heels. She had to stall Elton, to buy herself some time. Quinton would come. Somehow it'd all work out. She had to believe that.

Shaking her head, Ashley said, "Told me what? That you're my father?" She looked up at Elton. "That's old news."

Glaring, Elton took an aggressive step toward her. "You knew?"

"Why does everyone keep insisting I'm an idiot? I have eyes, don't I? I can see the resemblance, and knowing Stuart's . . . proclivity for catting around, along with my mother's less than conservative lifestyle, it didn't take a genius to figure it out."

And someone said, "You sure hid it well, brat."

Both she and Elton jumped at the intrusion of Denny's voice. He'd come up behind her, but Ashley had been so intent on Elton, she hadn't heard him.

Raising the pipe, Elton started toward Denny.

Ashley quickly came to her feet, and from be-hind Elton, Tim snarled, "I wouldn't."

Ashley blinked at him. *"Tim?"*

"Hush, Ashley," he said. "It's all right now."

No friggin' way. But she couldn't deny her own eyes: that was Tim with a man's voice, a man's con-viction.

A damn parade had come through and she hadn't heard a thing. Tim didn't look particularly shocked by the news that she was his half sister. No, if any-thing, he looked very determined to take Elton apart.

Ashley prayed he'd leave that to Denny, because although Tim had been training hard, she didn't want her fate in his hands.

Eyes wild with fear and insanity, Elton turned on him. That damn pipe gleamed in the moonlight. "Are you going to stop me, boy?"

"No." Quinton spoke from the side of Elton. "I am." And before Elton could even acknowledge him, Quinton's left hand clamped onto Elton's wrist, squeezing hard to keep him from detonating the bomb. With his right fist, he landed one solid jab to Elton's chin, and the lunatic slumped in his hold.

Quinton relieved him of the bomb, handed it to Denny, and hauled Elton back up again. "Bastard." Elevating Elton by the front of his ragged, dirty shirt, Quinton struck him again and again. Denny and Tim stood there, arms crossed, just watching. Stuart groaned and crawled into a sitting position, and then he, too, watched.

Approaching sirens shook Ashley out of her stu-por. "Quinton?" He struck Elton again, even though

Elton had long since passed out. She ran to him. "Quinton, stop it."

He hovered over Elton, heaving in anger, rage pulsing off him.

Denny patted her on the shoulder, and she moved to the side. He caught Quinton's arm, saying, "I got this, son. Go take care of Ashley."

Eyes on Quinton, Ashley muttered, "I can take care of myself." And she could, damn it, but . . She needed him. She wanted him.

Quinton relinquished his hold on Elton, but he didn't reach for Ashley. He took a step back.

Her heart almost broke.

Until he said, "I love you, Ashley."

Because he still sounded furious, the declaration was odd indeed. She started shaking all over and tears welled up in her eyes.

"All right." Gulping down her tears, Ashley nodded and opened her arms to him.

He took one gigantic step toward her, enraged larger than life, and everything she ever wanted.

He crushed her close, saying into her hair, "No it's not all right. *You're mine.* The baby is mine."

Cars pulled up, people swarmed around them but Ashley barely paid any attention to them.

Quinton inhaled a deep breath, let it out, the did it again. He tipped her chin up, and thoug he didn't smile, he didn't look as fierce, either.

"Children of my own . . . They were never in n plans, but then, you weren't in my plans, either He turned his hand to brush his knuckles over h bruised cheek. "I'm finding plans have a way changing pretty quickly."

She choked on a laugh. "Tell me about it."

"I love you. I want you in my life, with kids

our own, and kids that we sponsor and care for, and . . . I want everything."

She nodded. "I want that, too."

Hands shaking, he cupped her face. "God, honey, you almost scared me to death. Right after you left, I decided to hell with Warren and his mess and anything else that was on the agenda for the day. I wanted to see you. Then the guards called and said you'd gone to your apartment. At first, I thought you were still mad, then I saw you rushing across the back lot and you disappeared out of sight before I could stop you—"

"I knew you'd come."

His eyes closed and he sucked more air before continuing. "I told the guards to call Denny and the cops, but I swear, I died a dozen deaths, praying and hoping and more frantic than any man should ever have to be."

Ashley smiled at him. "I didn't know what to do. I was afraid he'd kill Stuart—"

"*I love you.*" He held her back the length of his arms, staring down at her, breathing hard. "Admit that you love me too, tell me that you'll marry me, and let me have some peace."

She couldn't help it. She started to laugh, but because she was still crying, too, the sound was bent and pathetic.

Quinton looked appalled and scared all over again before she blurted, "I love you, too, and as to marriage, sure, Murphy, whatever you want. Now console me, damn it. I've been through hell."

And with a bomb squad, an ambulance, and various police and ATF agents surrounding them, Quinton did just that.

* * *

Quinton came into the kitchen and found Ashley seated at the table, books spread out around her, papers everywhere. "Hey, babe." He smiled, bent and kissed her on top of the head, and said, "How's the studying?"

"Slow." She finished writing something, laid aside a pencil, and pushed out of her chair to waddle toward him.

She'd rounded out with the pregnancy, and she still had nearly two months to go. She raised her arms, put them around his neck, and planted a long warm smooch on him.

Quinton automatically filled his hands with her newly voluptuous rump and lifted her up into him. "Mmmmm."

Ashley laughed. "Letch. I'm as big as a house and here you are, copping a feel."

"You're beautiful, so I can't help myself." He kissed her again, lingering, lazy, loving her more with each day. "I suspect when we're ninety-five I'll still totter over with my walker and get a handful every now and then."

Ashley nestled her breasts against him. "Well, at least with the pregnancy I have some boob for you to grab."

Quinton shook his head. He started to laugh—and something jabbed him in the ribs. Overcome with emotions, he spread his hand out on her abdomen and felt their child squirming around. "How are you feeling?"

"Fat and content. How about you?"

"I love you."

"I know." She squeezed him tight. "I got some news today."

"About?"

She waved him into a seat while she went to the fridge and got out a juice. "You want coffee?"

"Thank you." Quinton removed his suit coat and sprawled in a chair. "The news?"

After pouring his coffee, Ashley reseated herself, too. "The detective called to tell me that they have pretty solid proof that Elton committed another murder to steal some poor woman's car." She shuddered. "I am so glad he's out of our lives."

Quinton reached for her, and pulled her from her seat and into his lap. "I don't want you worrying about him."

"I'm not. It's just that too many innocent people were hurt by him."

"I know." To give her something better to think about, Quinton told her, "The new hearing aid we got for Oliver? He loves it. It's so small that the other kids can't even see it, and he says it's more comfortable."

"Wonderful! And that reminds me, Rupert's birthday is coming around. He wants to have a party at the pizza place."

"All right." Quinton smoothed back her hair. Now that she no longer insisted on working while attending school, she'd dedicated extra time to the boys. And they all loved her, almost as much as did Quinton.

She took a sip of her juice, then turned her face up to his. "May, Jude, Denny, and Tim are coming to dinner tonight."

"Should be fun."

Ashley tried not to laugh.

"What's so funny?"

"I never suspected that anyone who leg-shackled himself to me would also be chained to such a big family."

"I adore May, and Jude's a great guy. Denny's funny at the worst of times, even when he doesn't mean to be. And even Tim is growing on me."

May had accepted Ashley as her sister with tearful glee. She'd told Ashley that to her heart, she'd always been her sister. The two women didn't treat each other any differently, except that Quinton had noticed how they'd sometimes lock gazes, then burst out laughing. He credited that to an excess of happiness for both of them, which made him feel damn good.

And Tim, having gained a lot of maturity in his time with Denny, now behaved more as a brother should, instead of being a liability. He teased May and Ashley mercilessly, tried to protect them even when they didn't need it, and he'd already started talking to Ashley's abdomen, calling himself "Uncle Tim."

To May's parents, nothing much had changed—but then, that mattered little to Ashley, so it didn't bother Quinton. For their wedding, Denny had walked her down the aisle. He'd been as proud as any father could be.

"I was thinking," Ashley said, "maybe we should invite Warren and Adrianna, too."

Quinton almost groaned. His uncle had finally worked up the backbone to end his sham marriage with Ivana. Far from brokenhearted, Aunt Ivana had complained only long enough to get the house, the furnishings, and a hefty cash settlement

Since then, Warren had been begging Adrianna to marry him, but she said they needed time.

It drove Quinton nuts to see Warren kowtowing to Adrianna, but . . . He smiled at Ashley. "Whatever makes you happy, sweetheart."

Her smile went lopsided. "*You* make me happy, happier than I ever dreamed possible."

"Ah well, that'd be Murphy's Law, you know. You have to be happy." He lifted her hand and kissed her knuckles. "I insist."

We don't think you will want to miss Lori's story,
DO YOU HEAR WHAT I HEAR
in the anthology A VERY MERRY CHRISTMAS
coming in October, 2006, from Brava.
Here's a sneak peak.

He was thinking of warm Christmas cookies, songs on the piano and strings of popcorn when he spotted the confusion in front of the funeral home. Lights from a police car flashed blue and red and an elderly couple, bundled in coats over pajamas, gestured with excitement.

Ozzie pulled up behind the cruiser and parked. It only took him moments to identify himself to the officer and to find out that someone had stolen a donkey from the nativity scene erected on the funeral home lawn.

Marci.

Somehow he just knew she was behind this. She'd probably claim the damned donkey was shy, or that he didn't like the colored lights, or God knew what. But Ozzie's instincts screamed and so, with a few more words to the officer, he gave up on the idea of sleep and instead headed to Marci's apartment.

Lucius used to live in the apartment across from

Marci, but thankfully he and Bethany had purchased a home of their own. They'd recently moved out, so Ozzie didn't have to worry about Lucius finding him at Marci's door. Lucius still owned the apartment building, but he left Marci in charge of it.

Not a good idea, in Ozzie's opinion, given that Marci was a kook. But far be it for him to tell Lucius how to run his business.

When he parked in front of the building, Ozzie looked toward Marci's porch window, and sure enough, her inside lights were on. Okay, so it was seven-thirty and she was maybe getting ready for work.

Or hiding a donkey.

Ozzie slammed his truck door, trudged through the crunchy snow and ice, and went up the walk, inside, and up to Marci's door. He knocked twice.

Breathless, Marci yelled, "Just a moment!"

His body twitched. More specifically, his cock sat up and took notice of her proximity. *Damn it.*

A full minute later, Marci opened the door. A look of pleasure replaced her formal politeness. "Osbourne. What a surprise."

He stared down at her and thought, if she'd just not talk about animals, if she'd just smile at him like that, he'd be happy to ravish her for oh . . . a few hours maybe.

When he said nothing, her smile widened, affecting him like a hot lick. She wore a soft pink chenille robe, belted tight around her tiny waist. Her small feet were bare, crossed one over the other to ward off the chill. Her baby fine straight brown hair had the mussed look of a woman fresh out of bed—or fresh inside from the blustery outdoors.

Shaking himself out of his stupor, Ozzie looked

beyond her. He saw nothing out of the ordinary in her tiny apartment, but that didn't clear her.

She took a step closer to him, staring up in what seemed like provocation to him, a heated come-on, a . . .

She tilted her head and said, "Osbourne?"

Lust tied knots in his muscles. He cleared his throat. "Busy?"

Big blue eyes blinked at him, eyes so soft with such thick long lashes, she didn't need makeup. "I just got out of the shower, actually." She patted back a delicate yawn. "It's early. Would you like some coffee?"

He'd like her.

By Best-selling Author
Fern Michaels

Weekend Warriors	0-8217-7589-8	$6.99US/$9.99CAN
Listen to Your Heart	0-8217-7463-8	$6.99US/$9.99CAN
The Future Scrolls	0-8217-7586-3	$6.99US/$9.99CAN
About Face	0-8217-7020-9	$7.99US/$10.99CAN
Kentucky Sunrise	0-8217-7462-X	$7.99US/$10.99CAN
Kentucky Rich	0-8217-7234-1	$7.99US/$10.99CAN
Kentucky Heat	0-8217-7368-2	$7.99US/$10.99CAN
Plain Jane	0-8217-6927-8	$7.99US/$10.99CAN
Wish List	0-8217-7363-1	$7.50US/$10.50CAN
Yesterday	0-8217-6785-2	$7.50US/$10.50CAN
The Guest List	0-8217-6657-0	$7.50US/$10.50CAN
Finders Keepers	0-8217-7364-X	$7.50US/$10.50CAN
Annie's Rainbow	0-8217-7366-6	$7.50US/$10.50CAN
Dear Emily	0-8217-7316-X	$7.50US/$10.50CAN
Sara's Song	0-8217-7480-8	$7.50US/$10.50CAN
Celebration	0-8217-7434-4	$7.50US/$10.50CAN
Vegas Heat	0-8217-7207-4	$7.50US/$10.50CAN
Vegas Rich	0-8217-7206-6	$7.50US/$10.50CAN
Vegas Sunrise	0-8217-7208-2	$7.50US/$10.50CAN
What You Wish For	0-8217-6828-X	$7.99US/$10.99CAN
Charming Lily	0-8217-7019-5	$7.99US/$10.99CAN

Available Wherever Books Are Sold!